THE

BAD

KITTY

LOUNGE

IN THE JOSEPH KOZMARSKI SERIES

The Last Striptease

NONFICTION

Romantic Migrations: Local, National, and Transnational Dispositions

Romantic Geography: Wordsworth and Anglo-European Spaces

THE

BAD

KITTY

LOUNGE

MICHAEL

WILEY

MINOTAUR BOOKS

A THOMAS DUNNE BOOK
NEW YORK

A THOMAS DUNNE BOOKS FOR MINOTAUR BOOKS.
An imprint of St. Martin's Publishing Group.

THE BAD KITTY LOUNGE. Copyright © 2010 by Michael Wiley. All rights reserved. Printed in the United States of America. For information, address St. Martin's Press, 175 Fifth Avenue, New York, N.Y. 10010.

www.thomasdunnebooks.com
www.minotaurbooks.com

Library of Congress Cataloging-in-Publication Data

Wiley, Michael, 1961–
    The bad kitty lounge / Michael Wiley. — 1st ed.
        p. cm.
    ISBN 978-0-312-59300-1
    1. Private investigators—Illinois—Chicago—Fiction.
2. Nuns—Crimes against—Fiction. 3. Murder—Investigation—
Fiction. 4. Chicago (Ill.)—Fiction. I. Title.
    PS3623.I5433B33 2010
    813'.6—dc22

                                                    2009041134

First Edition: March 2010

10 9 8 7 6 5 4 3 2 1

Por los niños

ACKNOWLEDGMENTS

I'm grateful to those who've made the party happen at the Bad Kitty Lounge:

Toni Plummer at St. Martin's, whose editorial insights have been unerringly true, and Ruth Cavin, who prodded me first and hard.

Philip Spitzer, Lukas Ortiz, and Luc Hunt, whose goodwill, good-spiritedness, and good sense are all that I could hope for.

Julia Burns and Sam Kimball, who've helped me past many rough beginnings.

Beryl Satter, who knows these streets and yards.

THE

BAD

KITTY

LOUNGE

ONE

I SAT IN TOMMY Cheng's Chinese Restaurant facing a window onto North LaSalle Street and watched a four-story condo complex where Eric Stone was screwing another man's wife. Not the kind of work I look for, but it always seems to find me. I kept my eyes on my client's condo and ate egg foo yong.

Behind me in the kitchen, Mr. Cheng cooked something that sizzled in the wok. He wore an apron and a white baseball cap. My Pentax, its telephoto screwed into focus, rested on the counter in case Eric Stone showed his face outside.

I squinted into the glare. The little birch trees that the city had dumped into sidewalk planters flared October yellow. The condo complex was stucco and had the kind of Spanish arches and wide balconies that belonged far from Chicago in a place where the sea was always clear and the breeze blew as warm as a woman's breath.

A man walked onto the balcony in front of the condo.

Eric Stone.

I dropped my chopsticks, readjusted the lens on the Pentax,

and snapped a photo. The man had a caterpillar of a beard under his bottom lip. The rest of his head was shaved. He looked somewhere in his early fifties but his arms and body were thick—all muscle. He flexed the arms over his head. He wore white shorts and a white T-shirt on a forty-degree autumn day. He looked like a pirate in tennis whites.

A woman joined him on the balcony.

Amy Samuelson. My client Greg Samuelson's wife.

She was dressed in khakis and a sweater, her blond hair in a ponytail. She wrapped her arms around Eric Stone from behind.

Mr. Cheng came from the kitchen and stood next to me. "Every day the same thing," he said, laughing. "She never gets enough of him."

She slid her hands down the man's stomach. One hand disappeared into the front of his shorts. Stone looked proud of himself.

Mr. Cheng said, "Some people've got no decency," and I snapped more photos. "What do you do?" he asked. "Blackmail them?"

I pulled out my wallet, let him read my detective's license.

"Joe Kozmarski?" he said.

"I'm helping her husband get a divorce."

He laughed. "You blackmail them."

Amy Samuelson and the man went back into the condo, closing the door behind them.

I ate more egg foo yong. The bean sprouts were fresh, the shrimp as big as walnuts. Mr. Cheng stood and watched the balcony as if he expected them to come back out naked and screw in the open air.

Another man walked across a parking lot next to the condos. He was thin, wearing blue jeans, an oxford shirt, and a navy blue jacket, no tie. He carried a two-gallon gas can. He looked in no hurry. He crossed to a yellow Mercedes convertible that was parked facing the street.

I knew the car. Eric Stone drove it when he wasn't flexing his muscles on the Samuelsons' balcony in his tennis shorts.

The man set the gas can on the hood of the Mercedes and undid the cap. He screwed a spout onto the can. He poured gasoline over the car's hood, over the convertible roof, onto the trunk.

Mr. Cheng said, "What the hell—"

The man shook gasoline onto the car doors. He stooped by the tires and poured gas over them. He took his time.

"Take—pictures," Mr. Cheng sputtered. I left my camera on the counter.

The man splashed the rest of the gasoline under the Mercedes, then stepped back to appraise his work.

He touched the fabric convertible roof with a lighter and leaped away. The car burst into flames. Thick black smoke fingered into the air. The convertible top flared and fell into the interior.

The man with the gas can watched the fire, then pulled a cell phone from his pocket, dialed, and talked into it. When he hung up, he walked slowly away. The empty gas can dangled in his fingers. The car made a hollow popping sound and the windshield fell into the front seat.

Mr. Cheng glared. "Why don't you take pictures?"

I looked him up and down. "That was the husband—my client."

Mr. Cheng stared at me with blank eyes and nodded, then returned to the kitchen and called 911. He told the operator that a car was burning and gave the street address. When he hung up, he came back and sat on the stool next to mine. "You like the egg foo yong?" he asked.

"Best egg foo yong I ever ate," I said.

"Thank you," he said. "It's my mother's recipe. It gives you long life."

We sat together and watched the Mercedes burn. Giant flames angled out of the interior. The car roared like an open furnace. Heavy black smoke, dense as dirt, clouded above it. The smell of burning rubber and something worse—the leather interior, something that once was living—made its way into the restaurant. By the time we heard sirens, the fire had blackened the car's exterior, and whatever was feeding it from inside was gone. The flames shortened. Then the gas tank exploded and the fire roared again.

I pushed away the egg foo yong. Long life it would give me, said Mr. Cheng. I'd lost my appetite.

TWO

THREE FIRE TRUCKS AND a squad car crowded the curb in front of the Samuelsons' condo. A couple of firefighters sprayed foam on the burning car. The hot metal smoked and steamed. A young uniformed cop with a notepad talked to Eric Stone on the sidewalk. The October air was cold and Stone was still in his tennis whites, but he looked like he was sweating.

I waited until the cop left him and then I wandered across the street. Stone pulled out a cell phone, punched some buttons, and yelled into it. Up close he still looked like a pirate, but I added five years to the young fifties I'd estimated from a distance. He was driving hard at sixty, but he was sixty years of muscle. I was forty-three years old, six foot one, and just under two hundred pounds, but I didn't want to bounce my muscles off of his.

I stepped next to him and we watched the firefighters deal with the remains of his car. It looked like a burned carcass, a large grazing animal, a buffalo, maybe a small elephant—bury it in a pit with hot coals for a week, buy buns, invite the neighbors. Stone didn't seem to notice me.

"I used to be a cop," I said.

He glanced at me like I was an innocent nuisance. "That so?" He looked back at the car.

"Yeah. Got fired. I plowed my cruiser into a newsstand at three in the morning. I was drunk—I did that back then—so something had to give. No one was hurt and my car, unlike yours, didn't burn. But magazines and newspapers filled the air like a blizzard."

He glanced at me again, barely tolerating me. "Do you mind?"

"Sorry," I said. I nodded at his car. "Tough luck."

He nodded once, apology accepted.

"I'll tell you a story, though," I said and he grimaced. "I knew this guy in the department—"

"Look," he said, "I'm sure you're a fine guy but my car burned and there's nothing you're gonna tell me that'll make me want to talk with you."

"Got it," I said.

We stood together and watched the firemen and the smoking car. "So this guy in the department," I said and Stone's shoulders tensed. "This guy had a problem. He played in a department softball league and every time he had a game a fellow in the neighborhood was screwing his wife."

Stone turned slowly from the car to my face. His eyes were cold, hard, dark.

"Now, this cop kept a Taser in his trunk. Against department regulations at the time, but he kept it. So his problem was this. He came home early from a game and found the neighbor in bed with his wife. Well, not in bed—they were in the kitchen, the wife on the kitchen counter and the neighbor—you get the picture."

Stone got the picture. He'd balled his hands into fists. Nice fists and only a couple of knuckles looked like they'd been broken, probably hitting the jaws of guys like me.

"The cop faced a hard question. Should he Taser the fellow, knowing one hundred percent he would lose his job in the department and spend the next four years working night shift as a security guard at Sears? Would it be worth it?"

"Listen, you fuck," Stone said. "I don't know what—"

"I'm Joe Kozmarski, Mr. Stone. Amy Samuelson's husband hired me to keep an eye on you."

That startled him about as much as a poke in the eye. But he said, "That asshole burned my car."

"Doesn't seem like something a guy like him would do," I said. "He's a regular altar boy." It was true, or almost. Greg Samuelson worked at Holy Trinity Church. When he wasn't burning cars, he surrounded himself with saints and saints-in-training.

Stone showed me one of his fists. "Tell your altar boy I'm going to fuckin' kill him."

The cop with the notebook returned. "Everything all right here?" He probably saved Stone and me from going a couple rounds.

As I crossed the street to my car, a Mercedes convertible that looked like Eric Stone's, but silver and without the flames, whipped around the corner. The driver was a thin man with a ponytail. A woman sat next to him in the passenger's seat in a bright red vest, looking like a fancy fishing lure. The Mercedes sped toward me, swerved a few feet away, and swung to the curb beside a fire truck.

THREE

LATELY I'D BEEN DREAMING of escape. From Chicago. From the camera I kept in front of me on the counters of cheap Chinese restaurants. From the trouble I got myself into. From my life. I'd heard about a shrimping village just south of the Florida-Georgia border, a place where the sun shined soft through the ocean mist and the air smelled like salt and engine oil and the life that trawl nets raised out of the sea.

I drove down LaSalle, a wide soulless street, banked by soulless residential towers. Downtown, the street dropped into a canyon of dark office buildings and dead-ended into the Chicago Board of Trade, a pyramid-roofed concrete giant that looked like it could rise and march up LaSalle, crushing everything that fell under its feet.

I turned and drove west to the Kennedy Expressway, headed north, and exited at Division, then turned toward Holy Trinity Church, where Greg Samuelson worked when he wasn't lighting Mercedes-Benzes on fire.

Holy Trinity was in an old Polish neighborhood that was

THE BAD KITTY LOUNGE

sliding fast to Mexican. A teamsters local, a Duks Red Hots hot-dog stand, and a school of cosmetology shouldered up to La Pasadita Taqueria and little *tiendas* in dirty old brick buildings. Depending on the weather and the mood, everyone might dance or everyone might fight. Holy Trinity Church stood at the edge of the neighborhood with a partial view of the expressway, its Polish name spelled out in gold letters over the door to the sanctuary—*Kościół Świętej Trójcy.*

Holy Trinity High School stuck out behind the church. A courtyard garden, dying in the cold October air, separated the church from three housing blocks for the priests and nuns who taught at the school. I parked on the street, climbed the steps, and tried the heavy steel doors that led to the sanctuary. They swung open. I had no excuse not to walk through them.

The chapel was bright and painted as fancy as a twelve-year-old in mascara. A painter had climbed a scaffold and covered the vaulted ceiling with fat, rosy-skinned angels frolicking in heavenly blue skies. A portrait showed Jesus and Mary wearing crowns, Jesus dressed like a little prince, Mary in a red and gold getup that made her look like a model from an old Imperial margarine commercial. Still, the place took your breath away—all the color and light in the middle of the graying neighborhood. I hadn't been inside a church since Dad died, but I crossed myself. Old habits and all, I couldn't help it.

A couple of women sat in the pinewood pews, praying or staring into the air. A thin, bald priest with a short beard was fiddling with a lighting fixture embedded in the ornate pulpit.

I went to him and asked if Greg Samuelson was around.

"In his office. Next to Sister Terrano's." He pointed to a door that led away from the pulpit.

The door opened into a narrow hall with a room on either side. A man in priest's black worked at a computer in one of them. At the end of the hall, another door led to a stairwell that went down to an undercroft and then more offices. The first office door, open a crack and marked by a brass name-plate, was Sister Judy Terrano's. The next door was Samuelson's.

I went in without knocking.

He sat at his desk working at a computer. He'd hung his blue jacket on a coat hook. A picture of Amy Samuelson, taken when she still had something to smile about with her husband, watched over him from on top of a file cabinet. The room smelled like the fruit and ammonia of a hundred years of furniture polish and floor scrubbing. Samuelson looked up from the computer and smiled with the innocence of a man who shared an office wall with a nun. "What's the news?" he said.

"News is that arson gets idiots like you thrown in jail. What were you thinking?"

"Oh," he said. "You saw that?"

"You paid me to watch your condo."

"I didn't see you there."

"You weren't supposed to."

He brightened. "Did you get pictures of my wife and Eric Stone?"

"I wouldn't worry about the pictures right now. I would worry about torching the Mercedes."

He put on the innocent face. "I've been here all morning."

"Stone knows you did it. The cops will figure it out if he doesn't kill you first."

He was crazy enough to laugh at that. "So, do you have the pictures?"

"I quit," I said. "I'll send you back your check. Find someone else to take the pictures."

"Come on," he said. "What else are you going to do with them?"

"Buy a gallon of gas and make a fire of my own."

I turned, ready to get back to my dreams of the Florida shrimping village, but Samuelson's boss, Sister Judy Terrano, stepped into the door. She was a light-skinned black woman, a couple years short of sixty, and wore a dress that, for a nun, showed plenty of leg. She had startling green eyes and tightly trimmed black hair curling gray.

Everyone in the city knew her. She kept herself in the news as the founder of a sexual abstinence program for inner-city girls. The press called her the Virginity Nun. A lot of people thought she was a nut, though some thought she deserved the Nobel Peace Prize. She served on the Mayor's Youth Commission and a half-dozen other city committees that dealt with teenagers and young adults. No matter who led the committees, the news cameras always went to her.

Now she stepped into the office, carrying a stack of file folders. She nodded to me and placed the folders on Samuelson's desk. "The clinic proposal and property records," she said to him. Then to me, "Sorry to interrupt," and moved again toward the door.

I said, "I have a question."

She turned and looked at me with her green eyes. They held me like she'd traveled miles just to see me.

"I used to be a cop," I said, "and a guy in the department had a problem." I told her the story that I'd told Eric Stone about the man, his wife, and their neighbor. She took it all in like it was a biblical parable. Samuelson sat at his desk with his mouth open. I ended with the same question I'd asked Stone. "The cop had to decide if he should Taser his fellow citizen. Should he have done it?"

She thought for a moment and said, "Absolutely."

I turned to Samuelson and said, "Forgiveness to the avenger, I guess." I followed the nun into the hall.

She paused by her door and turned with a sly smile. "Did your friend Taser the man?"

I shook my head. "He left the Taser in his trunk, packed a bag, and divorced his wife quietly."

Her smile dropped at the corners of her mouth. "Sad," she said.

"Is it?"

"Absolutely." She turned again to her door.

"I've got another question," I said.

Again the green eyes and the sly smile, as if she'd come to work hoping only to see me.

"Out of all the fights you could take on," I said, "why sex? Aren't there worse things?"

Her smile widened. "I have nothing against sex," she said. She put her hand on my arm. "But these girls don't know how to do it right. If a man isn't willing to lose his job as a policeman, if he isn't willing to humiliate himself for a woman he's having sex with, then why should she bother with him? If a woman isn't willing to die for her lover, she should stay home and take a hot bath. These girls don't understand that."

I blinked. "That's an unusual attitude for a nun."

She squeezed my wrist. "Is it?" she said, and she disappeared into her office.

FOUR

I DROVE EAST TOWARD Lake Michigan. If I turned south into the Loop, I could go to my office and write a refund check to Greg Samuelson. If I turned north, I could stop by the storefront where my ex-wife Corrine ran an urban landscaping business. We needed to talk. In the last couple months, we'd been picking up the pieces, seeing what we looked like together again. Then I'd screwed up and spent a night with my friend Lucinda and, though Corrine didn't know about it, I was pretty sure we were going to fall apart again.

Maybe Corrine needed to Taser Lucinda. Maybe she needed to Taser me.

I kept driving east. A strong wind was blowing into the city from the lake. That meant whitecaps would be battering the limestone slabs that the parks department had dumped to keep storms from undermining the lakefront luxury high-rises. On days like this, I sometimes drove to the lake to watch someone else take a hit. My car was a 1989 Skylark, with 165,000 miles and too little tread on the tires. It felt like home the way only an old car can. The heater hardly worked, but the afternoon sun on the vinyl felt fine. No place better to watch the lake pound on the city. No place better to dream of escape.

As I merged onto Lake Shore Drive, my phone rang. When I ran away to the Florida shrimping village, I would drop it in the ocean.

I answered and my ex-client Greg Samuelson said, "Can you come back?" His voice was quiet, worried.

"Huh? I told you, I'm done with you."

"You've—I'm in trouble—"

"Yeah, you're in trouble. You torched a Mercedes."

"You've—"

"Plenty of people to help you at the church. The priests. The Virginity Nun. The monks—Do you have monks? You can confess your arson if you want."

"Oh fuck!" he said.

The line went dead.

Yeah, I thought, oh fuck. He'd gotten that much right.

I kept driving. I could ignore the call. I'd already quit. I owed Greg Samuelson nothing.

But he'd sounded scared. Desperate.

Not my problem, I thought.

But I exited Lake Shore Drive.

Twenty-five minutes later, I knocked on Samuelson's office door at Holy Trinity.

Silence.

I knocked again and opened the door. His desk was clean, his computer off. He was gone—to a bar, home, out for a walk, wherever scared, desperate arsonists go when they leave work. That meant I could leave, too. I'd done my duty, more than it.

But I went to Sister Terrano's door and knocked on it.

More silence. So I walked in.

The sun shined through a window well covered by a sheer white curtain. A floor lamp and a desk lamp were on. Faded red carpet covered the floor. A large wooden desk stood in the middle of the room with a leather chair behind it. Papers, anti-abortion bumper stickers, posters, and T-shirts that said VIR-GINS ARE COOL were piled on top of the desk.

On one of the stacks of posters there was a head.

Greg Samuelson's.

Lying on its side the way you might rest your head to take a nap.

But a hole hung through the side of his face where he should have had a cheek. His bottom jaw was gone, God knows where. The rest of his body slumped forward onto the desk from the desk chair. His right hand was lying on a pile of T-shirts. So was a large pistol.

"Shit," I said.

I started toward him but couldn't get myself to go near. I went to the window, pulled away the sheer curtain, and looked through the window well at the blue sky. The window had been painted shut. My eyes teared. Samuelson was dead. I thought about Eric Stone threatening to kill him. I'd figured the threat was heat-of-the-moment. Why kill someone over a car? I took a couple of deep breaths and turned.

What I saw made me turn away again.

I took more deep breaths. Twenty, thirty, I don't know how many. I stood at the window a long time, but it wasn't enough—no amount of time ever would be. Then, because I knew I had to, I turned back to the room and looked.

A crucifix hung on the opposite wall, a wooden cross with a

carved Jesus in agony. Nails were hammered through his hands and feet. A crown of thorns stabbed into his forehead. Painted blood ran down his face like tears. He'd cocked his head to the side, his eyes looking to heaven, his mouth open in a huge *O*. A blue cloth covered his middle, exposing a bony left hip.

I lowered my eyes from the crucifix.

Judy Terrano was lying on the carpet. The Virginity Nun. She looked nothing like Jesus. Her dress was shoved up to her neck. Her underwear was beside her. She wore one black shoe. I didn't see the other. Her pubic hair was gray and bushy. She had no blood on her at all.

I forced myself to go to her.

She had great legs, legs that on a living woman would have drawn me close, and now, on a dead woman, terrified me. Her face was a bruised mask. Her green eyes were frozen, staring at the ceiling like she was looking for heaven but could see only hell. The whites of her eyes were marbled with the lines of broken blood vessels. I figured I knew what her neck would look like if I cleared her clothing from it. It would show the bruises of strangulation. Eyes don't bleed from reading in bad light.

Her chest was thrust up toward the ceiling and her breasts looked like heaven and desire. But on her belly, she had a big, fine-lined tattoo of a cat, its back arched, its tail raised like a furry *S*, its legs taut. The ink had faded, but the lines were sharp and clear. It looked like a cat in heat. Under the tattoo someone had scrawled two words in black marker: BAD KITTY.

I snorted. I couldn't help it. Then I sat on the floor by the dead nun and my eyes filled again with tears.

When I could stand up, I used my cell phone to call 911. The operator answered, and I rasped something about two bodies, a woman and a man.

"Yes," I said, "I'm sure they're dead. I'm very sure."

I stumbled back toward the desk where Greg Samuelson's head rested on a stack of bloody posters.

"Yes," I said, "I'll stay calm. Yes, I'll stay on the line."

Then Samuelson's hand moved, the one on the pile of T-shirts, the one by the gun.

I yelled and threw the cell phone at it, that hand which was attached to a man I was sure was dead. How could he be alive with the bottom half of his face missing?

Less than five minutes later paramedics and cops ran in. After the first of them arrived, a priest peeked around the door frame. His face paled. Sweat broke on his forehead. He disappeared from the doorway. But in the hallway, beyond the noise of the police and paramedics, he sobbed for the dead nun. Maybe for the rest of us, too.

FIVE

DETECTIVE STAN FLEMING LED the investigation. He came ten minutes after the first cops arrived. I knew him well. He'd dated Corrine before we'd gotten married and he'd started calling her again as soon as we'd divorced. We were friends so it was okay, right? he'd said when he'd told me he was still interested in her. No hard feelings, right? I couldn't blame him for his taste, and Corrine and I had split up so what business of mine were his calls? But still I'd wanted to punch him in the teeth. "Yeah," I'd said, "no hard feelings."

Stan had on a gray windbreaker over a blue shirt that he'd buttoned tight over his chest. He had a strong chin and cheekbones that I'd heard women say made him look like Hugh Jackman. Not only was he good-looking, he was smart. The department sent only their best for big-press events like this.

A bunch of other cops were in the room along with the paramedics. Two of them had Greg Samuelson on the floor and were working on his vitals. Another was injecting something into his leg. A cop standing close to Samuelson kept brushing his hand against his service pistol. Samuelson moaned softly and rasped into the plastic respirator cup that the paramedics had fixed over what remained of his face.

Stan Fleming glanced around the room, made sure the other cops were keeping Judy Terrano's body secure, and ambled over. He held out his hand and gave me a grim smile. "Hey, Joe."

"Hey."

He asked what had happened and how I was involved, and I gave him the short version and admitted that I'd called in the killings.

He moved close. "I know you, Joe, and I know you like to freelance. But you've got to tell me everything you know, what you did, and what you saw."

I nodded. "Okay. Every detail."

He smiled warmer. For the next twenty minutes, I described everything I could remember of the hour or so between when Greg Samuelson lit Eric Stone's Mercedes on fire and when I threw a cell phone at him after calling 911. Stan nodded when I told him that Eric Stone threatened to kill Samuelson. Maybe this would be one of the easy ones.

But I said, "I don't see why Stone would kill the nun."

Stan grimaced and thought. "Fine. Then Stone didn't do it. Greg Samuelson killed the nun and attempted suicide."

The forensics team arrived. They wore no bulletproof vests and their skin had a look that said they spent more time inside smelling rotting corpses than out on the streets. A clean-faced man in olive pants, an olive button-down shirt, and a big watch led the team. He looked like a forest ranger.

He stepped into the middle of the room and looked at Sister Terrano. "This, ladies and gentlemen, is a fucking mess," he said. Another forensics cop took photographs of Terrano's body, the desk where Samuelson had been sitting, and almost everything else in the room.

A third cop shouldered between the paramedics and used a glue-lift kit on Samuelson's hands and fingertips. The paramedics watched him, astounded. "What?" the cop said. "You swab this boy down, there's no more residue, no fibers, no nothing but shit."

"Get the hell out of the way," said one of the paramedics.

The cop took his time.

There were procedures for moments like this, step-by-step protocols that everyone should follow. But in the excitement and fear of a high-profile murder, even the best cops were getting sloppy.

The man in olive went to work on Sister Terrano. He tracked up and down her body with a penlight like he was counting her moles. Seven or eight times he stopped and called the photographer over to take photos.

I went to watch him.

He peeled the nun's dress down from her neck. A deep bruise ringed her throat. He measured the width of the bruise, brushed the skin for fiber residue, and let her dress rest around her neck again. He shined a light into her nostrils, her mouth, her throat, and each of her ears, and he made notes in a notepad. He spent some time with the black cat tattoo and the scrawled words on her belly, but if they offered him anything he didn't show it. Then he parted her legs.

"Makes you want to cry," I said.

He looked up. "Who the hell are you?"

"Joe Kozmarski," I said. "I found her and Samuelson."

"So?"

"So I didn't ask to find them."

"Get out," he said.

I gestured toward Judy Terrano's chest, thrust up slightly toward the ceiling. "When you roll her over, you'll find her missing shoe."

He gave the idea about a moment's thought, then pointed at the door. "Out."

I could take a hint.

I was ducking under the crime-scene tape when Stan Fleming put a hand on my shoulder and squeezed.

"Where are you going?"

I pointed my thumb at the man in olive. "Smokey the Bear told me to get out."

"Stay awhile in case I need you."

"I feel very conflicted," I said.

"Don't be a smart-ass, all right?" He turned away.

"I need some air," I told him.

"Fine," he said over his shoulder. "Go out in the hall with the dogs. But don't go far."

I ducked under the tape and stepped out of the room.

Cops and clergy crowded the hall, but the sobbing priest was gone. The air felt good away from Judy Terrano's office. I leaned against a wall as far from the others as I could get and ran through my memory, trying to remember anything I'd missed when I'd told Stan my story. I'd gotten to the point of approaching the nun's body when a loud commotion started inside the room. Two men were shouting. Heavy furniture tipped. I made my way to the door. Inside, a cop was arguing with the paramedics about removing Samuelson. He was holding a set of handcuffs, trying to reach around a paramedic. The paramedic kept blocking him. The desk chair was lying on its side. The posters and T-shirts were scattered across the floor. Who needed protocols?

Stan stepped in and got the paramedics to agree to let an officer ride in the ambulance with them and Samuelson. No handcuffs. Then a couple of cops moved the desk out of the way, and the paramedics carried Samuelson out of the room and down the hall. His face was pale and bloody and looked like it already had started the final decay.

Stan appeared beside me. "How the hell did you know about the shoe?" Smokey the Bear had reported our conversation.

"No woman sticks her chest out like that unless she's excited, and one thing Sister Terrano isn't is excited. I'm guessing she fell on the shoe or got strangled on top of it."

"And the significance of that is?"

"I don't see any. You?"

He breathed out long and shook his head. "None that I see."

"How about the tattoo and the Magic Marker on her belly?"

Stan screwed up his lips. "I've seen stranger things but not many. Looks to me like the killer went hunting for the tattoo and then put a caption on it."

"Like a sick joke."

"The tattoo's old. It says the Virginity Nun had a history. Our forensics guy figures she got it thirty or forty years ago. He says it's first-class work. Fine detailing. Great application. She would've paid top dollar. He says only a handful of artists in the city could do it now, probably less back then. The penned letters were made with a Sharpie Permanent Fine Point, and they're new, no more than an hour old."

"He can tell a lot with his magnifying glass."

"He's into tattoos," Stan said. "And we found the marker on the floor."

"How about the rest?" I asked. "Was she raped?"

He shrugged. "Forensics says there's no evidence of it." He glanced around to make sure no one else was listening. "But he also says the Virginity Nun was no virgin. Not for a long time."

"She'll have some confused followers. What about Samuelson?"

"What about him? Like I said, attempted suicide. Either he found the nun or more likely he did her himself and then put the gun in his mouth."

I shook my head. "If he had a gun, why go through the trouble of strangling her? Why not shoot her, then himself?"

"Could be he didn't plan to kill her. He got mad. It happened."

"Could be," I said.

"No?"

"He's a calm guy even when others would get stressed."

"A calm guy who shoots himself?"

"After he torched Eric Stone's car, he made a telephone call and then walked away, no rush, no worry."

"So, what happened? Stone strangled the nun, scribbled on her stomach, shot Samuelson, and left the gun on the desk?"

"Hell, I don't know," I said.

Stan told me again to stick around, then disappeared back into Judy Terrano's office.

But I'd had enough. I shouldered past a priest who was standing in the hall exit and found my way to a side door.

Outside, a dozen news vans lined the street. Their remote-broadcast masts extended high into the air, cables snaking to the top. Orange and white police barricades with yellow tape strung between them blocked the church entrances. Streetlights were on, fighting against the sinking sunlight. A late afternoon wind whipped cold. Clusters of neighborhood residents stood together, talking excitedly or watching the cops at the barricades like they were waiting for a parade. Reporters huddled near the vans, bouncing on their toes, their hands shoved deep in their pockets. Others sat inside the vans drinking coffee from Styrofoam cups. A couple of the younger ones schmoozed with the cops, looking for tips that the cops either didn't have or weren't going to share, though the rumors about what had happened inside were hot enough to keep everyone anxious.

Attention turned to me when I came out the door, and three reporters scurried over to talk as I ducked under the tape. They all spoke at once, asking if the man they'd seen carried out on a stretcher worked for Sister Terrano, if Sister Terrano had shot the man, if the man had shot Sister Terrano.

"I can't even save myself," I said. "I don't know why you think I can help you." They exchanged quick, nervous looks and backed away as quickly as they'd come.

I climbed into my car and turned on the engine. News vans had boxed me in on three sides. I hit the horn and waited. No one moved toward the vans. I hit the horn again. Again nothing.

I shifted into reverse and backed the car until it tapped the bumper of the van behind me. Top-heavy with the broadcast mast, the van wobbled. I cut the wheel, shifted, and tapped the van in front. I went back and forth like that for a while, gaining a couple of inches each time and making the masts sway like trees in a heavy wind. The guy who drove the van in front of me eventually noticed and ran over from where he'd been standing with a reporter and a cop. He yelled at me through the window. I waved at him and cleared the van bumper, pulled my Skylark onto the sidewalk, drove it half a block, and dropped back off the curb onto the street.

I breathed in and filled my lungs with the sweet, musty air of the old car. But deep as I breathed, I tasted the salt and metal of Samuelson's blood and Judy Terrano's nakedness. The street stretched in front of me, but in my mind I saw the jawless face of a man who'd shot himself and a tattoo of a big black cat in the grip of pleasure and pain.

SIX

THE LAST OF THE sun was dying from the sky when I drove over the crumbling asphalt in the alley next to my house. An old elm grew over the garage. Disease had wiped out most of the elms in Chicago when I was a kid, and I bought the house as much for this tree that had survived when city workers chainsawed the others as for the building I lived in. As I walked to the house, the tree swayed over me in the cold wind and blanketed the yard in darkness.

But inside the house the lights and television were on as I unlocked the back door. I closed my eyes and made my face calm, at peace with my life and the world.

A tall, dark-eyed eleven-year-old boy came around the corner into the kitchen and skidded into me in his socks. He had a smile that could make arsonists and dead nuns blush and hide their heads. "Hey, Joe," he said.

I gave him a hug. "Hey, Jason."

He was my cousin's son. She'd run off with a guy who worked at the Jacksonville Port Authority. Jason's dad was long gone.

Everyone else in the family thought Jason would benefit from the good influence of living with a man in the family: me—though why they thought I was a good influence, I didn't know.

He told me about his day at school. I didn't tell him about Holy Trinity. He said a kid named Tim Naley had been holding a lighter under the butts of classmates as they worked the combinations on their lockers. I didn't tell him about Greg Samuelson using a Bic to torch a $65,000 Mercedes. I said, "Tim Naley's a jerk, and one day someone's going to let him know it."

He nodded, tight-lipped, like he knew it, and went to get his backpack. He pulled out a rubber-banded roll of yellow paper. It was a painting of a face that I recognized as a skewed version of his mom. "Hey," I said, "that's great."

He smiled at the picture. "We had Picasso Day in art."

He sat at the kitchen table and did his homework while I thawed hamburger meat in the microwave and turned on the burner under a skillet. I'd gotten out the buns and put a pad of butter on the skillet when the phone rang. I'd been having bad luck with phones, so I let it ring until Jason looked at me. I answered and my mom said, "You're on TV. Again." She said it the way she might have said, "Your mug shot's in the post office. Again."

I said, "Did the shirt I was wearing make me look fat?"

"Come for dinner tonight."

"I just started burgers."

"Joe?"

"Yes?"

"Come for dinner."

"The news cameras caught me walking out of the church, huh?"

"And ramming your car into two news vans."

"I didn't ram them. I tapped them."

"You rammed them. And then you made your getaway down the sidewalk."

"It wasn't a getaway."

"What time will you be here?"

I glanced at Jason scribbling answers on a worksheet. "We're leaving the house right now."

Mom lived in a yellow, one-story bungalow on Leland, the house where I grew up. When we pulled into her driveway, knob-shaped boxwoods along the path leading to the front door shimmered silver in the headlights. The skinny white pine by the street leaned south in the October wind like it knew better than to stick around for winter.

When Mom opened the door, the smell of simmering meat and vegetables drifted out. A loaf of bread, a salad, and a pot of *golonka* stew waited for us on the dining room table.

"Two days it takes to make this right," she said as she ladled the *golonka* into bowls.

"But you managed it in the hour and a half since you saw the news," I said.

"I work wonders. Anyway, I didn't say I made it right."

Jason picked a piece of meat out of his bowl. "Is this a foot?"

"It's a hock," Mom said. "Eat it."

He did.

She said nothing about Holy Trinity during dinner, but I caught her watching me like she'd seen cracks in my surface and worried about them getting bigger. After we cleared the plates, she poured coffee and asked Jason to take out the garbage.

She put both elbows on the table and rested her chin on the

backs of her hands. "Why were you at the church when Judy Terrano got killed?"

I sighed and leaned back in my chair. "I wasn't. I came afterward. I was working for her assistant, the man who shot himself. A divorce case."

She sighed, too, like that relieved her. But she said, "Did you have your gun?"

My Glock 23 had been sleeping in my glove compartment all day. "This was a divorce—"

"Your father would have had his."

"Please don't," I said.

"He would have."

"He wouldn't, because cops don't work divorce cases."

"He worked North Side, South Side, and West Side, but wherever he worked he took his gun."

"Can we change the subject?"

"No, we can't. These people—these people you're working with are dangerous."

"Mom," I said, trying my best, "these people are a nun and her assistant. Something went wrong today, and it's sad and ugly and all that, but it didn't happen because they're dangerous."

She glared at me like I was mocking her. "I know who they are. Do you know Judy Terrano's background?"

"I was working for her assistant, not her."

"And what do you know about him?"

I knew a large caliber bullet had taken off the bottom half of his face. I knew he shot himself, or, if he didn't, Eric Stone did. I knew he burned a $65,000 Mercedes. I knew he loved his wife. "Nothing," I said. "But Judy Terrano was a nun."

"I know what she was."

Jason came in from dumping the garbage, and our talk ended.

Over dessert, Mom went back to watching my face for cracks. When she kissed me good night, she whispered, "Always carry your weapon."

"Come for dinner on Friday," I answered.

"I don't eat takeout," she said.

"I'll cook."

She kissed me again. "I'll eat beforehand."

Jason and I got back to my house a little after 10:30. As soon as he'd changed into his pajamas, I made a show of looking at my watch and announced, "Bedtime."

He shook his head. "From now on I'm going to stay awake at night."

"Like an owl?"

He nodded.

"And for your two A.M. lunch, you'll eat what?—mice?"

"I'll call out for pizza."

I picked him up over my shoulder.

He laughed. "What are you doing?"

"I'm carrying you to your room. It's time."

I dropped him on his bed and turned out the light. When I got to his door, he said, "Did you know aphids can have babies thirty times in one summer?"

"Good night, Jason," I said.

"I saw you on TV this afternoon."

I flipped back on the light. "You and everyone else." I sat on his bed and told him what had happened at the church, told him how sad it was when such things happened, reassured him that he was safe. He took it all in and his eyes said he understood it the way I would have hoped.

I flipped off his light and said good night again. When I reached his door, he said, "Joe?"

"Yes?"

"Can I ask you a question?"

"Anytime."

"Why did you ram those news vans?"

I ROLLED AROUND IN bed, sleepless. When I closed my eyes, I saw Greg Samuelson, bloodier than a dead man, stretched across Judy Terrano's desk, a gun inches from his fingers. I saw Judy Terrano stretched across the floor, a big black cat tattooed on her belly, graffiti under it.

I tried to change the topic. I thought about the women who'd made love to me. My ex, Corrine, who I loved and who loved me, though we'd broken every promise we'd ever made to each other. A twenty-year-old with black hair and blue eyes, whose name I barely knew. Lucinda Juarez, though we'd spent only one night together.

But as I drifted toward sleep, as I approached the edge where I would fall into the warm hole where consciousness would shed like a dirty second skin, flashes of a naked, brutalized woman, her dress pulled up around her neck, and a man with a hole in his head raced through my mind. I jerked awake and turned on the light.

When we were married, Corrine had talked me down at times like this. I grabbed the phone and dialed her number. The phone rang and rang. Maybe she was lying awake in the dark, listening to it ring. Maybe she was lying in some guy's arms, ignoring the sound. Maybe she was making love with him and they heard nothing but each other. Maybe the guy was Detective Stan Fleming.

Ah shit, I thought, and I turned out the light. I thought about the burning Mercedes. I thought about Samuelson and his gun, and about Sister Terrano, her tattoo, and the inked words, BAD KITTY. I thought about the forensics man who dressed like Smokey the Bear and inspected the skin cells of a dead nun, all in a day's work.

I thought about a lot. All of it exhausted me, and none of it made me tired enough to sleep.

At 2:00 A.M., I considered ordering out for mice. I smiled at Jason sleeping a room away. The last time I looked at the clock, it said 2:13 A.M. I slept then and dreamed of nothing at all—a deep nothingness—and woke up frightened.

SEVEN

THE CLOCK SAID 6:40, and the first light was glowing through the window blinds. I pulled up the covers and fought against the morning. When that didn't work, I put on shorts, a hooded sweatshirt, and running shoes. I checked on Jason, who was sleeping the sleep envied by guys like me, and ducked outside into the morning chill.

I ran north to Montrose and west toward the North Branch of the Chicago River. The wind had dropped overnight and I ran hard until I broke a sweat. I stopped and stretched on the bridge over the river. The river keepers had been scrubbing a hundred and fifty years of chemicals from the riverbed, and a fish or two had been spotted testing itself against the sluggish current. Now and then a pleasure boat motored past on summer days. Signs for luxury apartments were advertising river views. But the water still looked as brown and dirty as the city was old.

I ran south into Horner Park. The park was fine for a run in the early morning, great for an afternoon softball game, and not a bad place to buy crack after dark. By the field house, a granite bas relief of ex–Governor Horner, with a crowd of orphans and widows around him and an image of Justice behind him, watched over the park. On cold, windy evenings, the crack dealers set up shop in the shelter of the monument.

I picked up my pace and ran home.

At the curb in front of my house, a couple of guys in baseball caps sat in an idling Lexus SUV. The driver had licorice black skin, and the guy on the passenger side had skin a couple of shades lighter. I nodded to them. The passenger nodded back and unrolled his window. He gave me a smile and I slowed to see what he had to say.

He said nothing.

He lifted a nine-millimeter pistol and pointed the barrel at my belly.

His smile fell, and then he said, "Bang!"

EIGHT

AFTER THE BURNED RUBBER of spinning tires faded
into the cold air, I swallowed my heart and let myself into my
house. "What kind of jerk-ass stunt was that?" I muttered, and
Jason answered, "What kind of jerk-ass stunt was what?"

I joined him for a bowl of cereal, shaved and showered, and,
good son that I was, tucked my Glock into an over-the-shoulder
rig as I got dressed. No more neighborly fellowship for me this
morning.

After dropping off Jason at school, I drove downtown to my
office on South Wabash. My office was on the eighth floor of an
eight-story building, the only office on a floor occupied by a
secretarial school. The school taught inner-city women who'd
received federal education grants or state assistance to get off
welfare. It took the government checks, gave the women a few
lessons on a PC, then kicked them out the door back to the
streets.

I parked in the alley next to the building, bought a newspaper out of a box, and went inside. The two guys who'd pulled

a pistol on me in front of my house were standing next to the elevator. They were good-looking guys, one in his young twenties, the other a few years older. The younger one had three or four inches on me. I had an inch on the other one, the one who'd waved the nine-millimeter pistol at me. The tall one carried a knapsack.

I pulled out my Glock, nodded to them.

When the elevator came they stepped in and stood on either side of me. We rode up past the third floor in silence. Then I said, "You guys got names?"

"Robert," said the tall one.

"Jarik," said the other.

"My name's Joe Koz—"

"We know who you are," said the tall one.

"Of course you do."

We got off at the eighth. The secretarial school was between classes, and women filled the corridor, so I held my gun close. The women gave Robert and Jarik eyes that they'd never given me. Corrine used to tell me I looked like Lech Walesa from the Solidarity days but with abs and forget the moustache. Whatever I looked like, I didn't get the doe eyes that these guys got.

At the end of the corridor I unlocked my door and let us into my office. The single window looked east over the El tracks and, through a gap between the opposing buildings, toward Lake Michigan. The view made up for the cheap furniture. I went to the coffeemaker and made a point of taking my time about getting it started, then went around to the other side of my desk and sat down. I put my Glock on the desk to remind them that they should act nice.

The one who called himself Robert unzipped the top of the

knapsack and removed a stack of crisp twenty-dollar bills wrapped with a gold elastic band. He set it on the desk and we all looked at it as if it might get up and do a little dance. It wasn't the biggest stack of money I'd ever seen but it was big enough to interest me.

"That's for you to stop investigating Judy Terrano's death," Robert said.

The money surprised me about as much as the nine-millimeter they'd pointed at me. So I got up and stuck a coffee cup under the trickling coffeemaker spout and then went back to my desk. I didn't offer Robert and Jarik a cup.

I said, "I'm not investigating Judy Terrano's death."

"Right," said Robert. "Three thousand should help you remember that."

"What do you care about her?"

They exchanged glances. "Does it matter?" Robert asked.

"Probably. She seems to have had friends in a lot of places. I take it you know I was there yesterday."

Jarik laughed. "Yeah, the TV's been showing your ugly face night and day."

Robert smiled. "We're impressed by how you do business."

"What do you know about how I do business?"

"We know what you did to the TV vans."

"I didn't do anything to the vans!"

They grinned at each other.

I said, "What's it matter if I investigate Sister Terrano? The cops are all over this."

"They have the guy with the bullet in his face. They're not investigating anything."

"Greg Samuelson. Do *you* think he did it?"

Robert waved that off. "'Course not. If he's got a gun—and

we know he's got a gun—why strangle her? Why not shoot her, then shoot himself? It's a hell of a lot easier."

The point I'd made yesterday. "Maybe," I said. "So why did Samuelson shoot himself if he didn't kill the nun?"

Robert glanced at Jarik, then back at me. "You think he shot himself?"

I didn't necessarily. "If not him, who?"

Robert shrugged. "The guy his wife's fucking. Eric Stone."

I shook my head. "Stone in the news, too?"

"No," Robert said, "Stone's not in the news."

"Then how do you know—?"

"Look," said Jarik. "You want the money or not?"

"Sure I want the money. Who's backing you? Or did the two of you dig into your bank accounts on your own?"

Robert glanced at Jarik and said, "The man would rather not identify himself."

"So you're paying me off for someone whose motives I don't know?"

Robert nodded. "That's about it."

I nodded, too. "Five thousand."

Robert reached into his pack and pulled out two thinner stacks of twenties, each wrapped with another gold band. He put them side by side on the desk.

"What if I say six?"

He shrugged. "I reach into my bag and pull out more money."

"Tell me something. What was the point of your surprise visit outside my house this morning?"

"We want you to remember that we know who you are and where to find you."

I thought about that. "Nah. I won't take your money. Put it away and get the hell out of here."

Robert looked disappointed. Jarik looked angry. "I think you should reconsider," said Robert.

"Nothing to reconsider. It works like this. If someone comes to my office and makes an offer I don't like, I say, 'sorry.' I usually say it with a handshake and a smile but those are optional. So that's what I'm saying to you. 'Sorry.'" I smiled when I said it but I didn't offer them my hand.

They exchanged a look. Robert slipped the money into the knapsack, slung the knapsack over his shoulder, and turned toward the door. I felt pretty good about myself until Robert spun back. He held a pistol. He pointed it at my belly.

"No," he said. His voice was like a dry well. "It works like this. We make an offer, we give you the money, and you take it."

Jarik said, "Uh-huh."

My Glock was on my desk. If I grabbed it, I probably could squeeze off a shot before I died, but then two of us would be dead and that wouldn't help anyone.

Robert put the knapsack on the desk. "You do what you want with the money. You wipe your dick with it or you spend it getting drunk or high 'cause that's what the word on you is. Are you still into all that, Joe? Or maybe you're clean now, and you buy football tickets and take that little nephew of yours out for a nice afternoon."

I heard the threat in the last bit. They could roll down a window and point a pistol at Jason as easily as at me. "I don't like you knowing so much about me," I said.

"We don't want you to like it."

I thought about that. "Okay," I said.

"Okay what?"

"Okay, I'll take your money. I won't investigate Judy Terrano."

"Yeah?"

"Yeah."

"Okay, then."

Robert put the stacks of twenties on my desk again, and he and Jarik left. They didn't say another word. They didn't give me a phone number where I could reach them if I had questions or second thoughts. I didn't ask them for one.

The sensible thing would have been to put the money in the bank and take a vacation. I'd already quit working for Samuelson, and I'd never planned to investigate Judy Terrano. I could sign Jason out of school for a week and take him fishing in Florida. That would be safe. Sensible.

I tucked my Glock into my over-the-shoulder rig and slipped on my jacket, leaving the cash on my desk. The lights at the end of the hall said the elevator was at the fourth floor and heading down. A sign warned that if you opened the door to the emergency stairwell next to the elevator shaft an alarm would ring. It was a lie. I took the steps two at a time.

NINE

ROBERT AND JARIK DROVE fast through the morning
traffic, shifting lanes just before delivery trucks put on their
brakes in front of them, accelerating through intersections. I
followed a few car lengths back. There's no such thing as an
invisible tail. If a driver is looking for you, you'll be seen. Apparently Robert and Jarik weren't looking.

We went west out of the Loop, glided across three lanes onto
the entrance ramp to the Dan Ryan, and sped south. Ten minutes later we exited into Beverly, a tree-lined neighborhood,
once middle-class Irish, now mostly middle-class black.

I figured the money that Robert and Jarik put on my desk
came from someone who'd ordered them to persuade me to
take it as a payoff. Who was backing them? Who wanted Judy
Terrano's murder to be pinned on Greg Samuelson? The real
killer?

Robert and Jarik pulled up next to a large, yellow house and
climbed out of the SUV. I drove past and, a half block away,
swung to the curb. I gave them a minute and walked back to

the yellow house. The yard was clean and neat, the lawn raked and green, the trees bright with fall color. An autumn wreath hung on the front door.

I knocked on the door.

After a long time a very dark-skinned housekeeper in her eighties opened it. The edges of her eyes drooped like they'd been weighed down by a century of tears. She said, "Yeesss?"

"I'm here to see Robert and Jarik," I said.

Her jaw hardened. "Are you certain?"

I said I was.

"Very well." She stood aside, let me in, and closed the door.

The front hall was bright and tiled with slate. The air smelled like cedar smoke. A heavy mahogany sculpture of a naked girl stood to the left inside the entrance with breasts so perky you could hang hats on them.

The housekeeper led me up the hall and knocked on a closed door. The door opened a crack and the head of a kid in his late teens appeared. The woman said, "A man is here for Robert and Jarik."

The kid disappeared behind the door. I was tired of the show, so I reached for the knob, but the woman stepped in my way and hissed, "Patience."

The kid opened the door again.

A tall black man, dressed all in gray, his broad head shaved bald, stood by a large, dark-wood desk. He looked ninety or ninety-five years old at least, but his chest was broad and he stood straight and solid. Robert and Jarik stood behind the tall man. If they were surprised to see me, they didn't show it. Another man, about forty years old, sat in a wheelchair. He was an enormous man in vertically striped pants and a horizontally striped shirt. He stared at the tall man with dull eyes and a dull smile, and slowly and silently clapped big long hands. Saffron drapes, bunched at the bottom, were pulled shut over what must have been a large window. A black-and-gold-patterned mud cloth hung on the wall behind the desk. A stick of cedar incense wafted into the air from a tray on a sideboard. The room looked like a movie set for a 1970s film about an island dictator.

"Ah, Mr. Kozmarski," said the old man with a warm smile, as if he'd expected me.

I nodded. "And you are?"

"I'm William DuBuclet."

His name flashed back to me from when I was a kid. William DuBuclet had been a controversial leader in black Chicago from the early sixties until the eighties, starting in the civil rights movement when he'd pushed for a mix of violent and peaceful action, mostly violent. Later, if I remembered right, DuBuclet had gone back to school and written a book on ghetto politics. He'd eventually become a power broker who'd helped elect Chicago's first black mayor.

"I thought you were dead," I said.

With a gentle smile, he admitted, "A common misconception. Some mornings even I'm not certain. But as you see, I'm still here."

"And still stirring the pot."

He nodded. "When I think the pot's worth stirring and I have enough energy to stir it."

"Like now, for instance. Why are you concerned about Judy Terrano's death?" I asked.

With the same gentle smile, he asked, "Did you know her?"

"Barely," I admitted. "Mostly what I read in the paper. I take it you knew her?"

43

"Very well. She was an extraordinary woman, one of the most brilliant I've known. Her death is an enormous loss. Everyone loved her and not with a normal love either. With passion. I never knew a man who refused to give her what she asked for."

"You'll have to sign up to speak at her funeral."

He nodded once, ignoring my tone. "Yes, I may have to."

"Why don't you want me investigating her killing?"

"Like everyone else, Sister Terrano lived a complicated life." He emphasized the word *complicated* like it carried a history of grief. "In recent years, it became more complicated. It's sometimes better to be able to think about our heroes in simple terms."

"What exactly complicated her life?"

He gave me a knowing smile, like he figured I already was in on the secret. "This is my pot to stir," he said. "If too many people stick their hands in, everything gets messy. I want to resolve this my way."

"You'll have a hard time convincing the police to keep their hands out."

He shook his head impatiently. "They won't look further than Samuelson."

I looked at him unconvinced.

"I know that your father was a policeman and that you, for a time, were, too," he said, "but I—"

"How did you learn about me and my dad?"

"I have deep connections and old ones to this city. I make a few telephone calls and I find out what I need to know."

"I don't think I like your knowing about me."

He smiled a thin smile. "No disrespect, but I also know the police from a time when a dog could get more justice in this city than a black man—or a black woman, even a famous black woman. The police will take the fastest path, and that path is Greg Samuelson."

"How do you know Samuelson didn't do it?"

"I'm not naive. I made my calls and heard details that weren't widely reported. About the writing on her stomach. About the events leading up to the killing. And about the medical examiner's conclusions. The man they've charged had no history and no likelihood of doing this kind of—"

"He'd just torched a Mercedes."

"He burned the car so that he wouldn't have to confront his wife's lover. He didn't wish to hurt another person, or, if he did, he didn't have it in him to do so."

I said, "I don't know his psychology but it seems to me that you don't either."

"For similar reasons I don't believe he would have raped her."

"She wasn't raped."

"Have you read this morning's paper?"

"Robert and Jarik interrupted me before I got around to it."

"She was raped."

"Not from what I know."

He shrugged. "He would have shot her, not strangled her."

I nodded. "Robert's argument, too, and not a bad one."

"I'm confident in my assessment."

"Overconfident."

"What do *you* think, Mr. Kozmarski? Did Samuelson do it?"

I shrugged. "I don't know what to think."

He considered me for a while. "They say the bruising is consistent all the way around her neck. You don't get that from using the hands. Only a garrote will do that."

"So?"

"The police found nothing that could have made that bruise. Unless Samuelson raped and strangled her, left to hide the garrote, then came back to the office and shot—"

"Okay," I said, "so Samuelson didn't do it."

"But the DA will charge him."

"Maybe," I said. "I'm guessing you've also heard that Samuelson was threatened by Eric Stone."

"Of course. But what did Stone have against Sister Terrano?"

"I thought you might tell me."

He dismissed that with a wave.

"Why didn't you come to my office to see me yourself?" I asked.

"I'm ninety-six years old. I spend my days caring for my grandson." He gestured to the big, smiling man in the wheelchair. "I don't get out a lot."

I looked DuBuclet up and down. He wore the unworried expression of a man used to getting things his way. "I don't know who you are," I said.

"You can find out all you want to know about me from the newspaper files."

"And what's with the show here? The closed drapes. The incense. The staff opening and shutting your doors for you."

He smiled. "The sunlight troubles my old eyes, Mr. Kozmarski, and so the drapes remain closed at my optometrist's orders. The 'staff' are my family, biological and ideological. It means a great deal to me to have family near at this time in my life. As for the incense, it may be a pretension, but it's one I won't easily give up. I find that as I've grown older the city stinks to me. The South Side, and this neighborhood, and my neighbors—they smell like a rotting animal. If the incense doesn't cover the stink completely, it allows me to forget it for a while."

DuBuclet had plausible reasons for thinking Samuelson was innocent of Judy Terrano's killing. But I didn't trust him. He didn't fool me with his tired old-man act. His eyes were alive—he was thinking and scheming like he planned to be around for fifty more years. And like he planned to operate the city from behind the big closed curtain of his house. He was no Wizard of Oz who would shrink into a laughable midget once you pulled his curtain away. His smile scared me. But it also attracted me and I found myself wanting to get close to this man who, at ninety-six, saw reason to stir the pot of this big, stinking city and maybe had the energy and money to make things happen that could and should have happened years ago.

I said, "So you want me to forget about Judy Terrano?"

He nodded. "That's what I want."

"I'll try," I said.

The big man reached out a large hand and shook mine with a heavy grip. He said, "You do that."

TEN

THE SECRETARIAL SCHOOL STUDENTS kept their eyes to themselves when I walked back down the corridor alone to my office. Three stacks of twenties waited on my desk for me to riffle them, but I left them alone. The morning paper, its pages still creased, was lying on the desk near the money. The red light on my answering machine flashed but I ignored it.

I went to the window and looked east. Across the street through the crack between the insurance building and the building to the north of it, the waves on Lake Michigan danced in the late-morning sunlight. The wedge of light and water looked like a path to somewhere I would like to go if only I could step through my window and float through the gap without falling. Just looking at the wedge made me feel good. I stood watching the light and water for a long time until I noticed a man in the corner office across the street staring at me from his window. I waved. He flipped me off and went to his desk.

I figured that meant it was time for me to go to mine.

The front-page headline in the *Chicago Tribune* said,

VIRGINITY NUN KILLED, with a subhead, CHASTITY ADVOCATE AS-
SAULTED. In the article Stan Fleming got his name mentioned
twice along with some punchy lines about the shock this murder had caused to himself, the city, and the world. Without
using the word *rape*, he mentioned "an especially disturbing
sexual assault on Sister Terrano."

I trusted Stan but I wondered what he was up to. He'd said
that the forensics cop had told him that no rape had occurred.
Either the forensics cop had changed his mind or Stan had
figured on his own that Judy Terrano's naked body justified
the accusation. Or, with Greg Samuelson already lying in the
hospital in custody, he might have figured he could benefit
from the public thinking Samuelson was a sexual monster.

The article didn't mention the black cat tattoo or the Magic
Marker on Judy Terrano's body. I hadn't expected it to.

It did say Greg Samuelson was in critical condition at Rush
Medical Center, under police guard, and an unnamed source
said he might make it. He'd lost blood and he would stay in the
ICU for a couple of days, but they'd seen worse. With him in
that shape, the district attorney's office could take their time
about charging him. For now, the article described him as a
suspect and said the police weren't hunting for anyone else.
The article referred to me as an unnamed private investigator
who had discovered the nun and Samuelson.

I dropped the paper into the garbage and punched the Play
button on the answering machine. The machine said I had four
messages. Stan Fleming had left the first. He said, cheery as
morning coffee, "You're a friend, so I'm wondering why you
left the party early yesterday." I kicked my feet onto the desk
and listened. He yelled at me for leaving Holy Trinity before
he gave me permission to go, then calmed down again at the

end before adding, "You know, this case isn't about you and me and Corrine, so everything would go better if you didn't fuck around. Call me as soon as you get this message, okay? We've got more to talk about." More noise, I figured, and I deleted the message. I was curious if he planned to try to hang Judy Terrano's killing on Greg Samuelson, but he didn't sound like he was in a friendly and giving mood.

The second call was from Corrine. She said she'd seen me on television and was worried about me. She didn't mention Stan Fleming and I wondered if she knew he was heading the investigation. She also didn't mention my smacking my Skylark into the news vans.

The next message was a blank, a click followed by static and background traffic, then a hang-up.

The last message made me take my feet off the desk. "Hello, Mr. Kozmarski," the caller said. "This is Eric Stone. I'd like to talk with you." He was more polite than I would have thought he could manage and more than I deserved. I figured he still would want to sledgehammer me into the pavement. He left his number and hung up.

I dialed Corrine on her cell phone, but the call rang through to voice mail. "Yeah, hi," I said. "Thanks for the call. I'm okay—I'm all right." It wasn't quite true and it wasn't a love poem, but it told her what I needed it to. I added, "I would like to see you," and hung up.

Then I called the number Eric Stone had left me.

A receptionist answered, "LCR Real Estate."

I told her who I was and she made me listen to reruns of eighties pop music while I waited to talk to Stone.

He came to the phone with a voice full of concern. "Mr. Kozmarski, thank you for calling."

"What can I do for you, Mr. Stone?"

"Two things actually. I'd like to know what you said to the police about me yesterday."

"I told them you threatened to kill Greg Samuelson."

Unhappy now. "Why would you do that?"

"Because you did, and because Samuelson took a bullet in the face."

Less happy. "He burned my car. I was angry. I obviously didn't mean that I would kill him."

"So you didn't shoot him?"

"No."

"Have you told that to the police?"

"My lawyer and I are meeting with them in an hour."

"Okay."

"Anyway, Samuelson shot himself. That's what the paper says."

"Maybe. You said you wanted two things from me. What's the other?"

"Actually, I'd like to talk with you about working for me."

"Why would you want to do that?"

"Are you available to meet with me at my Loop office this afternoon?"

"Just talk? No brawling?"

"Just talk."

I sat at my desk and considered Eric Stone. No matter what he said about playing nice, he was throwing a surprise punch and I wondered what kind of fight he was looking for. No, he hadn't shot Samuelson, he said. Yes, I was curious to know where he was when Samuelson took the bullet and Judy Terrano got killed.

"I can be there at three thirty," I said.

"Fine," he said, and we hung up.

I sat at my desk and considered him. Maybe there wasn't a fight in him. Maybe he wanted to give me more stacks of twenties to stay away from the Sister Terrano investigation. Maybe I could retire from divorce work, skip-payment cases, and employee background investigations, and make a full-time gig of doing nothing after nun homicides.

Maybe I needed some lunch.

I peeled a twenty off one of the stacks William DuBuclet's helpers had given me and slid the rest of the money into a file drawer and locked it. Twenty dollars would buy a sandwich and a drink at Grandma's Kitchen just up the block and leave enough change for another lunch like it. I tapped my Glock in its holster, put on my jacket, and let myself out of the office. Then I stepped in again and went to the drawer with the cash in it. I took the twenty from my pocket, balled it up, and threw it in with the rest. Later I could put it in the bank and spend it with a smile. For now, I didn't want to eat on it.

ELEVEN

THREE GREEK BROTHERS RAN Grandma's Kitchen. If they had a grandma, she was dead, living in Greece, or doing dishes in the back. Alexandros, the oldest brother, said the Italian beef was good.

While he put together the sandwich, I thought about the past twenty-four hours.

Greg Samuelson was either an aggrieved husband who overreacted to his wife's affair by burning a car and then got shot, or he was a lunatic arsonist who murdered a nun and then tried to kill himself. Why would he murder Judy Terrano and scribble the words BAD KITTY on her belly? What could she mean to him that would lead him to kill her like that?

Eric Stone was either a jerk who screwed another guy's wife and then got payback in the form of a burned Mercedes, or he was a homicidal lunatic who shot the husband of the woman he was screwing and who killed and marked Judy Terrano. Why? Because she interrupted him while he was killing

Samuelson and setting up his body to look like a suicide? Because he had a history with the nun? But why would he?

William DuBuclet's motives were even foggier. He and his gun-swinging helpers were either overly enthusiastic about keeping outsiders away from business they considered their own, or they were playing a bigger game, where threatening a guy like me made sense. I figured they were playing a bigger game. What did Judy Terrano mean to them?

Who was she? The Virginity Nun. A woman with a complicated past, DuBuclet had said. But everyone's past was complicated in one way or another. What did the words BAD KITTY mean? What did the cat tattoo mean?

It was none of my business. No one had hired me to find out. DuBuclet had paid me to turn my back on the nun's corpse. Stan Fleming had told me not to interfere. I knew I should take the advice seriously.

Alexandros didn't object when I changed my order from one to two sandwiches with drinks and fries to go. He handed me the bag and my change, then formed a pretend camera with his hands and snapped a picture of me. "You lookin' good on TV, Joe."

I dropped the coins in the tip jar. "Not all publicity is good."

"I don't know. I got a cousin who see you and want to meet you."

I laughed. "I'll get back to you on that," I said.

"She's twenty-three and very pretty."

If his cousin was like him she wore a sleeveless white T-shirt and had hairy shoulders.

I drove to Lucinda Juarez's apartment. She lived in Edgewater on the second floor of a gray stone two-flat squeezed between brick-fronted apartment buildings. The neighborhood had improved in the past five years but still had one of the highest violent crime rates in the city. High enough that Lucinda should have worried about the broken lock on the door leading to the interior stairway to her apartment. High enough that when I found her front door open at the top of the stairs a shiver ran down my back.

Until a month ago, Lucinda had been a newly minted detective rising through the department ranks. Then she'd gotten involved with me and had shot a man with her service pistol when she shouldn't have. The department had suspended her and would have fired her if the union had let them. After that, we'd had a night together. It was too early to know whether that night had helped or would end up causing a terrible scar. Odds looked good for the scar.

Now I stepped inside her apartment and called, "Lucinda?"

The furniture was where it belonged and the place was neat except for an empty Absolut vodka bottle under the living room coffee table.

"Lucinda!" I called again and walked up the hall. I poked my head into her bedroom, which was almost as neat as the living room. She wasn't there. On the dining room table a thin layer of dust caught the sunlight from the window. By the sink in the kitchen, a cardboard case held six empty Sierra Nevada Pale Ale bottles. The back door, leading to the wooden porch and downstairs to a fenced backyard, stood open. I went through it.

Lucinda sat on the porch in a lawn chair. She was short and heavy boned but she had olive skin and black eyes that made you forget that you ever questioned if she was beautiful, though now her eyes had an alcohol glaze and looked like they'd been crying. She wore sweatpants and a sweatshirt, no shoes or socks against the cold. She had another half-full bottle of Absolut in her hand. A Beretta M9 pistol was lying on her lap.

"Hi," I said.

She looked only slightly surprised to see me. "Hey."

I nodded at the bottle and the gun. "What are you doing out here?"

"Enjoying the lazy days of October. Silver linings and all that," she said. "First time I've ever been able to do this." Something caught her attention in the backyard—a squirrel jumping between branches on an oak tree. "Did you know we have possums in the city?"

"That's a squirrel."

She screwed her eyes at me. "I know that's a fucking squirrel. I mean last night. I was out here and possums tried to get into the garbage cans."

"No," I said, "I didn't know we had possums." I nodded again at the gun. "You planning to shoot them?"

She laughed at that. "What would I do with a dead possum?"

"Can I have the gun?"

She set the vodka bottle on the wooden porch floor and picked up the Beretta. "No," she said matter-of-factly. "They can take my job. They can leave me at home watching fucking possums. But no one will take my gun."

I held my hand toward her. "Please."

A grin formed on her lips. "You afraid I'm going to shoot myself like that guy?"

"Greg Samuelson. No, you're drunk. You'd miss."

The grin widened. "I never miss. I'm the best shot."

"Yeah," I said. "You're the best. Now give it to me. Please."

She waved her hand toward the backyard oak. "You see that blue jay?"

About sixty feet away through the branches, a little brown bird sat on a telephone wire. "I see a sparrow."

"Whatever." She lifted the gun, squinted her left eye closed, blinked both eyes, and pulled the trigger. The blast of the gun cracked off the wooden porch structure, threw me back, stunned my ears. Twenty yards away the sparrow disintegrated in a tiny storm of feathers and blood.

"Jesus!" I yelled and I grabbed for the gun. She let go and it fell into my hands. "What are you—"

But then she was crying. Tears rolled down her cheeks. She didn't make a sound but the tears kept coming. I tucked her gun into my belt, reached for her, took her under her legs and around her back, and lifted her. She didn't resist. She was small but she felt like she was made of something denser than skin and bones. I carried her inside to her bedroom and laid her on her bed, covered her with a quilt that looked older than either of us. I kissed her on the cheek and tasted the salt of her tears.

"Sleep," I said.

She grabbed upward and pulled me toward her, lifted her head, and kissed me on the lips, a soft, wet kiss that tasted like alcohol and felt like freedom to do whatever I wanted with her. "Get in with me," she said.

I pulled away. "Sleep now."

Her eyes got furious but only for a moment. Then she let me go and relaxed into the pillow.

I threw away the empty bottles from the living room and kitchen and brought in the half-drunk vodka from the porch. My house had looked like this plenty of times until I'd lined up my bottles and poured them down the drain. I didn't pour out Lucinda's vodka.

I sat at the kitchen table and unwrapped one of the sandwiches from Grandma's Kitchen. I'd finished half of it when Lucinda wandered back in and sat across from me. She looked ragged head to toe.

"Can't sleep," she said.

I pushed the other sandwich across the table to her. "Eat. Absolut doesn't count as a balanced diet."

She looked at the white paper wrapping suspiciously, like it might jump if she touched it. "What is it?"

"Italian beef from Grandma's."

She stood fast and headed to the bathroom.

When she returned she said, "You trying to kill me?" But then she ate the sandwich. I sat across from her and watched her eat, and when she was done I watched her some more. She blew a strand of hair out of her face and drank her Coke. She didn't return my gaze.

I took her pistol out of my belt and put it on the table in front of her. "That was the best shooting I've ever seen. Drunk or sober."

Still nothing.

"Why don't you work for me?" I said.

Nothing.

"Just for now," I said. "A week or two, until you figure out what you want to do."

Another sip of Coke. She said, "You won't get in bed with me but you want to hire me?"

"I didn't say I wouldn't get in bed with you. The timing wasn't good. But yeah, I want to hire you."

Like the Coke cup was the only thing in the room worth looking at. "So you want to get in bed with me *and* hire me?"

I gave her silence.

She thought about it for a while. "'Cause I'd never have sex with my boss."

I expected a smile with that but didn't get it. "Work *with* me, not *for* me."

For the first time, she looked up. "What're you working on, the Virginity Nun?"

I nodded.

She considered that for a while. "What's the story?"

I told her the story.

She reached across the table and took the crusts from my wrapper. "First solid food I've had in two days." She ate the crusts. Then she sat back in her chair and said, "Okay."

"Yeah? Good."

"When do I start?"

"I'm going to poke around at Holy Trinity and then talk to Eric Stone," I said. "You want to see what you can find out about William DuBuclet?"

"Yeah, I can do that."

"And anything you can pick up on Judy Terrano. I want to know who she was that made her worth killing."

"Yeah, me too," she said. She stared at the Coke cup again, then closed her eyes and her whole body seemed to relax. "But first I've got to get some sleep."

I closed Lucinda's door tight behind me on my way out and allowed myself to smile. I liked having her in on this.

But as I drove to Holy Trinity, I tried Corrine on my cell phone, and I wondered if I was calling her out of guilt. Her voice mail answered again and I listened to her voice, which I loved and which had hurt me as much as I'd hurt her. I hung up without leaving a message.

TWELVE

I DUCKED UNDER THE yellow police tape blocking the doors to the church. No cops stood guard, and I figured they'd left the tape to slow down reporters and ghouls hoping to look death in the eyes. But they'd failed. A television reporter spoke softly into a camera about the history of the church and Sister Terrano's role in making it famous. A still photographer was snapping shots near the pulpit where a priest had given me directions to Greg Samuelson's office.

Men and women sat by themselves in the pews. A heavy man in black was explaining to a group of four other men that they couldn't enter the door that led to the narrow hallway I'd taken the day before when I was looking for Samuelson. The man took the elbow of one of them like he was the father of the bride and steered them down the aisle toward the exit.

I stepped into the narrow hall and went downstairs to the undercroft. In the big room a group of about thirty teenaged girls, some of them in VIRGINS ARE COOL T-shirts, sat on the carpet watching a video on a television screen. A couple of nuns stood at the side, nervously watching the video and glancing at the girls.

The video showed some of these girls talking with Sister Terrano. She laughed easily with them on the screen. After some small talk she asked, "How many of us are ready to embrace chastity?" A round-faced, blond-haired girl about fourteen said, "'Embrace chastity.' What's that mean?" The girl next to her, no older, said, "You know, embrace being a virgin." The blonde girl smirked at the other one. "I know what chastity is, bitch. What's it mean to 'embrace' it?" Another girl, maybe thirteen, said from across the circle, "It means 'hug.'" A sixteen-year-old with acne added, "It sometimes means 'fuck.'" Sister Terrano listened with a smile, her arms folded over her stomach. The blonde said, "It don't mean 'fuck.'" "It does some of the time," the sixteen-year-old said. The youngest one said, "I can get into that. 'Fuck chastity.'" The blonde smiled and raised her arms in the air. "See what I mean? Embrace chastity's confusing." Sister Terrano laughed. "Ladies? I appreciate your enthusiasm, but—"

The girls in the undercroft watched the video quietly, though every time Sister Terrano talked, one of them sobbed—the thirteen-year-old who'd said embracing meant hugging.

I felt a hand on my shoulder and turned to find one of the nuns who'd been standing watch over the girls. She gave me a stony face and beckoned me with an index finger. We walked out of the undercroft into another hall. She led me to an office and guided me inside. She stood close to me and said, "You're intruding on a private moment."

"I'm sorry," I said, and meant it.

The nun seemed to think she still needed to convince me. "Sister Terrano connected with these girls in ways that no one else could. She *touched* them and her touch was like—" For a weird moment I thought she was going to say *sex*. "Like the touch of God," she said.

"I'm the one who found Sister Terrano's body," I said. I pulled a business card from my wallet and gave it to her. "I'm looking into the murder."

Knowing who I was didn't impress her. "What's there to look into? The police have Greg Samuelson."

"He didn't kill her," I said.

"No?"

"Why would he want to?"

"I don't know why anyone would want to. Everyone loved her. I never knew anyone who wished her harm. She was the purest person I've ever known, the—"

I thought about DuBuclet's comment on her *complicated* life. "Except when the cameras were off?"

She adjusted her eyes and mouth. "You're going to have to leave." She was a small woman but looked ready to pick me up and throw me out.

I stepped toward the door to the office. "I understand."

We walked up the hall toward the undercroft together. I asked, "Who controls the finances for Sister Terrano's abstinence program?"

The nun considered me for a moment. "She did, with some help from Greg Samuelson."

"Was there any oversight?"

"Of course. We have annual audits."

"And everything added up for her?"

I was beginning to annoy her again. "I'm not an auditor."

"Of course not," I said. "Do you know, when was the last time anyone saw Sister Terrano alive?"

"No idea."

"Who would know?"

"Greg organized her schedule."

"Do you mind if I look at his office computer?"

She looked liked I'd slapped her. "Yes, I mind. Anyway, the police have it. Judy's, too." She put her hand on my shoulder, guiding me toward the door to the undercroft.

"Anyone come to visit her lately who's not in the church?"

"Out," she said.

"Did she have a cat?"

"No. Come on. Out!" She stopped at the door. "You aren't welcome here now." She forced a smile. "Her funeral will be early next week. You can come back then."

I shook my head. "I've gone to too many funerals."

As we walked through the undercroft the girls on the video were continuing to give Sister Terrano a hard time. One said to her, "You don't know what you're missing, lady." The thirteen-year-old looked triumphant. "Yeah, you don't know." Sister Terrano interrupted, now without a laugh. "Yes," she said. "Oh yes, I do." Something in the way she said it—something sad and longing—silenced the girls in the video. A few of them even nodded in sympathy.

THIRTEEN

THE SMART THING TO do would have been to drive downtown, find a coffee shop near Eric Stone's office, and kick back
until our 3:30 appointment. That also would have been the respectful thing to do. The priests and nuns who promoted teenage virginity would have approved. But Judy Terrano still
would have been lying on a stainless-steel shelf in the Cook
County morgue, awaiting release to a funeral that even a poor
sinner like me could attend. Greg Samuelson still would have
been lying in a hospital with half a face. Stone still would
have been screwing Samuelson's wife. William DuBuclet still
would have been holed up in his curtained house on the South
Side, stirring the pot slowly.

I took a side door out of the sanctuary into the courtyard
garden that separated the church from the buildings that
housed the nuns and priests who taught at the parish school. A
statue of St. Joseph, dedicated to a long-dead pastor, stood
near the front fence.

The mailboxes in the entrance to the second faculty building included 1-H. SISTER JUDITH TERRANO. The door into the building was locked but it was like a toy lock. I slipped a card between the door and the frame, slid it upward, and eased the spring bolt into its housing. The door swung open into a hall carpeted with the thin, outdoor-grade stuff you find on the greens of miniature golf courses, but red, fading to pink. The wall sconces held dimly lighted bulbs.

The fourth door on the right was 1-H. It opened more easily than the front door. It had no lock. The room measured about twice the size of a prison cell but had a closet and a separate bathroom. The bed was plain and institutional, and at the foot of it a white sink with old fixtures was attached to the wall, probably left over from a time when the room had no private bathroom. A medicine cabinet hung above the sink. A crucifix with a figure of Jesus looked over the sink and the bed. In front of a window, a steam radiator was propped up on one end with a brick. More bricks were stacked beside it. A plain wooden desk and chair stood in a corner. A telephone and a well-thumbed Bible rested on top. A thinly upholstered chair with a floral print stood in another corner with a dresser next to it.

I was looking for evidence of who Sister Terrano was, the kind that wouldn't appear in the news clipping files or the obituaries. If Greg Samuelson had killed her because his separation from his wife had driven him over the edge, I probably would find nothing. Same thing if someone else had gone nuts and killed her. But some people who kill aren't nuts. They're like everyone else, plus a weapon and a cause.

I started with the desk. The top drawer contained blank stationery, a roll of tape, and pens. A side drawer held a stapler, rubber bands, paper clips, and another roll of tape. The drawer under it contained three books on theology, a loosely bound national report on teenage sexuality, and a book called *A Short History of Medieval Architecture*. The bottom drawer contained a pair of binoculars, which would have been good for watching birds and small animals outside the window in the courtyard garden, a Swiss Army knife, an unopened pack of AA batteries, a flashlight, matches, and a box of candles.

I opened the closet door. The floor was a mess. Someone had pulled two cardboard boxes off the shelf and dumped them, rummaged through the contents, and then swept the mess back inside before closing the closet door.

The stuff was the debris of an almost possession-free life. A little wooden model of a Swiss chalet lay on top. It could have sat on a bookshelf or hung in the window of a young girl's room but now its roof was broken and attached to the rest of the building by a bent staple. Most of the rest had to do with Judy Terrano's service as a nun. There were diplomas and testaments printed on heavy paper, some in Latin, some English.

At the bottom of the pile three photographs were held together by a paper clip. The first two were black and white, and looked fifty or sixty years old. One showed a handsome-faced man wearing a hat. The other showed a serious-faced woman. Their faces had something of Judy Terrano's, and I figured they were her parents.

The third picture was in color and showed Judy Terrano when she was the age of the older teenagers who were watching the video in the undercroft. Everything about the picture amazed me. It looked like a dirty picture without the nakedness. She had an Afro, green eyes full of desire, and a wicked smile that said she was thinking darker thoughts than ever had crossed the minds of the girls she would later try to convince to remain virgins. She wore a blouse unbuttoned to show plenty of breast.

A teenaged boy would be afraid to bring a girl like her home to his parents. She looked like an angel but an angel of sex. I slipped the photo into my jacket pocket, shoved the wooden chalet and the papers back into the closet, and closed the door.

I glanced around the room.

Who had dumped the boxes on the nun's closet floor? Did she do it herself? Only if she was in a rush and only if she did it just before she died. Her office was cluttered, but, except for the closet, her bedroom was clean, down to the books stacked in the desk drawer. She wouldn't have left the mess. If not her, who? Someone who'd come in after she died, looking for something she might have hidden in a box in the closet. I wondered what that person had found.

Nothing unusual fell out of the dresser drawers when I emptied them onto the bed. Nothing was taped behind the drawers or behind the dresser. I checked under the bed and along the underside of the bed frame. I lifted the thin mattress and checked for rips where Sister Terrano might have stuffed a notebook or a small box. The medicine cabinet over the sink at the foot of the bed was empty except for a coat button.

I crawled under the desk and glanced under the desk chair. The upholstered chair had nothing tucked into its cushions or springs. I went back to the desk and thumbed through the Bible and the books in the desk drawer. No secret letters fell from between the pages. Breaking the binding of *A Short History of Medieval Architecture* seemed like overkill. But I opened the cover.

"Damn!" I said. Judy Terrano had cut out the inside of the book the way a kid might after reading an article on spy secrets in a magazine. A stack of twenty-dollar bills rested inside the cavity. The bills were as crisp as the ones Robert and

Jarik had delivered to me. The elastic band wrapped around the bills was gold.

William DuBuclet seemed to have been paying off Judy Terrano, too. For what?

I left the money in the book and tucked it back in the drawer.

The bathroom was next. In almost every way, it was a normal bathroom. It had a toilet, a sink with a medicine cabinet, and a bathtub. But when I flipped on the light, I stumbled back into the bedroom. A priest was lying in the tub. He was dressed all in black and was thin and bald with a little brown beard. Just over twenty-four hours earlier, he had sobbed in the hallway outside Judy Terrano's door after the police and paramedics arrived.

One of his thick black shoes hung over the side of the tub. He had a deep, almost bloodless gash in the side of his head. A brick was lying on top of the drain.

I didn't like touching the dead. But I made myself go to him and I put my hands on him. I patted him down from his shoulders to his feet. I found a wallet that had thirty-two dollars in it and a driver's license that named him Jerold Terwicki. I found a half-spent roll of Lifesavers. I found nothing that looked as if it might have come from the boxes in Judy Terrano's closet.

I washed my hands in the bathroom sink, using the soap of a dead woman, then dried them against my pants. The vanilla smell of Judy Terrano's soap caught in my nostrils and throat, and I ran from the bathroom.

The bedroom closed in on me. Sweat broke inside my shirt and pants. I slipped into the hall. It was empty and I ran down it to the outside door, fought to keep myself to a casual walk as I crossed the courtyard garden, went through the gate, and climbed into my car.

FOURTEEN

WHEN I WAS TRYING to break my bad habits, Corrine convinced me to do Chinese breathing exercises. I would inhale three short breaths through my nose, lifting my arms in front of me on the first, sticking them out to the sides on the second, raising them above my head on the third. Next I would exhale long and slow, lowering my arms in a big arc. The exercises didn't help much then and they didn't help much now, probably because I was gripping the steering wheel like I hung from it over the edge of the world.

When I relaxed enough to let blood flow back into my knuckles, I knew what I had to do. I called Stan Fleming at the District Thirteen station house. Calling him felt about as good as putting my hands on a dead priest.

He answered the phone, cheery. "You're gone, Joe. You're out of the picture. You're no longer my friend. I'm a reasonable guy. If you'd stuck around when I asked you to—Hell, if you'd called me back when I called you—"

"I know. I'm gone. I'm water under the bridge. I'm yesterday's news. I'm—"

"Then why are you bothering me?"

I inhaled three short breaths. "To tell you that you've got another body at Holy Trinity."

That quieted him. When he found words, they weren't much. "What are you talking about?"

"A dead priest. His name's Jerold Terwicki. You'll find him in Judy Terrano's bathtub." Now when the police found my fingerprints in the nun's apartment, Stan couldn't say I hadn't told him I was there.

"How did he get there?"

"Looks to me like he was dragged over the floor—not very gently."

"Jesus, Joe, you're dangerous. You can't go near that church without a body dying in front of you."

"They usually die before I arrive." It was a minor point but it seemed worth making.

"You in the room with the priest right now?"

"I'm driving in my car."

"Turn around. Meet me there."

"Sorry, can't do it. I've got an appointment."

"Don't test me, Joe."

"There's a book in the nun's room that you might want to read, too."

"Huh?"

"It's called *A Short History of Medieval Architecture*. I guarantee it'll keep you up at night."

"What the hell are you talking about?"

"You'll find the book in her desk."

"You're not going to meet me in Terrano's room, are you?"

I tried changing topics again. "Are you going to charge Greg Samuelson with her murder?"

"I'm hanging up, Joe."

"Did Samuelson kill her?"

"Who else?"

"You talk to Eric Stone?" I said.

"What's his motive?"

"Samuelson burned his car."

Stan sighed into the phone. "The man's got insurance. And he's got Samuelson's wife. Why bother chasing him? Why kill a nun?"

"What's Samuelson's motive?"

"Why should I talk to you about it?"

"I always call you when I find a body."

He made a sound somewhere between a laugh and a groan. "Samuelson's home life is fucked, obviously. His professional life, too, apparently. A priest we've talked to says church accounting recently turned up some questionable money transfers involving the nun's work—transfers that Samuelson controlled. He knows he's about to be caught and, with his wife leaving him, he has nothing to live for outside work, so he takes out the nun and shoots himself in the head."

"Maybe," I said, "but I don't think so."

"But it doesn't really matter what you think, does it?" he said.

I admitted, "Probably not."

Next I called Lucinda. She'd napped and sounded mostly sober. She was getting dressed and planned to head downtown to the library to look up Judy Terrano and William DuBuclet in the archives. I told her about the dead priest and she sounded more concerned about me than him. "Dangerous business working at that church," Lucinda said.

"Right up there with commercial fishing."

She said softly and bitterly, "Or becoming a drunk ex-cop."

"Drinking for a few days after you lose your job makes you human, not a drunk."

"Problem is, those were my best days."

"Just don't make that kind of good day a habit."

"Mmm," she said. She didn't sound certain but she added, "Thanks for bringing me in, Joe."

"Not a lot of people would thank me for getting them into a mess like this."

"Yeah, I know," she said. "But thanks."

I exited from the Kennedy at Ohio Street, drove to Orleans, and searched for a parking space. At the curb I looked at my watch. It was 3:35, and I was five minutes late for my date with Eric Stone.

I dialed the phone once more.

Corrine answered. The slight hoarseness of her voice tugged at me, though I'd heard it thousands of times. It relieved me in ways that three inhaled breaths didn't.

"Hey," I said, "I tried you earlier."

"I got your message. I'm glad you're okay."

"Stan Fleming's leading the investigation."

"Yeah?" She sounded only vaguely interested.

"Yeah. I'm supposed to stay out of it. He's warned me."

She laughed. "That'll make a difference."

"What are you up to?"

"I'm teaching a class on winter mulching at the Botanical Garden. Nothing very exciting." She ran a landscaping business and made things bloom while I worried about them dying.

"It gets me excited," I said.

Her voice got warm. "What excites you about mulch?"

I cradled the phone close to my neck. "It's not the mulch. It's *you* and the mulch. I fantasize about you and mulch."

"You're kind of weird, Joe."

"You do that to me. You want to have dinner tonight?"

She gave that a moment. "With you, or with you and the kid?"

The kid. "With me and Jason. If you want to wait for the weekend, it could be just us."

"I've got plans tonight."

"Because I asked if you wanted to have dinner with Jason and me?"

"No, because I've got plans."

"Okay."

"But this weekend?"

"Yeah," I said. "I'll call."

Her voice softened again. "Take care of yourself until you do."

Hundreds of couples had conversations like that. The trouble was, we weren't a couple anymore.

I rode the elevator to Eric Stone's office at 3:40. Lakeview Commercial and Residential Real Estate Development, or LCR as most people knew them, had an office suite on the twelfth floor of a white-faced office tower. The reception area had plush gray carpet and paneling that passed as teak. The receptionist buzzed Stone to tell him I was there.

The corridor to Stone's office took me past a glass-walled conference room. Inside, two women stood by a conference table and argued. One was in her late seventies at least, thin and dressed in a tight red skirt and jacket. Her hair was auburn, pointing at bronze, and she'd drawn on a thin line of red lipstick. The other was Greg Samuelson's wife, Amy. The glass deadened the sound of their argument. The older woman felt my eyes on her, and she and Amy Samuelson stopped talking and stared at me. Amy Samuelson looked embarrassed, but the other woman's gaze was hard, like she'd never experienced embarrassment in her life.

I stepped close to the glass and exhaled steam on it. Amy Samuelson's mouth fell open.

Then, from behind me, a woman's hand reached past my shoulder, and her index finger drew a little heart on the steamed glass.

The skin on the woman's hand was tan, though the sun hadn't shined solid in Chicago since Labor Day. Her fingernails glittered like semiprecious gems. I turned and saw the rest of her. She looked like she was in her mid-thirties but with a lot of wear. She had wheat-brown hair, tinted blond, and wore tight jeans and a little shirt that showed belly on the bottom and breast on top. I'd seen her once before, as the passenger riding in the silver Mercedes that almost ran me down after Greg Samuelson burned Eric Stone's car. She'd changed her clothes but she still looked like a fancy fishing lure.

I held my hand to shake hers and smiled. "I'm Joe Kozmarski."

She smiled back with bleached teeth. "Pleased to meet you, Joe."

"And you are—?"

"Cassie," she said. "Cassie Stone."

"This is a family business," I observed.

"Family is everything," she said. She didn't sound happy about it. She turned and walked away.

I called after her, "You ever go fishing?"

She stopped without turning to look at me. "No, Joe, I've never gone fishing."

"You should try it. You look like you would be good."

"Give me a call," she said. "I'll try anything once." She disappeared down the hall.

Eric Stone's office was next to the conference room. It had a large glass-topped desk and, on the walls, framed paintings of buildings that LCR had constructed—a mix of office and residential skyscrapers, all high-end.

He stood when I came in, and we shook hands, friendly, and sat down together. He wore a tailored charcoal gray suit and a tie. His bald head showed the healthy pink skin of a man who spent time exercising outdoors.

"Mr. Kozmarski," he said, "you saw me yesterday at an embarrassing moment. I'd just left Amy's house, and I was watching my car burn." He gave me a wink that could sell real estate at a thousand dollars a square foot. "But you know all that."

I agreed that I did.

"I apologize for my brusqueness. I don't usually behave that way."

"You behaved understandably, considering everything."

"And you provoked me," he said. "What happened later—to the nun at the church—was terrible. And I have a hard time believing Greg would do it. I've known him and, of course, Amy for over two years. He's a gentle man"—he gave an ironic smile—"if you keep him away from gasoline and matches."

I showed him my palms. "The police are convinced he did it."

"I can't believe that's true," he said.

"Did *you* do it?"

The ironic smile. "If I understand the sequence of events,

I was sitting at my desk when Sister Terrano died and Greg shot himself. My brother and his daughter picked me up at Amy's condo and we came straight here."

"I'm sure that others saw you here and can verify your story."

"I've given all of that information to the police." He leaned back in his chair. "If they want to talk with me, my lawyer and I are available."

I nodded. "Did you know Judy Terrano?"

"I did, but not well. Three months ago, before Amy and I started seeing each other, Greg introduced us. I don't necessarily agree with her principles, but she seemed like a good woman. And tough, very tough."

I nodded some more. I would describe her as tough, too, though I didn't know how good she was. "So why did you call me?" I asked. "What do you want?"

His smile dropped and he leaned forward. "Do you know of a man named William DuBuclet?" He probably saw my surprise. He said, "Last summer, I had dinner with Greg and Amy. This was right before Amy and I got together. Something was bothering Greg that night, and it came out that DuBuclet had visited Judy Terrano's office in the afternoon and threatened her. When Greg intervened, DuBuclet threatened him, too—'him and his family' was what Greg said. Apparently DuBuclet and the nun knew each other from way back—they met in the sixties on the South Side—but Greg took the threat seriously. He was scared that night."

"Why did DuBuclet threaten Sister Terrano?"

"Greg wouldn't say. I'm not sure he knew."

"Yesterday *you* threatened Samuelson after he burned your car."

"If he'd heard me, he would've laughed. He knows I'm harmless. He didn't laugh when DuBuclet said it."

Stone was right. Samuelson *had* laughed when I'd told him that Stone said he would kill him. "So you're saying DuBuclet killed Judy Terrano or had her killed."

"I don't know. I'm saying he threatened her and now she's dead."

"Did you tell the police?"

He hesitated. "No."

"Why not?"

"DuBuclet's a very powerful man, and he influences most decisions involving commercial property on the South Side. If word got back to him that I pointed the police at him, he would become a quick enemy. If he turned out to be innocent, his anger could have a lasting effect on my business. As a land developer I can't afford to have that kind of enemy."

"So why are you telling me?"

"I'd like to hire you to keep an eye on DuBuclet. Quietly. I don't want you to talk to him, but I want to know what he's doing. If he had Judy Terrano killed and if he's responsible for Greg getting shot, I want to know whether he really meant he'd get Greg *and his family*. I want to know that Amy's safe. Me too, to tell the truth. I spend a lot of time with Amy, and I want to know if DuBuclet's people are coming."

I thought about all he'd told me. "Okay," I said. "Write me a check."

He looked relieved. "How much?"

Usually I charged fifteen hundred up front. But I didn't like Eric Stone. Or what he did. Or how he did it. "Five thousand," I said.

Five thousand was no problem for him. He nodded and

pulled a checkbook from his desk. I would put the check in the drawer with the cash from William DuBuclet and decide what to do with it later.

I WAS FINDING MY own way out when the receptionist said, "Mr. Kozmarski? If you have a minute, Mrs. Stone also would like a word with you."

That stopped me. "Stone is married?"

The receptionist found me funny. "Mrs. Stone is Eric's mother." She directed me through another door, which led down a short hallway to a single office. The woman who had been arguing with Amy Samuelson in the conference room sat at the desk having another argument, this time with the pony-tailed man who had been driving the silver Mercedes that almost hit me outside of Samuelson's condo. I saw no reason to listen to the argument, so I knocked on the door frame.

The woman glanced at me with the same cold, impassive eyes she'd shown me before and touched the man's hand with her fingertips. "We can continue this later," she said quietly.

The man pulled his hand away. He stood and cocked his head to the side like he was sizing me up. I guess he thought I was small enough. He bowed his head slightly and knocked my shoulder with his as he pushed through the door.

Mrs. Stone offered me his chair. Her office looked a lot like Eric Stone's, but the walls were tinted pink and she had framed pastel renderings of a project called Stone Tower that the company seemed to be working on. A small vase of roses stood on her blond-wood desk. The soft colors didn't fool me. She was the hardest thing in the place.

She said, "Never go into business with your family, Mr.

Kozmarski. My son David"—she gestured to the door that the ponytailed man had passed through—"is fifty-six this month and Eric is fifty-eight, but I treat them like badly behaved thirteen-year-olds and they respond by acting like badly behaved thirteen-year-olds. They bring their girlfriends home and give them jobs. They hire their friends with or without qualifications."

I gave her a straight face.

She waved impatiently. "Nothing but trouble. But what choice do I have? I won't put them out on the street. Did you know that both of my boys live in my house? They're almost sixty and they live with their mother. David's daughter Cassie, too. I raised the girl myself. What do you think of that, Mr. Kozmarski?"

"It's nice to be close to your family."

She laughed sharply at that. "It's nice to be close to this," she said, and she gestured at the framed renderings of the Stone Tower project. "Without the buildings my boys would live in the holes where they probably belong. Me too. But with the buildings they get to play tennis and drive nice cars and hire the girls they're dating. And I get to play queen over it all." Her cold eyes watched mine. "What do you think of that?"

"Like I said, family is nice."

She leaned back in her chair. "That's my story, Mr. Kozmarski. What's yours?"

"Which story do you want?"

"The one that explains why you're here talking to my son."

"He called me because he thinks you're having an affair."

"Pardon me?"

"He's paying me to follow you around, watch who you park next to at the Motel 6, snap some pictures. He thinks you've been getting together with the eighteen-year-old kid who delivers mail to your office."

She gazed at me with her hard eyes. "I have very little patience and less of a sense of humor."

"Why don't you ask Eric?"

"Are you saying you won't tell me?"

"That's what I'm saying, yes."

"Very well," she said. "I'll tell you, though, I protect what's mine. I'll do whatever I need to do. I have lawyers and other resources that can stop you and crush you."

I had no idea what she was talking about. "If they crush me, they'll probably get Eric, too."

She shook her head. "Just you." But her voice quivered.

I tried to see into her eyes but saw only a rocky hard place.

ON THE SIDEWALK OUTSIDE, I thought about the Stones. I wondered what they were up to and how they tied in to Judy Terrano. I wasn't sure how much I bought Eric Stone's worries about William DuBuclet. Robert and Jarik had threatened me. They'd pulled a gun on me to make the threat stick. But even if DuBuclet was responsible for killing Judy Terrano, Amy Samuelson seemed too far out of the nun's circle to need protection. Still, if DuBuclet and his flunkies were on the prowl, I wanted to keep my eyes open for them.

I wanted Lucinda to watch out for them, too. I pulled out my cell phone to check in with her. But the screen said someone had left voice mail while I was chatting with the Stones. The number was Stan Fleming's and his three-word message sounded unhappy—"Call me please." *Please?* Who was teaching him manners? I called the District Thirteen station and they told me how to reach him in Judy Terrano's room at Holy Trinity.

His voice was flat when he answered the phone. "Look, it seems Greg Samuelson got up and walked out of intensive care at Rush Med."

"Huh? When?"

"A couple hours ago. But I just heard."

"He 'got up'?"

"And left."

"With half a face?"

"The injury's not quite as bad as it looks. He shot off part of his jaw. But, yeah, half a jaw, half a face, he left."

"I thought you had him under guard."

"Of course I had him under guard. But you know what he looked like. The guard took a break and—"

"Yeah, I get it."

"With the bandages, he shouldn't be hard to find," Stan said. "We can stake out every Dairy Queen in the city. He's not eating anything chewier than a milkshake."

"You think he killed the priest?"

"The church is just a mile away from the hospital."

"Yeah, but it's hard to believe he could have done it."

"It's hard to believe he didn't. Who else?"

Exactly, I thought, who else? I said, "What can I do for you?"

He said, "I need your help on this." He must have had a hard time saying those words.

I said, "I'll be there in twenty minutes."

FIFTEEN

I CALLED LUCINDA WHILE I drove. She was on her way to play reference librarian. I told her about Stan Fleming's call and Greg Samuelson walking out of his hospital room. I warned her about William DuBuclet's threats and told her about the check I was carrying from Eric Stone.

"Do you trust Stone?" she asked.

"Are you kidding? But he interests me. Yesterday he was waving his fists around and promising he would draw blood. Today he's playing the calm, concerned boyfriend. He even sounds worried about Greg Samuelson."

"I'll check the newspaper file for articles about him and his family."

"Thanks," I said. "You want to catch up over dinner with me and Jason?"

She said she would pick up Thai on her way back from the archives and meet us at my house.

A LITTLE BEFORE FIVE I pulled into a parking spot a block and a half away from Holy Trinity, locked my gun in the glove compartment, and eased myself out of the car. The afternoon sky had turned gray, and a cold wind was rising again from the west. Six police cruisers and an ambulance lined the curb in front of the church. News vans had parked across the street. A neighborhood crowd watched the church buildings as if Moses himself would walk out and deliver ten new commandments. If the killings kept up, concession stands would come next.

A cop at the garden gate radioed inside to Stan Fleming, then let me in. In Judy Terrano's room, a forensics man was working on the brick that the killer had taken from the stack next to the radiator and used to crush the priest's head. A bunch of cops were squeezed into the nun's bathroom. Stan was one of them. The forensics detective who dressed like Smokey the Bear was another. "We're looking at early rigor," Smokey was saying. "Better put a couple sheets over him, 'cause this guy's coming out of the Virginity Nun's room stiff."

"Can't blame him," said one of the other cops. "I get off on old nuns, too."

"Sickos, all of you," said Stan, and he came into the bedroom, followed by the other cops' laughter. He brushed past me and went into the hall. I followed him. "There are days," he said. "There are—" He stopped again. His eyes were dry but I knew better.

"Yeah," I said, "there are."

He shook his head. "Samuelson worked for the church eleven years, the last eight of them for Judy Terrano. Quiet as a fucking rat." His dry eyes moistened.

"You don't really think he killed the priest, do you?" I asked.

His eyes got stony again. "He's got priors, did you know that?"

I admitted that I didn't.

"Nothing official anymore. The Mercedes he torched yesterday—that's not the first car he's burned. When he was fifteen he burned his mother's station wagon. A 1979 Buick Century. Might even have deserved burning, I don't know. They adjudicated him and he took four months in juvenile corrections.

"He got in trouble again when he was twenty-nine. He worked for a small accounting firm and was directing company checks into his own account. The firm dropped charges when he agreed to pay back the stolen money."

"Anything else?"

He looked incredulous. "What else do you want? We never arrested him for spray-painting BAD KITTY on the sides of subway cars if that's what you're looking for."

"Burning his mom's car and dipping his fingers into the company bank account isn't homicide."

He looked at me hard. "The cash in Judy Terrano's architecture book says this is about money, too. Eric Stone's burning Mercedes says Samuelson's still a bad boy."

"So Samuelson strangled Judy Terrano, shot himself, and then climbed out of his hospital bed to kill a priest?"

"Who else?"

I knew I should tell him about the similarly banded cash that DuBuclet gave me. But instead I said, "If you put this out on the street, a patrolman might think he's doing his church duty to put another bullet in Samuelson's head."

Stan shrugged. "I might have to agree with him."

I looked at him, unconvinced.

"Why else would he escape from a locked-down hospital room?" he said.

"A room without a lock or a guard."

"Still."

"Did he know you planned to arrest him?"

He looked angry. "Of course he did."

"Samuelson was unconscious when he went to the hospital. Did anyone tell him? Or did he just wake up and walk out of the hospital without necessarily knowing everyone in the city thought he was a killer?"

Stan considered that. "Okay. But the guy has a major head injury. Why would he leave?"

"Like you said before, he tried to kill himself in Judy Terrano's office. I would drag the river near the hospital and keep an eye open for floaters downstream. He might have left the hospital to finish the job."

"We've got a little problem with that, too. We did glue-lifts on his hands and they came out clean. No gunshot residue."

"He didn't shoot himself?"

"I'm not saying that. Not yet. We traced the gun. It's his. And there were powder burns on his face. We're retesting the glue-lifts."

I shook my head. "He didn't kill the priest in Judy Terrano's room. In the shape he was in, he'd be lucky to have enough strength to flag down a cab to take him to the morgue."

"A dying man could drop a brick on a guy's head."

"And kill him?"

"Sure, why not?"

"A dying man couldn't drag him into the bathtub afterward."

Stan crossed his arms over his chest. "Okay, how do *you* figure it?"

I said, "The priest worked closely with Judy Terrano and might have known her secrets. I figure he was looking for the same thing his killer was looking for and he surprised him in the nun's room. The killer had made a mess of the closet but hadn't gotten further. He was by the desk when the priest came in. He picked up a brick, hit the priest with it, dragged his body into the bathtub, swept the mess back into the closet, and left."

Stan nodded. "Okay, that fits the scene. What were they looking for?"

"Let's go with your theory. Money. Not robbery, though. Bigger money than we found in the architecture book. Enough to kill for."

"A nun with big money?"

"A nun with cash stashed in her desk?"

"Okay," he said. "Where's the money from?"

I considered the connections to DuBuclet—the gold elastic bands around the cash, the threats Eric Stone had told me about, and the gun Robert and Jarik had pulled on me. "I don't know. Look at the audit books."

"All right. Who's the killer?"

I figured the killer was one of DuBuclet's followers, but I wanted to know more about DuBuclet before I turned him over. "I don't know," I said again.

Stan thought about it. "It was Samuelson," he said.

I shook my head. "What else have you found out about Judy Terrano?"

"Grew up on the South Side, one brother now deceased, both parents deceased. Poster child for famous activist nuns. What do you want to know?"

"Any ideas about the 'Bad Kitty' and the tattoo?"

"No ideas, but that stuff got to me. I dreamed about the tattoo last night."

"I don't want to know about your dreams."

"*I* don't want to know my dreams," he said.

"So what can I do for you?" I asked.

That was easy. "Tell me where to find Samuelson."

I shrugged. "Try his condo on LaSalle," I said, "but I'm guessing you've already done that."

He looked disappointed.

I said, "If he calls me, I'll do what I can to bring him in."

He nodded. That would have to do.

"I doubt he'll call me," I added.

He turned back to Judy Terrano's room, then asked, "You find anything other than the book full of money when you searched?"

Denying that I'd dug through her belongings was pointless. "Nothing," I said. The picture in my pocket of a teenaged Judith Terrano called me a liar, but I wasn't ready to give it up.

Stan looked at me close, like he could hear the picture calling. "You move or remove anything?"

"Of course not," I said. "Why are you telling the news that she was raped?"

"Huh? I'm not telling them she—"

"You're saying she was sexually assaulted, but you told me that your forensics guy said she wasn't."

"She *was* assaulted. Her dress was around her neck. Her panties were off. That looks like sexual assault."

"It looks like it was about to be," I admitted. "Has forensics found any evidence?"

He shook his head a little. "Not even a hair."

"So maybe it wasn't sexual assault."

"What else?"

"I don't know." I shrugged. "Maybe someone wanted to give you bad dreams."

SIXTEEN

I WATCHED STAN WORK and tried to stay out of the way until 7:30, then slipped out of the housing block into the cold evening. The news camera lights glared like ice.

I cranked the heat in my Skylark and drove. The wind was whipping through the side streets, and the pavement and lawns looked dark as rain-slicked tar. A couple blocks from my house I came around a corner and hit the brakes when something that looked like a red snake slithered halfway across the street. I squinted at it. The headlights shined on a red party streamer. Happy birthday to someone, I thought, and give me dinner and a full night's sleep.

I drove over the streamer and less than a minute later rolled into the alley by my house. The familiar crunch of the asphalt under the tires made me laugh. Snakes. I was seeing snakes.

I pulled into the garage and stepped outside into the dark shadow of the old elm tree. Then two men were beside me in the dark. I reached for my gun but I was too late, much too late.

The men took hold of my arms and turned me back toward the alley. "Come on," said one of them. I knew the voice—it was of one of DuBuclet's helpers. Robert. I glanced to the other side. Jarik. In his hand, pressing against my neck, black gun-metal glinted in the dark. He and Robert had told me they would come gunning for me if they thought they needed to. Sweat slid down the insides of my legs.

They marched me out of the alley toward the street. "You know," I said, "you guys spend too much time lurking outside my house. If you'd knocked on the front door, I would've asked you in. If you'd called, I would've invited you for dinner."

"Shut up," said Jarik.

"I've got a friend coming over. She's bringing Thai food. Probably not enough for all of us, but we could microwave—"

Jarik stuck the gun deeper into my neck. "Shut up!"

"You must have already eaten," I mumbled.

Their Lexus was across the street at the curb. Robert patted me down and took my gun.

"In," he said, and as I climbed into the backseat, Jarik smacked the back of my head with the gun butt. Hard enough to draw blood. Hard enough to make me think of a dead priest lying in a bathtub with a head wound.

Robert climbed in next to me. Jarik drove.

I held a hand to the cut. "Are we going to see DuBuclet again?"

They said nothing.

We went east toward Lake Michigan, crossed under Lake Shore Drive, and cruised into the park at Montrose Harbor. The harbor was a liquid shadow surrounded on three sides by a horseshoe road. The fourth side opened to the deeper shadow of the lake. We circled the harbor until we reached the end of a rock-and-sand landfill that kept million-dollar yachts safe from storms all summer. Now the docks and mooring cans were empty. The orange glow of the harbor-road streetlights shined on the blank pavement and told me I was all alone except for two guys who'd bloodied the back of my head and forced me at gunpoint into their car. Jarik parked and turned off the headlights but left the motor running. Outside, waves rolled in over the invisible dark of the lake and slammed into the blocks of limestone that protected the shore, then drew away with a hush and a hiss. I started to wish I was in a little boat bouncing on those waves.

Robert spoke again and his voice was calm, businesslike. "If we'd wanted you to work with the cops, we wouldn't have paid you five thousand dollars."

"How'd you find out so fast?"

"Don't talk. Listen," said Jarik to the windshield.

Robert said, "William DuBuclet has a long history in Chicago. Not just in politics—a personal history. He'll do anything he needs to do to protect his interests."

"Do his interests include killing Judy Terrano?"

Jarik shook his head like he couldn't believe I still was talking.

Robert said, "His interests are none of your business."

"They're worth handing out stacks of twenty-dollar bills."

"Yes."

"And killing for?" I asked again.

"I don't think you get what we're saying." Jarik sounded exasperated.

"I think I do," I said. "You're telling me to forget about Judy Terrano's death. It has nothing to do with me. Same goes for Greg Samuelson's shooting. Same for the murder of the priest.

I'm supposed to ignore all that. It's someone else's problem—William DuBuclet's, not mine."

Jarik clapped quietly in the front seat. "Good work, Joe."

"You know I'm not exactly the only one investigating this."

Robert's voice was calm. "The cops think they've know the guy who did it. Why do anything to change their minds?"

"It's possible the cops are right."

"Okay. Then you can sleep good, too."

"But I don't think they are."

In a flash, Robert held a gun to my head.

I raised my hands. "But I could change my mind."

"We don't really care what you think," Robert said. "We care what you do. So, what are you going to do?"

"Drop out of sight?"

Jarik sounded doubtful. "You said you'd do that the first time we talked with you."

"You're making a stronger argument now," I said.

"Yeah? Because we don't want to have to tell you again."

"Yeah."

"Okay, then," Jarik said, and he flipped on the headlights and shifted into drive.

I grinned a little. "You're not going to kill me?"

Jarik shrugged. "Not yet."

Robert said, "You're an asshole, but when it matters you make the right decisions."

I had nothing to say to that, so I kept my mouth shut and fingered the sticky blood where Jarik had hit me.

Fifteen minutes later we pulled up in front of my house. I had one other question I needed to ask. Eric Stone had paid me five thousand dollars to ask it.

I said, "Is William DuBuclet planning to hurt Greg Samuelson's wife?"

Jarik gave me a look like I'd lost my mind. "Why the hell would he want to do something like that?"

"I guess he wouldn't," I said.

Robert and Jarik got out with me at my house.

I touched the back of my head. I said, "Was the thugs-in-the-night routine really necessary?"

"We want you to know what we can do to you," Robert said.

"Can I have my gun?"

Robert laughed. "Sure." He handed me my gun.

Jarik said, "No hard feelings?"

I took my Glock by the barrel. "No," I agreed. "No hard feelings."

I swung the gun so its grip hit Robert square in the face, between his nose and his upper lip. He went down on the sidewalk.

Jarik grabbed for his gun but I swung on him, too. I caught him above his left ear and he crumpled on top of Robert. "No hard feelings," I said. Now we all had blood on our heads.

SEVENTEEN

JASON AND LUCINDA WERE sitting at the dining room table when I came in. I'd bought the house in the Ravenswood neighborhood after my divorce from Corrine. The ad had called it a handyman special, and I'd figured I should keep my fingers busy doing something healthier than unscrewing the caps from whiskey bottles. Now Jason and Lucinda had shoved the tools I was using to one end of the table, and they'd made the place look like home—if home was plaster dust, aluminum foil, take-out containers, mismatched glasses, and paper towels for napkins, which is what home was for me. They were chatting and laughing and if you didn't know better you could've mistaken them for a mother and son eating together and welcoming home a father who'd been kept late at the office. But we all knew better.

Lucinda had showered and put on jeans and a soft green wool sweater and looked like someone you'd want to cozy up to on a couch. Jason looked like the tall, grinning eleven-year-old he was, except he had a deep bruise on his right cheek.

"What happened to you?" I said as I walked into the room.

They looked at me and their laughter broke. Lucinda said, "What happened to *you*?"

I looked at my jacket, at my hand. Blood had stained them. More blood streaked the top of my jeans. "Oh, this," I said. I tried a smile, but got back blank faces. "Give me a minute."

I went to the kitchen, soaked a dish towel, and tamped the skin and hair around the wound, rinsed the towel, and touched it again and again, until the towel came away pink and then clear. I went to my bedroom and put my Glock on the dresser, emptied my jacket pockets, leaned the picture of the teenaged Judy Terrano against the mirror, balled up the jacket to soak in the sink, and changed into new jeans.

Jason and Lucinda gave me the same blank faces when I returned. "Bumped my head," I explained, and took a seat. They'd finished the tom yum soup and pad see yew but had left a few bites of red curry with shrimp. So I poured the remaining jasmine rice onto my plate and ate. My head hurt when I chewed. They watched me in silence. I swallowed a bite and looked up. "What?" I said.

Jason gave a little shrug. "You're still bleeding."

I tried the smile again. "A lot?"

A couple of quick shakes of his head.

"Then it will stop," I said, and ate another bite. "What happened to the cheek?"

Again the shrug. "I bumped it."

"Don't be a smart-ass. What happened?"

He hesitated, then said, "You remember that guy I told you about who burns other kids' butts with a lighter?"

I nodded.

"You remember how you said guys like him don't get away with that forever?"

I didn't like the direction this was taking. "Yes."

"I decided he shouldn't get away with it."

I took another bite, chewed, and thought. If my head hurt when I chewed, it hurt worse when I thought. "You pick the fight with him?"

The little shrug. "Kind of."

"Could you have stopped him without fighting?"

The question surprised him. "I don't know."

"You should have thought about it," I said.

He looked distressed but only a little and only for a moment. Then he ducked his head under the table.

"What are you doing?" I asked him.

His head reappeared. "Seeing if you had on sandals."

"Huh?"

"I thought you might have turned into Gandhi."

I shook my fork at him. "I'll Gandhi *you*."

He laughed.

I laughed, too, then said, "This really isn't funny. You'll hurt someone or you'll get hurt yourself. You'll get kicked out of school."

He looked like he was considering that. "Okay," he said.

"You're too smart for that. No more fighting."

"No more fighting," he agreed.

Lucinda leaned back and gazed at me wide-eyed. "How's it different from you coming in with a bump on your head?"

I glared at her. "It's different." As if saying it could make it true.

Jason leaned back, too. "How?"

"You're eleven. I'm forty-three."

Jason looked bewildered. I couldn't blame him.

"It's no different," Lucinda said.

Jason nodded.

I asked, "What do we have for dessert?"

Lucinda smiled. "You're not going to eat the rest of your dinner?"

"No," I said. "What do we have for dessert?"

"It's your house. You tell us."

I brought in a container of orange sherbet and three bowls, and I let them laugh at me while I finished my red curry with the sherbet. When Jason got up to clear his dishes, I saw a singe mark on the back pocket of his jeans.

Lucinda motioned at the wound on my head. "Let me guess," she said. "William DuBuclet?"

I blinked once at her. "How'd you know?"

"I spent the afternoon reading about him. He has a messy background. In the sixties, he led a radical leftist group. When the Black Panthers were still serving hot lunches to hungry kids and setting up inner-city community centers, DuBuclet's group pushed for immediate change, no matter the cost. That included armed violence.

"One of DuBuclet's sons died in a police raid, a kid named Anthony. He was a young guy, but he'd already taken a leading role in his dad's organization and in a more violent splinter group. The official story is that Anthony's death was too much for DuBuclet and he got religion. He went back to school and got a job teaching at Chicago State, and by that time he was all about peaceful action. That's the man you're going to see on the statues if they ever make them.

"But last December, the *Sun-Times* ran an article that said the old William DuBuclet was rumbling again. He'd made a couple of wild speeches and thrown around some violent language. Mostly the article took the angle that he's a soft-headed old man who isn't a danger to anyone but himself. But it also said his group is suspected in vandalism against businesses on the South Side and a couple attacks on the owners."

"DuBuclet isn't soft-headed."

She gestured toward the gash on my skull. "So what was this about?"

"They paid me five thousand dollars to lay off the Judy Terrano investigation, but they found out I was still involved." I ran my fingers over my matted hair. "This was their second request for me to get out."

"And you told them . . . ?"

I smiled. "I said, 'Okay.'"

She smiled, too, and gave that some thought. "You know that's also what Jason said when you told him to stop fighting."

"Damn."

"He's a smart kid, Joe. He'll learn whatever you teach him."

"That's what I'm afraid of."

"Yeah, you should be." Then, "You want to know about Judy Terrano?"

"What did you find?"

She went to the kitchen and came back with a small notebook. "Not much before 1989. In December '82 she got arrested along with three other nuns during a march protesting Reagan's policies in Nicaragua. This was liberation theology stuff—you know, the clergy on the front lines. The *Sun-Times* ran a photo of her and the other nuns carrying a pro-Sandinista banner and another of them in handcuffs. She got arrested twice more—in '84 and '85. Similar stuff.

"In '89, she started the abstinence campaign, and the *Tribune* ran a short article on her in the religion pages. They said she was a well-known figure in civil rights battles and Latin

American social rights, though I don't remember hearing her name back then. Six months later a *Sun-Times* editorial praised her for her plain speech about sex, though she'd apparently gotten into trouble with the archdiocese. By '94, she'd gone more extreme and the papers started calling her the Virginity Nun. She collected a bunch of awards and a bunch of ridicule. She made big claims about the success of her programs. The people who wanted to believe them did, and the people who didn't like her said she was full of it. No one doubted her commitment, though. She appeared at hundreds of school assemblies, church conferences, fund-raising banquets, and youth rallies."

"What about more recently?"

She flipped the page in the notebook. "Three years ago she got in trouble again, or almost. The *Trib* ran an article that said the Diocesan Finance Council, which is the group that keeps an eye on church finances, was looking at her after a hundred ninety thousand dollars went missing at Holy Trinity. There was no follow-up in the paper, so I'm guessing the money turned up or the Council realized they'd made a mistake. Or," she added, "the Church decided a cover-up was cheaper than bad publicity."

I considered that. "The room she was living in says she wasn't skimming from the offering plates. She was the kind of woman who saved soap slivers so she could pack them together and make a new bar."

"Yeah," Lucinda said, "but she also hid a stack of twenties in her desk. That doesn't look like a vow of poverty. What was she up to?"

I shrugged. "Something with William DuBuclet. If he was paying her off, she probably knew one of his secrets. Maybe that secret was worth killing for."

"Okay, but what was it?"

"Don't know," I said.

"I also Googled Judy Terrano's name," Lucinda said. "I got eleven thousand hits, so I didn't look too deep."

"Did you Google her name along with 'Bad Kitty'?"

She nodded. "Came up dry. What else did *you* come up with?"

I went to the bedroom for the picture and placed it on the dining room table in front of her.

"Who's that?" she said.

"Judy Terrano as a teenager."

"Wow." She ran a finger down the picture. "When I was eighteen, I wanted to look like that. Why the hell did she become a nun?"

"It's not like good-looking girls never do."

"She's more than good-looking," she said, and she held the picture close. "She's a sex kitten. I bet a lot of guys fell in love with her."

"Yeah," I said.

"How about William DuBuclet?"

"In love with her? He's thirty-five years older than she is."

"*You're* twenty-five years older than she was in this picture. Don't you want to sleep with her?"

"You're talking about a dead nun," I said.

She nodded like she knew it. "You do. Jesus, *I* almost want to."

I cocked my head at her. "You get a chance to research Eric Stone?"

"Not yet. The archives were closing. You think he's involved?"

"I wouldn't swear it, but yeah. Something's strange about him paying me five thousand dollars to keep an eye on DuBuclet.

He could afford one of the big security firms. The only reason to hire me is I'm already in the middle of this mess. I think he wants to keep a leash on me."

She nodded. "So what's next?"

"Tomorrow one of us looks at the archives for Eric Stone and one of us talks to Amy Samuelson to find out what she sees in Stone and what she's after."

"I'll take the librarians. I don't like ex-wives." The way she said it made me think there was something in it for me. We sat quiet for a moment and I felt her eyes on me. "Are we done?" she said.

"I suppose so."

She gave that a few seconds and then said, "You want to go to bed?" Like a surprise gift in the mail.

"Now?"

"If we're done talking, what else is there?"

"Jason's in his room."

She took my hand in hers. "He'll go to sleep sooner or later."

Three weeks earlier we'd spent the night together, the night she'd heard that she could either leave the department or spend the fourteen years leading up to pension in a police warehouse repairing radios, so far behind-the-scenes she wouldn't even hear sirens. She'd shot a man to death. It didn't matter that the man she'd killed was a killer himself. She'd used her service revolver and shot him outside city limits, breaking seven department regulations along the way. She was too hot for the higher-ups ever to put back on the street.

"Corrine is still—" I started, but I didn't know where I was going, so I shut up.

She pushed her chair back from the table and stood. "I told you I don't like ex-wives."

I stood, too, and reached for her, but she picked up her dishes and walked into the kitchen. I left mine on the table and followed her. When she turned from the counter I was there in front of her. I could hardly stand looking into those eyes. There was pain in them. I wondered if there was pain in mine.

Then she came to me and kissed me. She lifted herself onto the counter, opened her legs, and I moved close. I kissed her forehead, her eyes, her neck.

"I don't care about Corrine," she said.

"Shh," I said. We kissed. But then her eyes got big and she pulled away. "What?" I said.

An eleven-year-old boy's voice answered from behind me. "Can I have more orange sherbet?"

Jason stood in the hall doorway. I looked at my watch. It was 10:25. "Too late for dessert. You should be in bed."

He pointed at Lucinda. "Not until I see what happens here."

"Jason!"

He gave me innocent eyes and said calmly, "Joe?"

Lucinda climbed off the counter and straightened her shirt. She put a hand on my arm. "I should go home and let you get this guy into bed."

"I should lock this guy in—"

She stopped me with a quick kiss. Then she scooped her jacket and car keys from the counter and headed for the front door. I shook my finger at Jason and followed her.

"We've got plenty of time," she whispered as she slipped into her jacket. "Tomorrow night. The next night. Long drawn-out school days when we should be working."

She stepped outside into the cold.

When I went back into the kitchen, Jason had disappeared into his room. I went down the hall after him and knocked on his door. He was in bed, covers over his head, the lights still on. I sat on the edge of the bed.

"That was a rotten thing to do," I said.

From under the covers. "You could have told her to stay."

"You pretty much ruined that possibility."

"Sorry," he said.

"You'll understand in a few years," I said.

His head emerged from the covers. "I already understand."

"You do? Well, good, then—"

"I probably know more about it than you do."

I raised my eyebrows. "I don't doubt it."

"Yes, you do," he said.

"Look, you're eleven years old and—"

He propped himself on his elbows. "Some kids in my class are doing it."

I thought about that. "You?"

He looked disgusted. "Who would I do it with?"

This was making me sweat. "I don't know. Any of the girls you like." He narrowed his eyes and smirked. "Or boys . . . I mean, whatever you—"

He laughed at me. "You're so weird."

I shrugged. "I guess so."

"Did you know female aphids can have babies without mating with a male?"

"No," I said, "I didn't know that."

"See?"

"See what?"

"I told you I know more about it than you."

"I think you know a lot about a lot of things," I said, and I flipped off his light.

When I got to his door, he said, "Did you know aphids start having babies when they're one week old?"

"Good night, Jason," I said.

"I told you so."

EIGHTEEN

I GOT INTO BED at 11:00 and tried to take my mind off Lucinda. Thinking about Corrine was no better. I wanted to get back together with Corrine, but I screwed up every chance I got. Being with Lucinda was good and easy, or at least easier. Maybe I should wake up Jason and ask his advice.

I thought about Judy Terrano, dead with a black-cat tattoo and black-marker graffiti on her belly. That didn't help me sleep. I imagined her at age eighteen or nineteen, looking like she did in the picture propped on my dresser. What did she think about when she stood in front of a mirror, knowing that boys and men would do anything—anything at all—to be close to her? No matter what she did, she could have them all.

Sometime after midnight, I slept. I dreamed that Lucinda and I were in my kitchen having sex, her on the counter, me standing on the floor. I heard a noise behind me. A teenaged Judy Terrano stood in the hall doorway. She was naked and she laughed at us with the laughter of an angel. I jarred awake in the middle of the night.

The phone was ringing. My bedroom was dark and the glowing red on the clock said 2:23. In my night fear, I felt sure that a phone ringing at two in the morning must bring news of a death.

I grabbed at the receiver and said hello.

A voice mumbled at me.

I started to hang up, then returned the phone to my ear. "Who is this?" I said.

"Geg Sanuelson." A voice sputtered out of half a mouth.

"Greg Samuelson! What the hell—Where are you?"

"You office."

"Mine? How did you get in?"

He said nothing.

"What do you want?" I asked.

"Talk—to you."

"Fine. Talk to me about Judy Terrano."

"Need—to—talk."

"About what?"

"Noney."

Nunny? Judy Terrano? Then I realized—"Money?" With no bottom lip, he couldn't say *M*.

"I need."

I thought about the five thousand dollars I'd locked in a file drawer. If Samuelson had broken into my office, why hadn't he found it, too? "Stay where you are. I'll be there in half an hour."

When I hung up, I sat in bed half-awake. I'd told Stan Fleming that I would call him if I heard from Greg Samuelson. No reason that I shouldn't call him now. I was pretty sure he was smarter than I was and would handle Samuelson better. But I didn't call him.

I got up and put on jeans and a sweatshirt, strapped on my

shoulder holster, popped a loaded clip into my Glock, and slid the gun into the holster. I saw plenty of reasons to think Greg Samuelson was innocent, and I saw just as many to be ready to put a second bullet in his head.

I left a note on the kitchen counter telling Jason that I needed to go out but promising to be back in time to make him breakfast before school. I'd broken promises like that before and I wondered what they meant to him and why I made them. I wondered what breaking them made me. I grabbed a four pack of Red Bull from the refrigerator and slipped through the back door into the night. The night was quiet. After exchanging head wounds with me, Robert and Jarik had apparently gone home to put on Band-Aids. I sighed in the night air and felt my body come awake and alert.

I cruised east on Montrose under the El tracks and past Teldan's Bail-Bond Agency and a string of Mexican restaurants that stayed open every night until 2:00 A.M., then snapped closed, lights out. I popped the tab on a can of Red Bull, downed it, waited for the rush of caffeine. At the corner of Clark Street, the wind whipped from the north and made a metal road-repair sign shudder. I turned south on Lake Shore Drive and punched the gas. Ten minutes later I pulled to the curb outside my office. Eight stories up, my office light was on, the only light in the building.

I drew my gun and rode the elevator.

Samuelson sat behind my desk, like he was moving in. He'd torn away most of the bandages the hospital had put on him, but he'd left a packing of white gauze, which hung to his face with drying blood and something yellow and oily. His mouth, what was left of it, trembled. His glazed eyes turned slowly to look at me. His skin glistened with sickly sweat.

"If you stay out of prison and out of the mental ward," I said, "a reconstructive surgeon is going to put a kid through college on that face."

He responded with a grunt that was half liquid.

The file drawer with the five thousand dollars in it was closed. It didn't look like he'd broken into it. On top of the file cabinet, my coffeemaker steamed. Maybe Samuelson really was planning to move in. I poured myself a cup and sat in one of my client chairs.

"You're going to die if you don't get to a doctor."

He shrugged like it didn't matter.

"If you don't care, why are you haunting me in the middle of the night?"

He gave me a glassy stare and managed to spit out a noise that again sounded like "Noney."

"Money."

He nodded.

"For what?"

He said nothing.

I said, "You know where you should go? The police. They'll take care of you, get your chin fixed up, and you won't need money."

He shook his head.

"I don't get it. It's not like you're booking a flight to Mexico. What do you want?"

He struggled and said it again. "Noney." His mouth trembled. Talking hurt.

I wanted to hit him. "Yeah, money. What for?"

The glassy stare.

I took a deep drink of coffee. It tasted bitter but not as bad as I'd sometimes drunk.

"No one's giving you money, Greg. How'd you get here anyway? You've got to have cash to get around the city."

He raised his hands and held an imaginary steering wheel.

"You steal a car?"

He managed to say, "Ai—ny."

Amy. A shiver ran down my neck. Samuelson's wife. He'd burned her boyfriend's car. I didn't know what he would do to her. "You went to her house?"

He sputtered, "Ny—house."

"Okay, your house. What did you do to her? You hurt her?"

Hate shined through the glassy eyes. "Ass-hole." His face shook in pain. He closed his eyes until the worst seemed to pass. Then he managed, "Gone."

"She was gone?"

He nodded.

"Without taking her car?"

He shrugged.

I shook my head, and my exhaustion was dizzying. I should've brought another Red Bull from the car. "So you went to the condo and got, what, some clothes, the car, and, by the look in your eyes, something from the medicine cabinet?"

"Co"—he rested—"deine."

"And then you hung out all day waiting for her so you could hit her up for cash. But she didn't come home, and so you called me?"

He nodded.

I shook my head again, sipped from the coffee. "Okay," I said, "my advice is we arrange for you to turn yourself in. You're in more danger out than in. It's your best—"

"No."

The clarity of his voice stopped me short. I looked at him closely. "Did you kill Judy Terrano?"

Again clear. "No."

I watched to see if he was lying. But his glassy eyes and trembling face told me only that he was hurting.

"Did you shoot yourself?"

The smallest focus remained in his eyes, and the focus looked like hate. "'uck"—he trembled—"you."

"Yeah? Fuck you, too," I said. His glassy eyes were like mirrors. I felt a buzzing rush but steadied myself. "Tell me about the hundred ninety thousand dollars she stole from the church."

He shook his head like he was disgusted with me, but he didn't tell me to fuck off—he flipped his middle finger at me.

"Okay, then tell me about her tattoo."

He looked confused, but he might be faking stupid.

"The black cat tattoo," I told him.

His shaking head said he had no idea what I was talking about.

"The bad kitty on her belly."

The confusion lifted and he trembled. He smiled. It's possible for a man with only an upper jaw to smile but it's nothing you ever want to see.

"You know about the tattoo?" I asked.

He shook his head.

"You know about the BAD KITTY?"

He ignored the question. He struggled to get up from the desk chair but failed.

I shook my head and felt another buzzing rush. "I'm going to drive you to the hospital. You'll be safer off the street."

This time he managed to get out of the chair. He stumbled

around the desk. A dying nun could tackle him in the shape he was in. All I needed to do was stand up and block the door out of my office.

I stood and my head spun. My vision narrowed. I would pass out if I didn't sit. I sat. My vision cleared, some of it, and my head got off the carnival ride. Samuelson stood at the edge of the desk and watched me like he was a kid and I was a bug whose wings he'd clipped. I tried to stand again and got half-way up before I had to sit. He watched me and I shook my head. My head spun. I felt nauseous. "Damn," I said. "What's in the coffee?"

"Xan—ax. Lots."

"Xanax," I managed to repeat for no reason at all except I had no thoughts of my own and felt like I never would again.

He looked almost sorry.

"You bastard," I said, and tried to throw the rest of the coffee at him. I poured it down my leg.

The buzzing rushed through my head, then a fast, woozy calm.

My eyes closed themselves.

I fought to figure out what was happening. Samuelson looked sorry for something—tying up my mind in a knot, leaving me in a chair with drool running down my chin, serving me a bad cup of coffee. Whatever he was sorry for I was missing it. I'd disappeared down a drain into a hard, dreamless sleep. I was gone and I missed his apology.

I woke once with a shiver on the floor next to the chair and got sucked down the drain into sleep again. Later, I woke again, shivered—slept. A third time, I woke and fought clear of the drain, though it sucked at me like it wanted me forever. I felt a sock in my mouth and when I tried to spit it out it was my tongue. I needed my tongue. Or I would need it. Sometime. Some day.

I squinted at my watch. It was 5:20 in the morning. Less than two and a half hours had passed. Xanax still was pumping through my brain.

I peered around the office. Samuelson was gone. My ring of keys hung out from the lock on the file cabinet where I'd stashed the money that Robert and Jarik had paid me. I crawled to the cabinet and looked in. No surprise—the money was gone.

I felt my pockets. Samuelson had taken my wallet. I felt the rest of my clothes. He'd lied to me. He'd wanted more than money. He'd taken my gun, too.

I rested on the floor and tried to think clearly. After a few minutes I figured out that Samuelson hadn't taken my gun to shoot himself, at least not immediately. He could have killed himself a dozen ways without going to the trouble to get it. Who else would he use the gun on? His wife Amy? Eric Stone? William DuBuclet?

I figured DuBuclet could cover himself. Eric Stone was doubtful. Amy Samuelson more so.

Was Greg Samuelson a killer? With his back against the wall, maybe he would kill. And his back was definitely against a wall. Did he kill Judy Terrano? Did he kill the priest in her room? I couldn't see it. But I hadn't seen him drugging and robbing me either, not until it was too late. Why would he kill? Stan Fleming had said that his marriage was over, his job was about to go, and he had nothing to lose. Maybe he wanted company as the game ended.

I pushed myself onto my hands and knees. I needed to get to Amy Samuelson. If her husband was going after her, he was going after her with my gun.

I needed to move fast. But my body and mind were soaked blankets. So now would be a good time to call Stan. He could have a cruiser at the Samuelsons' condo in the time it took me to drag myself downstairs to my car. I stood up. Nausea swilled through my stomach and my vision narrowed but I held myself until my eyes cleared. I leaned against the desk. I squinted at it. My wallet was on it. Samuelson had removed fifty bucks and the credit cards.

He'd also removed the check Eric Stone had written to me. It sat next to the wallet on the desk. Ripped into eight pieces.

The credit cards might get him a one-way ticket to Mexico, the fifty bucks a plaster marker for his grave when he died there from his head wound. But the five thousand he'd taken from the file drawer would get him more, maybe a twelve-piece orchestra for the funeral.

I paced the room, leaning against the walls, panting, knees weak. The office couch looked like the best bed I'd ever seen. I wanted to lie on it and sleep until the day passed and then I wanted to sleep there until spring.

I paced some more.

I paced until I knew the pacing would do me no more good.

I stumbled out of the office and returned. I got the pot of coffee and poured it out the window, watching the steam rise into the dark.

NINETEEN

CIRCUS CLOWNS WERE SITTING on my feet, hugging my knees. I tried to kick them off, but they rode the elevator down with me and came with me to the car. I collapsed onto the driver's seat, slapped my cheeks, and guzzled a can of Red Bull.

My car rolled back up Wabash at a scary speed. The speed-ometer read twenty. The city lights glared as if stars had fallen from the sky and were burning cold on earth. Nausea tumbled through my belly as the Red Bull played with the Xanax. When the nausea passed, I got reckless and inched up to twenty-five.

A couple of minutes before six, I pulled into a fire lane in front of Samuelson's condo. Across the street, the window of Tommy Cheng's Chinese Restaurant was gray, the stools stacked upside down on the counter by the window. A few of Samuelson's early rising neighbors walked through the half light, freshly showered, wearing business suits, looking like they'd spent the night on something more comfortable than my office floor. After a while a middle-aged woman came out of the metal security gate to Samuelson's condo block. I wished her good morning and slipped through the gate into a bricked walkway. She hesitated, looking at me like I was a junkie.

Exterior stairs took me to a second-floor landing and a corridor that led to Samuelson's door. It was a nice door: solid wood, inlaid with parallel panels of frosted glass fitted together in a thin metal framework. There were two locks, one of them good. A jiggle of the door handle said at least one of the locks was doing its job. If my mind had been clear and I'd been carrying the right tools, I could have worked the locks in twenty or thirty minutes. I stumbled back down the stairs, found a chunk of decorative granite in the bushes by the walkway, and returned. I wrapped the stone in my jacket sleeve and punched the glass panel closest to the locks. The glass cracked, and the panel bent inward. Two more punches drew the metal framework from its wooden housing. I pushed the framework further, reached in, tumbled the locks, and let myself in.

Nothing about the place said murder might have happened.

I called, "Mrs. Samuelson?"

No one answered. That was either good or very bad.

I made my way through the front hall into the kitchen. Bloodied towels and bandages were scabbing brown in the stainless-steel sink. I stared at them and called louder, "Mrs. Samuelson?"

No answer.

I took a spatula from a container of kitchen utensils and pried the towels from the sink. I don't know what I expected to find under them. I found blood.

I moved deeper into the house. The living room shades were

closed over a set of glass doors that led to the balcony where I'd watched Eric Stone flex his muscles. I flipped on a light. Brown stains were smeared on a white sofa. Samuelson could have made those stains if he had rested while he waited for his wife. A large mailing envelope, marked with the LCR emblem and address of the Stones' real estate development company, sat on the coffee table in front of the sofa. I stepped into the doorway to the bedroom. "Mrs. Samuelson?"

The queen-sized bed was made, though its spread had more brown smears. No bodies tumbled out of the closet. Clothes, mostly a woman's, hung on the racks.

The bathroom was a mess. Bloody towels were in the tub and on the floor. The medicine cabinet door hung open, its shelves swept clean. Toothbrushes and a tube of toothpaste were scattered on the floor. Blood was smeared on the counter and on the toilet seat and mirror.

I found no dead bodies—no dead wife and no dead wife's dead boyfriend.

I went back into the living room. The sofa with the blood smears looked just right for an early morning nap. Maybe I could sit on it and recharge. Maybe I could rest my head on a bloodstained pillow.

A sharp, hard knock came at the front door.

I froze.

Another knock, followed by the beam of a flashlight through the hole I'd knocked in the window panel. A third knock and a loud voice. "Police!"

A patrolman strung out at the end of a night shift wouldn't like me breaking into Samuelson's condo, stoned on Xanax and Red Bull.

As the cop's gloved hand reached through the hole to the

doorknob, I moved to the balcony door and popped the lock, slid the door open, and stepped around the shades into the cold. The drop from the balcony to the grass was fifteen feet, maybe more. If I was lucky, on a straight fall I would break only my legs. I climbed onto the ledge and lowered myself until I could grab the vertical rails. My arm muscles burned and my head spun. I breathed deep, tried to get oxygen to my arms. My vision narrowed.

I fell.

I don't know how far, but I fell, and when I understood where I was, I was lying on the grass under the balcony. The grass felt good, good as a bed, good as a bloodstained sofa. But a tired patrolman would be interested in why I was camping on the lawn under a burglarized apartment, so I tried moving my arms, my neck and shoulders, my legs, my feet. I tried standing, and when I stood and felt no pain, I laughed. I laughed so loud that Samuelson's neighbors, eating their breakfasts, must have stopped and listened, a spoonful of oatmeal halfway to their mouths, wondering what could be so funny at 6:30 in the morning.

TWENTY

A CALL TO 411 got me the Stones' home phone number and address. They lived in a suburb west of the city. I knew the town. The first case I worked when I went private involved a missing teenaged boy who had lived there. The police chief walked between the redbrick police station and the bakery for his morning cup of coffee. The mayor chatted on the downtown sidewalks with the local ladies. But every path through the woods led to a little clearing where the kids got high. And watch out for what Aunt Bee was baking in the brownies. On the unincorporated edge of town a strip club called The Cheetah did hot business with the local men at lunchtime and again after the kids were tucked into their beds. One of the dirty secrets of the place was that the mayor and police chief owned shares in the club.

My investigation into the missing kid had uncovered a small-time drug dealing operation headed by the police chief's son. After that, the police chief and the mayor let me know the town was private property as far as I was concerned and if

I crossed the town line they would look at me as a trespasser—
and in that town, the mayor said, they shot trespassers.

I crossed the town line at 7:15 on a cold, clear morning. The
Stones lived in a large Georgian house with a plot of almost
treeless lawn that looked made for strolling barefoot on summer afternoons and for evening garden parties with open-
flapped tents and a string quartet. The garage would house
three Mercedes, burned or unburned.

A maid answered my knock. She wore black and white and
looked like an English servant but her voice was southwest
Chicago. I told her I needed to see Mrs. Stone and her boys,
and after closing the door on me for a couple of minutes she let
me in. The entrance hall expanded upward two stories to a
large glass chandelier, and a wide double stairway curved up
opposing walls to the second floor. At the base of the stairs,
backed by a curving marble bench, a fountain pulsed, the water braiding inside itself, tossing upward from a spout shaped
like a fish mouth. I would like to sleep away the day on the
bench, listening to water music.

The maid walked through a doorway into the living room.
We wound through several rooms until we came to a breakfast
nook. Mrs. Stone, her two sons, and Amy Samuelson sat at the
table with coffee and breakfast. At the back of the room a
glass door was propped open to an indoor swimming pool.
Morning light shined brightly into the room from the exterior
glass wall beyond the pool.

Mrs. Stone, her hair wet, wore a heavy terry-cloth robe. She
looked up at me and blinked. Eric Stone nodded. David Stone
and Amy Samuelson ate their breakfasts as if I wasn't there.

Mrs. Stone said, "Good morning, Mr. Kozmarski. I hadn't
expected to see you again so soon." The edge of her lips curled

upward. She kept her eyes on me but said to the maid, "Donna, please bring coffee for Mr. Kozmarski. And a chair."

I turned to Amy Samuelson. "Mrs. Samuelson, have you heard from your husband?"

She chewed a bite of toast and shook her head but didn't bother to look at me. "Should I have?"

"Have you been watching the news?"

A grimace crossed her lips. "As little as possible."

I said, "Greg walked out of his hospital room yesterday when the guard wasn't looking. He spent some time at your house, bleeding on the furniture and waiting for you. He has a gun, and I think he's looking for you."

Her face twitched but she said nothing. Eric placed a comforting hand on hers. He said, "The police called and warned Amy that Greg had escaped, but they mentioned nothing about a gun."

"They don't know." The maid brought the coffee, and I blew on it once and gulped.

Mrs. Stone watched me with her lips parted. "You think he's coming here?"

"It would make sense." I turned to Amy Samuelson. "He's got your car, so he must know you're riding around with Eric. And he knows you're not at home, so where else?"

David Stone pushed his chair back and stood up.

Mrs. Stone looked alarmed. "Where are you going?"

He was dressed in a blue tailored suit for a day at the office, his ponytail banded neatly behind him. He looked calm and mean. "If he shows up here, I'll shoot him."

"You'll do no such thing." She pointed at his chair.

He looked unhappy but he lowered himself into it. He mumbled, "The man's coming here with a gun to shoot us."

"Not in this house."

I asked David, "You've got a gun?"

He glanced at his mother and she shook her head. He said, "A couple of pistols."

I fixed on Mrs. Stone. "It wouldn't hurt to have them nearby."

"Not in this house."

A woman in a bikini came into the breakfast room from the hall, and the discussion stopped. I'd seen her twice before, when she and David Stone almost ran me down as Eric Stone's car burned and when she introduced herself as Cassie Stone after drawing a heart in the steam I'd blown on a glass wall in the Stones' office suite. But I hadn't seen her like this. She filled every centimeter of the bikini and more.

"Good morning, Daddy," she said to David Stone. She leaned over him farther than a daughter should lean over her father and kissed his cheek. Her bikinied hip brushed against me when she leaned.

Mrs. Stone spoke to her in the sweetest tone possible. "Cassie, would you please get the hell out of the breakfast room?"

Cassie gave her a wide-eyed look of mock surprise. "'Morning, Gram." She tucked her thumbs under the back of her bikini bottom and smoothed down the fabric, then sashayed through the open door to the pool. We sat in silence and listened to her hum a little tune, then splash into the water.

"Do you have children, Mr. Kozmarski?" Mrs. Stone said.

My heart jolted. I thought about Jason waking up to the note I'd written and finding me gone. I thought about the story of William DuBuclet changing his life of violence to peace because his son, Anthony, had died. And me? I couldn't even get home to cook Jason breakfast. "No," I said. "No kids."

"Then you might be smarter than you look," she said. She

sipped her coffee and added offhandedly, "The grandchildren are even worse. She's married three times already, and she's home again to her daddy and me."

A loud sound came from the room leading into the breakfast nook. Eric and David Stone started to rise from their chairs but sat hard as Greg Samuelson and the maid stepped through the doorway. Samuelson held the barrel of my Glock to the woman's cheek, and they stumbled forward together, the maid's eyes wild with fear.

He pushed her away from him. There wasn't much in the push, but she tumbled onto the table. Samuelson swung the gun side to side. David Stone leaned forward and looked ready to lunge from his chair. Samuelson's wife clung to Eric Stone's arm. Mrs. Stone watched with cold, closed lips.

Samuelson pointed the gun at Mrs. Stone. "Did—you—" He trembled.

Mrs. Stone interrupted him, her voice calm. "You'll get nothing by coming here."

That made Samuelson tremble some more. "Did—"

David Stone started to make his move, but Samuelson swung the gun on him and Stone sank back in his chair.

"And—*you*—" The gun fired and a terrific explosion sounded through the room. The shot went high and punched a softball-sized hole in the wall. The blast pushed Samuelson backward, but he stayed on his feet, and when he found his balance he looked as surprised as everyone else. The gruesome half smile he'd given me in my office formed on his face again and he laughed. The laugh made his face tremble with pain. Then David Stone laughed, too, and he leaned forward in his chair and rocked onto his feet.

Samuelson stopped laughing. He pointed the gun at David

Stone's chest. Stone went pale and inched down into his chair but Samuelson kept the gun on him. His eyes, which had been glassy, were clear and full of hate. "Not—yet." He caught his breath.

I figured the next one of us to move would take a bullet, but then Cassie Stone stepped into the doorway from the pool area. Her long hair fell in a twist behind her head. Water ran off her tanned skin. Her nipples protruded through her bikini top. She looked at the gun in the bloody man's hand and shook her head like she was disappointed.

She was the most amazing sight I could imagine on a cold October morning.

She stared at Samuelson and his gun, and a coy smile found her mouth. "Turn-ons?" she said, putting a finger to her lips. "Sunsets, sushi dinners, candlelight, sleepy-eyed men." She stepped toward Samuelson, dripping on the tile floor. He watched her, transfixed. We all did. "Turnoffs?" She pointed the finger at Samuelson's chest. "Ghouls."

She reached for him like she wanted to caress his groin. But instead she took the gun from his hand. The shock of her in a bikini seemed too much for him. She looked at the gun like it was a strange toy, turned it over and over in her hands, got bored of it, and dropped it on the breakfast table.

David Stone and I reached for it. He got there first. But I opened my palm to him.

"It's mine," I admitted. "Samuelson took it off me last night."

He looked me in the eyes, suspicious. He looked at the gun. He didn't want to but he gave it to me.

TWENTY-ONE

I DROVE TO THE District Thirteen police station with Samuelson in the passenger seat. Eric Stone had pulled me aside and asked if I could avoid mentioning that I'd picked up Samuelson at his mother's house. The family was about to announce the opening of Stone Tower, the luxury building that they'd been developing southwest of the Loop. News of their involvement in Judy Terrano's death could dent the sales.

"What does Samuelson want from you?" I'd said to him.

"He wants me dead. Me and Amy."

I shook my head. "I wouldn't blame him if he did, but he ignored you. He pointed his gun at your mother. Then he shot at David—more or less."

He frowned at that. "He shot at David because David's a fool and can't stay seated when he should. He pointed the gun at my mother, I'm guessing, because this is her house and his wife and I were in it."

I thought about the pieces of Stone's ripped-up check on my desk. I said, "You paid me to keep an eye on William DuBuclet, not to deal with Samuelson, but I can claim confidentiality. No guarantee, but I'll try to keep your name out of it."

"Have you done anything about DuBuclet?"

DuBuclet's helpers had laughed at me when I'd asked if he was interested in Amy Samuelson. "I think he's under control for now," I said.

Stone bound Samuelson's hands and feet with orange plastic twine, and his brother tied a cord from his wrists through the handle above the passenger door of my Skylark. He fashioned a gag for him but looked at Samuelson's face and thought better of it. They wrapped him like they wanted to send him securely to a faraway place.

I fished through his pockets until I found my credit cards. I checked the glove compartment of the car he'd been driving and found the five thousand dollars he'd taken from my file cabinet.

As we pulled out of the driveway my cell phone rang. It made me jump almost as high as Samuelson blowing a hole in the breakfast-room wall. The phone said the call was from my home number. I tried to shake the bad night from my voice and answered, "Good morning, Jason."

I pictured him sitting alone in my house, next to a note that had lied to him about the dependability of adults, or at least me, and I expected a morose eleven-year-old to reply. But he gave me cheer. "Morning, Joe. I know where you are."

I was driving through suburban streets in a town where the mayor and police chief had promised to shoot at me, sitting next to a man with half a face. "That's good because I hardly know where I am."

"Cool," he said, and he added with a note of mystery, "and I know who you're with."

Samuelson moaned quietly.

"I doubt that," I said.

Jason laughed, pleased with himself. "You like to kiss this person."

He thought I'd snuck over to Lucinda's apartment. I glanced at Samuelson. "Nope, not this one."

He laughed again. "I'm glad you went over there."

I saw no reason to explain. "You getting ready for school?"

"I'm not going to school," he said happily.

"Yes, you are," I growled. "Eat breakfast, put on your clothes—"

"Okay."

"And then go to school."

"I can't."

"You lose your shoes? Your legs stop working? You—"

"The principal suspended me for a day. For fighting Tim Naley."

"Jason!"

"Joe?"

Samuelson moaned louder. I shook my finger to quiet him. I said to Jason, "Why didn't you tell me last night?"

"I did tell you. When you asked me about my cheek."

"You told me you had a fight but you didn't tell me you got suspended."

"I thought you knew we weren't allowed to fight in school."

I gave myself a moment. "Get yourself some breakfast, okay? And get dressed. I'll be there as soon as I can."

"Okay."

Samuelson was leaning against the passenger door, eyes closed.

"It might be a couple hours."

"Okay," he said, and the pleasure of mystery returned to his voice as if he was imagining what Lucinda and I might be doing in those couple of hours. Then he added, "A man called and said it was important."

"He leave a name?"

Jason looked for the notepad where he'd written it. "Jarik."

DuBuclet's flunky. I figured he was nursing a headache as bad as mine this morning and that made me smile a little. "He leave a number?"

"He said he'll try you again later."

"All right," I said. "I'll see you in a while."

"Okay," he said. "Behave yourself."

"*You* behave yourself," I said.

He laughed and we hung up.

Samuelson moaned.

"Shut up," I said.

He opened his eyes. "Co—deine?" he managed.

"Yeah, right, I keep a quart of it in the glove compartment."

He gazed at the glove compartment like he wished it were true.

"Keep quiet for a minute," I said, and I dialed Lucinda's home number. It rang four times and the answering machine picked up. "Hey, it's me," I said. "I've got Samuelson. Long night, long story. I'm taking him to the Thirteenth. Can you do me a favor? Jason's home today. Can you swing by and check on him?"

I hung up and turned onto the on-ramp to the Eisenhower Expressway. Samuelson had become quiet but still breathed deep wet breaths.

"Now you get to tell me why you're doing what you're doing. It makes no sense to me—you, the Stones, Judy Terrano,

William DuBuclet, you're all part of a game, but I don't understand the rules and I don't know what you've been playing for."

He answered with more deep wet breaths.

"The clip in my gun holds thirteen rounds," I said to him. "I loaded it with ten. That's how many were in it when you took it from me in my office. You shot one into the Stones' wall. Did you plan to use the other nine on us?"

He stared through the front windshield at the morning traffic and said nothing.

"Your wife looked worried, clinging onto Eric Stone like that. But I don't think you planned to shoot her. You had the chance and you let it pass. Who else? Not me. You could've shot me in my office. You didn't want to shoot any of us, did you? 'Not yet.' That's what you said to David Stone. 'Not yet.'"

Again no answer.

"You wanted something, though, and I don't think it was to see Cassie Stone wandering around in her bikini. But she was worth the ticket price for me, a bit of sunshine on a cold fall day."

Nothing.

"Look, I don't think you killed Judy Terrano and I don't think you shot yourself. But the cops will hang this on you. They're so pissed off, you might never get to court. They'll find you dead in your cell—no one will argue it wasn't suicide."

He grunted.

"I figure you were in the room when Sister Terrano died. I figure whoever killed her shot you. Who did it? One of William DuBuclet's followers? One of the Stone brothers?—David?"

He said nothing. His eyes told me nothing.

I felt like hitting him. "What the hell do you get out of this?"

We rode like that: me making noise, him making silence. Then I snatched up my cell phone and punched in Lucinda's number again. It rang until the answering machine picked up, but I didn't have anything to add.

So I dialed Corrine.

"I've got a favor to ask," I said after we told each other hello. I told her about Jason's trouble at school.

"I've got appointments this morning, Joe. I can't cancel them."

"I know. Can you take him with you?"

She sighed. "How long?"

"Ten o'clock. Maybe eleven."

"Ten," she said. "No later. And you owe me."

"I'll pay you back anyway you like."

"Hmm," she said, and I heard desire in that sound.

I let myself think about ways I could repay her. Then I exited at Division, and before I could slow, the passenger door swung open. Samuelson had gotten to the door handle—I don't know how. He leaned his body out and hung like a hammock over the open pavement. He kicked his feet against the mat and his body lowered.

I hit the brakes and grabbed him by the belt. He struggled as much as a half-dead guy can struggle. I heaved him back into the car, pulled to the side, and stopped. "What the hell are you doing?" I yelled.

He stared out the front windshield.

I clenched my left fist and leaned in on him.

He closed his eyes like he was getting ready to sleep.

I climbed out, went around the car. "You want to die? Get the hell out of the car! I'll push you into the traffic!"

He sat where he was. Tears formed under his closed eyes and streamed down his face. He sobbed.

"Oh, Jesus!" I said, and I slammed his door.

We sat on the side of the exit ramp, him sobbing, me listening to his sobs and thinking I would prefer almost any other sound, even his moans. The sobbing made him human and I preferred to think of him as a crazed, sick animal.

"Tell me what this is all about," I said.

He sputtered but something less than words came out.

I kept myself from punching him, barely. "Fine. You can tell it to the cops," I said.

"No."

"Then tell it to me. What did you mean when David Stone stood up at his breakfast table and you said 'Not yet'? Did you mean you're going to shoot him later? Not yet, but soon? Did you mean something else?"

He stared at the windshield and looked like he was building energy to talk. He wasn't.

"Tell me," I yelled.

"Tired—" he said.

"Yeah, right, tired—me too." Then I brushed him away. "There's nothing I can do for you."

He looked at me, his eyes glazed with pain and grief and exhaustion, his face grislier than the faces of the dead priest and dead nun. He looked like he was about to plead with me for something no one could give him—a new life, a fresh start. Then he did it. He said, "Let—ne—go."

I laughed. "You've got to be kidding. Let you go? What happens then? You going to stumble down the highway until you get to the Stones' house? You going to stand on the shoulder with your gruesome face until a Good Samaritan stops and gives you a ride? Let's say by some miracle you manage to get to the house, what then? What could you possibly do that would make any difference?"

None of that changed his expression. "Let—ne—go," he repeated.

I shifted the car into drive. "No," I said.

THE STREET OUTSIDE THE District Thirteen station was lined with cop cars and a couple of news vans. The sky was bright, cold, and clear. The sun, glinting off the car polish and the pavement, threatened to make the morning happy. I parked behind a cruiser, untied Samuelson's feet, and marched him into the station. A couple of reporters were talking with tired-eyed video-cam operators who sat on the floor, backs against the wall. A heavy-set woman cop sat at the front desk. Four other uniformed cops were chatting by a soda machine. As we walked in, they glanced at us, did a double take, and surrounded us like I'd stepped onto a dock with the prize-winning fish.

I kept moving. "Detective Fleming?" I said to the woman at the desk.

She stood, flustered, and dialed the telephone, spoke into it, then came from behind her desk and showed us through a door that looked like more than one unruly prisoner had bounced against it. Stan Fleming jogged down the hall toward us, met us halfway. He grinned. "If it isn't Duane 'Dog' the bounty hunter and his half-faced quarry."

"Yeah, but you don't have to pay me for him."

He looked at me top to bottom. "You look like hell."

"Yeah," I said, "and feel like it."

He tipped his head toward some doors at the end of the hall.

"Come on." He took Samuelson by the wrists and tugged him along.

"Co—deine?" Samuelson pleaded as he stumbled down the hall.

"You're going to hear a lot of that," I said to Stan.

He stopped and got close to Samuelson. "You hurting?"

Samuelson nodded.

Stan said, "I'm sorry to inconvenience you, Mr. Samuelson, but we don't keep any painkillers in the station." There was real pleasure in his voice.

He took Samuelson to an interview room and left him there shackled to a steel table. We stepped into his office. On his desk he had a picture of a woman who, I noticed, wasn't Corrine. Other than the picture, he kept a lot of stacks of paper on his desk.

"Okay," he said. "Spill it."

TWENTY-TWO

I TOLD HIM A lot of it. I told him about Samuelson's call and about going to my office and having Samuelson hit me up for cash. I admitted to the Xanax and Samuelson rolling me for my gun and my money. I told him that dirty money seemed to be a common theme since Judy Terrano apparently had played loose with $190,000 a few years back. Stan nodded like he knew about the scandal. I told him that I'd grilled Samuelson about Judy Terrano, and Samuelson had given me nothing but tears, lies, and moans. I saw no reason to do the Stones any favors, no reason to help them pay the mortgage on their mansion and swimming pool, but I left out everything that happened west of the city. I said I'd tracked down Samuelson's wife early this morning and found him with her, which was close enough to the truth that I could live with it.

Stan took it all in, then looked at his watch. "It's five of nine. What happened between three and now?"

I shrugged. "Time slipped away. You know how it is."

His cheer fell from his face. "I've got no idea how it is. Tell me."

"Nothing to tell," I said.

"And you didn't call me when you first heard from Samuelson. Why?"

An honest answer probably would have included a long discussion about Corrine and maybe a short one about his promotion to lead detective in the Chicago Police Department while I was terminated without benefits. So I shrugged.

He drummed his fingers on his desktop, then made a decision. "Are we going to find any more dead nuns or priests?"

"Not that I know of."

"Any other bodies that mysteriously died during the night?"

"I don't think so."

He drummed his fingers some more. He looked at me like I deserved no more sympathy than Samuelson. "Okay," he said.

"Okay?"

"For now."

I watched through a one-way mirror as he went to talk to Samuelson. But as I expected, Samuelson wasn't talking. Stan raised his hand and threatened to hit his face and Samuelson shrunk away, but Stan didn't hit him and Samuelson soon learned the trick. After twenty minutes Stan came out without hearing a word, not even another request for codeine.

Stan sat in the chair next to mine and watched Samuelson through the viewing glass. "We're going to need to get him back to the hospital," he said. "Don't want him dying in the station house."

"Seems like a smart move," I said. "You mind if I go home?"

"You're not going to tell me where he was all night?"

"Are you charging him?" I said.

"Yeah, for burning the car," he said. "We don't have enough for the nun or the priest yet."

"Then last night is confidential. For now."

He shrugged and waved at the door. "Get the hell out of here." He was tired of me. I understood why. I was tired of myself.

I went out a back door at 9:30. If I headed straight home I would get there by Corrine's ten o'clock deadline. I could even stop for a take-out coffee and bagel. If I swung by my office, I would be a half hour late.

I dialed my home number on my cell phone. After three rings Corrine picked up.

I said, "Jason's a great kid, isn't he?"

She thought about that a moment. "Yeah," she said. "How much longer?"

"Another hour?"

She growled, "Joe!"

"Forty-five minutes?"

"This is what I hate about you."

"I know."

"Then why do you do it?" she asked.

"I don't know," I admitted. "People keep dying. I don't want them to. It happens."

She laughed. I didn't know if that was good or bad or if she was laughing with me or at me. So I laughed, too, and said, "I'll be there soon."

I DROVE DOWNTOWN TO my office, parked, and went into Grandma's Kitchen and ordered the three-egg breakfast special to go. Alexandros looked hard at my face and my hair, matted with blood from Robert and Jarik. He leaned over the counter and beckoned me close. "You know my cousin, the one that wants a date with you?"

I nodded.

He shook his head. "She changed her mind."

I took the breakfast up to my office, put my five thousand dollars back in a drawer, turned on my computer, glanced at the red light blinking on the answering machine, and ripped open the bags containing my food. I ate my scrambled eggs, toast, and sausage while the computer warmed up. I tickled the computer mouse and brought up Google, then stepped out of my office to the restroom across the hall. I ran water over my face and arms and shampooed the dried blood from my hair with soap from the dispenser. When I was done, the face that stared back at me from the mirror needed a good night's sleep, a three-week vacation, and a month in a woman's arms, but other than that it looked fine.

In my office, I sat and thought. I needed to know more about the Stones and their business. I Googled *LCR* and *Lakeview Commercial and Residential Real Estate Development*, and got twelve hundred hits. I sighed, pushed back my chair, looked at the screen, and thought about other terms I could add to narrow the search. *Judy Terrano* or *William DuBuclet* might be interesting. *Eric Stone* or *David Stone* would make sense. So would their mother's name, *Dorothy Stone*. I wondered what would happen if I typed the name of David Stone's daughter, *Cassie*, and added *bikini*.

I was too tired for this. I needed to go home and sleep, and I needed to let Corrine get to work. When I woke, I could play computer games all I liked.

I put on my jacket. But as I closed my office door behind me, the red answering machine light winked at me. I stepped back inside and hit the Play button.

Jarik spoke with a calm, quiet voice but it had danger in it. "Hey, Mr. Kozmarski," he said. "We picked up your girlfriend when she left your house last night. A little girl named Lucinda. She's doing fine, just fine, chilling with me and Robert. But she's missing you. And Robert and me, we are, too. We're all missing you. We'll be calling you soon, all right?"

The message ended. He left no phone number. He left nothing but the vague threat. They had Lucinda. And I no longer felt tired. I felt angry and cold.

TWENTY-THREE

I SPED SOUTH OUT of the Loop. The Dan Ryan Expressway had enough lanes to land a jet, and I used them all. On the
side of the highway, the shell of Sox Park was dead and would
be until the spring, the players flown south for the winter.
Brown low-rise apartments and warehouses always would look
abandoned, no matter how much life was in them.

I exited and shot through the streets of Beverly until I
reached William DuBuclet's brick house. The lights were off
but I pounded on the front door anyway, rattled the doorknob,
and pounded some more. I was reaching for my gun, figuring
the butt against the wooden door would get the attention of
anyone in the house and probably the neighbors' houses, too,
when the woman who had answered the door the last time I'd
been there opened it again and peered at me from sad, droop-
ing eyes. "Yeesss?" she said, like she'd never seen me before.

"I need to see William DuBuclet." I started inside without
an invitation.

She stood her ground and shook her head half a shake. "Mr. DuBuclet's not available," she said slowly.

I could knock her over. "He'll want to see me. It's about Jarik and Robert."

She stared at my mouth like I might have something more to say. I didn't. "Very well," she said, and she turned from the door. She led me up the hall to DuBuclet's office, knocked on the door, and cracked it open. "Joseph Kozmarski is here to see you," she said.

"Let him in," said DuBuclet.

He sat at his desk, reading a book bound in cracking black leather. His tall, dull-eyed, dully smiling grandson sat across the room from him in a wheelchair. Last time, the grandson had worn striped pants and a striped shirt and had clapped silently. He still clapped silently, though now he wore jeans and a sweatshirt.

DuBuclet opened the top drawer of the desk and slid the book into it. A stick of cedar incense burned on a metal tray in front of him. He motioned to a chair facing his.

"I've been following the news on TV and the radio," he said. "I understand that Greg Samuelson is back in custody."

I waved that away. "Robert and Jarik have my partner, Lucinda Juarez."

He looked at me, perplexed.

"Don't give me that look. They do what you tell them to do."

He shook his head. "I'm afraid that's not entirely true. Please explain what happened."

I said, "Last night they paid me a visit." He nodded like he knew that much. "They took me for a ride and told me again that they wanted me to stop investigating Judy Terrano's death. They'd found out I'd agreed to help the cops, and they didn't like that." DuBuclet frowned. He already knew about the cops and didn't like it either. "They said your interest in Judy Terrano was personal, a deep dark secret from an earlier life. They didn't like me digging into that. Jarik clubbed me on the head to make the message stick. Then I clubbed him and Robert to let them know I didn't appreciate that kind of reminder. Later, to remind me again, I suppose, they grabbed my partner as she left my house."

"I wasn't aware of that part of it," he said.

"They still have her. I don't like this kind of reminder either."

He put two fingers to his lips. "Are you planning to grab me to make the point?"

"The idea crossed my mind."

He looked down and shook his head. "Don't ever go into business with the people you love," he said.

"That's the second time in two days I've heard that."

"It's good advice."

I thought about what Lucinda had found in the files about DuBuclet's son, dead in a police raid. "How about Anthony? Was he in the family business?"

He flinched. "What do you know about my son?"

"Just that he got killed about forty years ago. And afterward, you changed your heart about the best ways to fight."

Fatigue seemed to weigh him down, the fatigue of a man who was pushing hard toward a hundred years old, the kind of fatigue that might stop an old man's heart. "It was 1969," he said. "December 4. Three days before Pearl Harbor Day. My boy was sleeping with some friends in an apartment on Fifty-ninth Street. If you want the truth, they had a gun, just one, and about a dozen lightbulbs and some kerosene. You can break the neck off a bulb, fill it with kerosene, and you've got a handy, little Molotov cocktail. They weren't innocent. None of us were. I'll never pretend we were.

"Four in the morning, the police broke into the apartment and shot my son dead. Ninety-nine shots. And you know how many shots my son's friends returned? One. One shot. You do the math. They shot my son in the doorway to his bedroom. His girlfriend was lying in bed behind him. Pregnant, you know. He was wearing boxer shorts, and the police shot him in the head. The newspapers showed the picture. Press conference the next day called him 'vicious,' called him 'violent,' like an animal. Maybe he was, I don't know. But I do know that if he was violent and vicious it was because the police made him so. Because I know where he came from. I know that much. And I know that this supposedly violent, vicious man died in boxer shorts, without a gun in his hand. Pitiful. He was twenty-one years old."

I watched him talk. I listened to a voice that had come through a pain that I thought I understood, a pain that smelled of infection and guilt. He was ninety-six years old and he'd come through that and there was something extraordinary about him sitting at his desk telling me his story, weighed down by decades of grief, but still talking. I said, "Where's my partner?"

He shrugged, picked up a telephone, and dialed. He listened to it ring. I watched him listen. He said, "Robert, call me right away." He hung up and dialed again. He left a similar message for Jarik. "They're not answering their cell phones."

"Not good enough," I said. "What are you going to do to find her?"

He looked at me level. "Not much else I can do. If I were thirty years younger, they wouldn't have done this. If I were your age, they wouldn't even have dared to *think* about doing it. But I'm old and sick, and when the boys don't listen to me there's not a lot I can do about it."

"You don't fool me. They do whatever you tell them. I want Lucinda Juarez now."

He nodded and a small smile crossed his lips. "Undoubtedly you do. But as you must have learned by now, we protect ourselves and our own first, and only then, if we're able to do so, we protect others."

"I'm amazed that you consider Robert and Jarik your own."

"They're what I have," he said. "Just as you have Lucinda Juarez—and that nephew of yours."

I heard the threat in that. He knew too much about me, about my family, about all I loved. "You won't have Robert and Jarik much longer if they've done anything to hurt her."

His smile turned grim. "I understand that, and it would sadden me terribly."

"Me too," I said. "Call me the moment you hear from them." I stood and turned to the door but stopped. "What's the connection between you and Judy Terrano?"

He looked astounded that I didn't already know. "She was my son's girlfriend."

The look on my face made his eyes glint with a small pleasure. "In 1969," he said. "She was involved."

I needed a moment to sort out what I was hearing. "You're saying Judy Terrano was the girl who was in the apartment when the cops shot your son?"

"Yes."

"And she was pregnant?"

"Hell, yes."

"Wow!" I said.

He laughed.

"Is the—Where's the child now?"

"He's sitting right behind you."

I turned and my eyes met the dull eyes of the tall, clapping man in the wheelchair.

DuBuclet spoke gently to his grandson, "Tony, say hello to Mr. Kozmarski."

The man said nothing, but a big baritone laugh erupted from his mouth.

William DuBuclet laughed, too, and said, "He's the love of my old age."

I needed a moment to think. "Then why would you want me to stop investigating his mother's murder?"

DuBuclet sighed. "You're part of the problem, not the solution." He said it gently, like he was easing me into bad news.

"Huh? Why? Because I'm white?"

"For a starter, yes. And because you were a cop and your daddy was a cop, and for all I know your daddy's daddy was a cop. And your friends are cops. You might not want to be, but you're blind."

"That's bullshit," I said. "It's worth pistol-whipping me and kidnapping my partner to get me to quit?"

He laughed at me. "You made the world, I didn't."

"Me? I'm just trying to survive in it."

He shrugged. "Like the rest of us, Mr. Kozmarski."

I said, "Seems to me you're still living in the past."

"The past is right here between you and me," he said. "I can feel it in this room. I can smell it. You're living in the past, too—you just don't know it."

His grandson clapped silently.

I said, "How did Anthony and Judy Terrano get together?"

He shook his head. "You don't quit, do you?" He considered me for a minute and said, "At twenty, anything's possible, isn't it? There was a hangout in the old Maxwell Street area. The whites—mostly Poles like you, Jews and Christians both—had moved out of the neighborhood, but they came back in to sell overpriced groceries from their grocery stores to the blacks who'd moved into their tenements. The '68 riots had come and gone. The West Side already had burned, a lot of it. So, early in the summer of '69, some kids in their teens and twenties started squatting in a vacant house. They filled it with old chairs, and sofas, and mattresses for those who wanted to spend the night. They'd come and drink, and party, and screw. Most of the guys my son was involved with stuck far away from the place. I don't know what my son was doing there. Curiosity, I guess. But he went and he met Judy Terrano. I can't say I blame him for falling for her. One thing led to another, and by Pearl Harbor Day my son was dead and Judy Terrano was carrying the child of a man the police had called a vicious animal."

If all that DuBuclet had told me was true, he'd told me a lot. But I didn't know how much of it to believe. I asked, "Is the building where they had the hangout still there?"

He shook his head. "It burned later the same year. Those were tough nights. Smoky ones, too. Now the rest of the neighborhood's gone, wiped out. Wrecking ball, bulldozer, backhoe, and steamroller—every machine that weighs ten tons or more has been through there."

I thought about that and asked, "Did the kids who hung out at the place call it the Bad Kitty?"

He smiled. "Now I'm impressed. Yes, the Bad Kitty. The Bad Kitty Lounge."

TWENTY-FOUR

I CALLED A MAN I hadn't seen or talked to in three and a half years, not since the day Corrine and I got married. He was one of those guys you see only when someone's walking down the aisle or lying in a casket, but you like more than half the people you see every day. "I need a favor," I said. "Maybe a lot of favors." Lucinda was gone and I didn't trust William DuBuclet to bring her back.

He said, "Come on over." Like we saw each other every day.

I drove through the South Side and cut east into Bronzeville. The mayor had been turning downtown Chicago into a garden city. Flower beds bloomed all summer and park fountains played until the winter ice threatened to break their pipes. But the South Side was outside of the garden, mostly. The streets needed repaving, the sidewalks, too. Trash and dead weeds covered the vacant lots. The downtown high-rises fell away to brick tenements, two-flats, apartment blocks, and empty store-fronts with ghostly windows covered by burglar bars. Developers had poured money into a few corners of Bronzeville but the rest of the neighborhood ate away at those corners like rust.

I found my way to Forty-fifth and Lawrence and parked at the curb outside a gray, one-story commercial building. In a vacant lot across the intersection, a dozen men sat on an assortment of chairs around a trash and wood fire. A couple of them were drinking. A couple smoked. The others just hung out. Across the intersection the other way, a toothless woman sat on the steps of a crumbling gray stone, taking in the sun.

I rolled down my window and took in the sun, too. The air was still cool but the bright light warmed my skin. The breeze tasted like lake air and wood smoke. I closed my eyes and tried not to worry about Lucinda.

"Hey," a deep voice said.

I opened my eyes. A man stood outside my window. He was huge—around six foot four and three hundred pounds so when he stood on a bathroom scale the needle would spin once around and land on zero. He carried most of the weight in his chest and shoulders. He wore a black baseball cap with a sunshade hanging from the back. He had a close-cropped goatee and his eyes were set a little too close together, which gave him an almost unimaginable gentleness.

I rolled up my window and got out of the car. The big man and I gave each other a big hug.

I said, "How've you been, Terrence?"

He gave me the gentlest of grins. "Getting by. You?"

"Same," I said. "Barely."

"That's enough, I figure. How's Corrine?"

I shrugged. "We split up."

He shook his head like he felt it. "Sorry."

"It's okay," I said. "We're still working on it. How about Darlene?"

The grin came back. "Better and better."

"That's what I want to hear."

"Come on," he said, and he led me through a trash-filled alley, around the side of the gray commercial building, across a McDonald's parking lot where seagulls were fighting over a scattered pack of French fries, and toward a redbrick apartment building with wooden stairs hanging off the back.

I'd met Terrence Messier when we were going through the academy together. He'd scored perfect or near perfect in every course from Crisis Prevention to Presentation of Evidence. He'd broken the academy record in the muscular endurance tests and scored near the top on the pistol range. Our instructors had called in their supervisors to watch what he could do. Then five weeks before graduation his younger brother was walking home from working minimum wage at a Pizza Hut and took a bullet in his forehead. The cops were on the street breaking up a small coke-dealing operation, and they thought Terrence's brother presented a clear danger. He'd come out of nowhere carrying a metallic object that turned out to be a foil-wrapped slice with pepperoni and mushrooms. The DA had ruled the shooting justifiable, and the next morning Terrence had cleaned out his locker at the academy. Since then he'd made his living by hustling.

Terrence led me up the wooden stairs. On the first landing, we stepped past a tangle of dirty tricycles and bikes. On the second landing, we stepped over cases of empty beer bottles. The third landing faced a door. Terrence unlocked it and we stepped into a courtyard garden. He'd nailed wooden lattices to the exterior vertical supports, leaving a gap of a couple feet to let in air and light. Roses, flowering vines, and ferns filled most of the rest of the space. The plants, fed by the heat of the building, still lived, though the October cold was killing everything outside. In the middle of all the plants two reclining chairs waited for Terrence and his girlfriend Darlene.

"Nice," I said.

"My island retreat."

He stepped past the plants to a large plate-glass door. He unlocked it, too, and we stepped inside. The inside looked nothing like the neighborhood. The sofa and chairs were leather. The rugs looked hand-loomed. The lighting was modern, with lots of exposed wires, halogen bulbs, and accents over the framed pictures, also modern.

"Nice," I said again. "And you got all this by doing what?"

He looked at me square. "By doing what I've got to do. You got a problem with that?"

"It's what I do every day."

"All right then." He allowed himself an appreciative glance at his possessions. "I decided I like high-end."

"Yeah, I'm feeling altitude sick."

He looked at me with those gentle eyes. "What can I do for you?"

I told him about Lucinda's kidnapping, then gave him the background, starting with William DuBuclet, Robert, and Jarik and ending with DuBuclet's connection to Judy Terrano and the Bad Kitty Lounge. He knew about DuBuclet but not about the link to Judy Terrano. He'd never heard of the Bad Kitty Lounge but he knew people who would know about it.

He got his phone and cupped the receiver in his big hand like it was a child's toy. He purred into it, hung up, and dialed again, then purred some more. Everyone he called seemed glad to hear from him, and if they didn't give him what he asked for he asked again, never raising his voice above a soft purr.

After he hung up the last time, he said, "They've got her in Chinatown." He looked at me hard. "DuBuclet's a dangerous old bastard. You know what you're getting into if you tangle with him?"

"I'm already tangled," I said. "Anyway, I kind of like him. He reminds me of another big tough man I know."

He shook his head. "Compared to him, I'm a violet. He wouldn't notice if he stepped on me."

"You sure *you* want to tangle with him?"

He laughed. "You know me. I've never been scared of getting stepped on."

"You have a gun?"

"Just a minute." He disappeared into a bedroom and reappeared cradling a FAMAS assault rifle. "Yeah," he said, "I've got a gun."

"You have anything smaller?"

"Yeah, if you insist." He disappeared and reappeared again, this time with a Smith & Wesson pistol that would have looked enormous in anyone else's hand but his. "Does this suit your delicate tastes better?"

"What if I said no?"

"Darlene's got a fingernail file somewhere. I could borrow it."

"Your fingernails look fine. Let's go."

TWENTY-FIVE

WE DROVE INTO CHINATOWN, Terrence's knees crammed against my glove compartment. The smell of ginger and garlic filtered into the car from outside. "If Robert and Jarik don't kill us, I buy lunch," I said.

Terrence grunted and kept his eyes on the street.

We turned off the main drag onto West Twenty-third and left the smell of lunch behind. At the far end of the street, narrow little houses stood shoulder to shoulder. Beyond them a chain-link fence rimmed an industrial park. I squeezed my car into a spot at the curb and we walked four houses back.

The house that Terrence took us to looked no different from any other on the street. Cheap, white gauze curtains covered the front window. A screen door that had seen too much winter hung loosely on its hinges, covering a wooden door that had seen the same. The window, the red brick, and even the roof and the front sidewalk looked clean but cheap and old and tired.

We walked up the front path and drew our guns. The window watched us like a cloudy eye.

"Should've let me bring my other gun," Terrence muttered.

"You should've offered me one, too."

"All you needed to do was ask."

I glanced at him to see if he really had extra assault rifles ready for a loan. He gave me nothing back.

On the front doorstep Terrence held the doorknob, squared his shoulder against the door, and pushed. The top of the door creaked quietly inward from the frame, and the lock bolt splintered the old wood that had held it. The door blew open with hardly a sound.

We stepped into a softly lighted living room. Old, floral-print couches, chairs, and a coffee table were all the furniture. I wondered for a moment if we'd broken into the wrong house and we would find an aging Chinese couple drinking tea in the kitchen, but hip-hop music played from somewhere in the back, so I figured the owner might have rented the place to a couple guys I'd exchanged head wounds with. The hall floor sagged underfoot. There were three closed doors on the left and an open doorway at the end of the hall, leading into a brightly lighted room with an exterior door visible on the far wall.

We stopped at the first closed door and Terrence held his pistol close to his chest like it was a small animal he'd rescued, then pointed it into the room as I eased the door open. The room was dark and smelled like sweat and musty sleep. A heavy curtain covered the window. Dirty clothes lay on the floor. Two unmade single beds stood against the walls. A man slept faceup on one of them. He had on sweatpants with one pant leg pushed up around his knee and a ribbed, sleeveless white T-shirt. He looked like he could have been Robert's brother. I eased the door shut again.

The second door was a foul-smelling bathroom.

The third door stuck when I tried to open it. I used Terrence's trick, holding the knob and leaning in. No lock held the door shut, just a damp, warped door frame. It sprang open with a loud crack.

Chairs scraped on the tile floor in the next room.

Terrence swung around and stepped into the bright room, gun first. I went through the door I'd forced open and into a dim bedroom. Lucinda sat inside on a metal-framed bed, her ankles chained to the foot posts, her wrists to the headboard, with just enough play to allow her to sit. She had a nasty bruise on her jaw and another under her left eye.

I closed the door behind me.

"Where the hell have you been?" she said, friendly enough.

I went to her and checked the chains and locks. They weren't coming off without help. "Do you know where the keys are?"

She nodded toward the room that Terrence had entered. "They've got them."

I looked at her face and touched her bruised jaw. She flinched. "How bad?" I asked.

"They barely touched me."

"Yeah?"

"Perfect gentlemen. They served me breakfast in bed."

There was a commotion in the next room, chairs tipping over, furniture sliding across the floor.

"I'll be right back, okay?" I started to the door.

"Come soon." She smiled but I heard the fear.

The bright room was a kitchen—a table, a couple of chairs, a sink, a refrigerator, and a stove and oven, nothing more except the remains of Chinese takeout on the table. Terrence had Robert and Jarik up against a wall. He held his pistol against

Robert's forehead. He had a hand on Jarik's chest. But our visit had awakened the man who'd been sleeping in the first bedroom. He stood behind Terrence and held a gun to his back. The four of them stood so still you could've painted them.

I stepped into the room and pointed my Glock at the man's back. "Put down the gun," I said.

They all looked at me at once. "I'm not putting down shit," the man said.

"I shoot you, you shoot my friend, and my friend shoots Robert. Who wins?" I said.

A crazy little smile crossed his face. "No one wins, but I'll tell you who loses. You do. You're the only one that seems to care. I don't give a shit if you shoot me. Your friend and Robert, they're dead, so it don't matter if they care. Who the hell cares?"

"You hear that, Terrence? This man doesn't care if you die."

"Yeah. No one's insulted me like that since I was thirteen years old."

"What did you do then?"

"I broke a couple of the kid's ribs. Didn't mean to. I just hit him too hard."

I spoke to the man with the gun. "So, what's the point of your speech other than you're asking for broken ribs?"

"Point is, if you don't want me to put any holes in this big, fucking black man, you'll put down your gun." He shoved the barrel of his pistol further into Terrence's back.

It was a good point but I held my gun on him.

His eyes twitched. He said, "I'm counting to three, and I shoot."

I let him get to two, then lowered my gun.

"Your turn, big guy," the man said to Terrence. "Put it down."

Terrence didn't put down his gun. He removed his hand from Jarik's chest and spun. His fist caught the man under the chin. The man's head snapped back, his body rose, and his feet lifted off the floor. When he came down, his feet were no longer feet. They were just floppy things that eased his fall.

Robert made a play for Terrence's gun. It was a big mistake, as all things were big when dealing with Terrence. Terrence brought his free hand forward, grabbed Robert under the chin, and lifted him in the air. Terrence pressed his lips together but other than that showed no sign that he was working. Robert kicked at him but Terrence squeezed his throat and lifted him higher. Robert stopped kicking. Jarik glanced at the gun that his friend had dropped when Terrence hit him, then glanced at Terrence, and thought better than to go for it. I picked it up and tucked it in my waistband. When Terrence lowered Robert, his feet did him as much good as the other man's. He fell on the floor and gasped.

I glanced around the room. Two more guns sat on the counter by the refrigerator. I loaded my waistband with more steel.

Then I aimed my Glock at Jarik's middle and said, "The keys?"

He pointed at Robert. "He's got them."

"Get them."

He stooped and tried three of Robert's pockets before he found a key ring.

I left Terrence with him and his unconscious pals, and returned to Lucinda. She stretched spread-eagle on the bed while I unlocked her hands and feet. She rubbed her wrists, then picked up one of the chains and lowered its links into an open palm. The chain clinked out music like falling rain.

She carried it with her into the kitchen. Terrence was relaxing in a chair at the table, and Jarik gave her an embarrassed smile. She swung the chain at him, missed, and wound up again. But she stopped herself short. "Nah," she said, "you're not worth it." She threw the chain onto the table, looked at Robert and the other man on the floor. She nudged them with her toes to see if they were breathing. They groaned.

I pointed at the man who'd threatened Terrence. "Who is he?"

Jarik gave another embarrassed smile. "Robert's cousin. Name's Johnny. Sometimes he gets carried away."

"Yeah, I noticed. What's he do in your organization?"

"Mostly humiliates himself. He's supposed to be a spokesman."

"Might do you some good if you could teach him to shut up."

Jarik got a glint in his eye. "See something of yourself in him?"

Terrence, Lucinda, and I hoisted Robert and Johnny into kitchen chairs and told Jarik to sit with them. I held my Glock on them and gave Lucinda one of their guns. A few slaps on the cheeks brought Robert around. His cousin, Johnny, needed more prodding.

The three of them looked at us, scowling, suspicious.

I put my arm around Lucinda's shoulders and said, "First lesson is never touch someone's friends or family. It's a losing game. Better to keep your hands to yourselves."

"Fuck off," said Johnny. Terrence might have loosened some of his teeth but he spoke clearly enough.

"Second lesson," I said, "is never say, 'Fuck off.'"

He let one eye droop at me. "Fuck off."

Lucinda put on a wry smile. "Hey, there's a lady present."

He turned to her. "Fuck off."

Terrence stepped over to him and hooked a foot around one of his chair legs. As gently as if he was scuffing the ground to clean a shoe, he kicked the chair out. Johnny crashed backward to the floor, sat for a few moments, set his chair upright, and sat again. He looked at Terrence and said, "Fuck off."

Terrence laughed at him.

I said to Robert, "What do you get from Judy Terrano being dead?"

He shrugged. "Nothing at all."

"You're too nervous about me looking into the killing. You've got to be getting something from it. Sometimes I get hired to do claims investigation work for insurance companies, and you want to know how the guys behave when they're trying to commit fraud? The amateurs, not the professionals? They behave like you. They run around like squirrels scared that someone's going to take their nuts. So what are you getting?"

"You tell us," spat Johnny. "You got all the ideas. You come in here with the Jolly Black Giant and you got your Tex-Mex girlfriend and all your United-fucking-Colors-of-Benetton shit. You tell us."

I looked at Robert. "You've got to get a new spokesman."

"I mean it," said Johnny with venom. "What the fuck do you think you know about it?" He pounded his fist on the table. "You haven't been here. You haven't sat at this fucking table." He saw the chain. He picked it up and flung it at me. It snaked past me and crashed into the wall. "You don't know anything."

His eyes were wild. He was panting. I could have shot him in the forehead. "Tell me then," I said.

He opened his mouth. Maybe to tell me about Judy Terrano.

Maybe to tell me to fuck off. But from the other side of the house, heavy, slow footsteps came up the hall. Lucinda slipped silently to one side of the doorway, Terrence behind her. I slipped to the other side.

William DuBuclet stepped into the doorway. He nodded hello and continued into the room, ignoring our guns. He wore a black overcoat and sunglasses. Robert, Jarik, and Johnny looked frightened to see him. He took off the overcoat and handed it to Jarik without looking at him. Then he smiled at Lucinda and tipped his head in a slight bow. "You must be Lucinda Juarez?"

She pointed Johnny's gun at him. "Yeah," she said. "And you're the one who forgot to teach your friends good manners?"

"I'm afraid that early in life I learned to equate good manners with submission and, where I came from, submission led to exploitation. So yes, I'm guilty of neglecting to teach good manners. Perhaps times have changed and I've failed." He looked around at the rest of us. "I don't think times have changed so much, though." He turned to Terrence. "I don't believe I've met you."

Terrence had already tucked his pistol back into his waistband. He gazed hard at DuBuclet. "Terrence Messier, Mr. DuBuclet," he said in a calm, respectful, but none-too-friendly voice, the voice of one big man speaking to another before he knows if he's going to do battle with him.

"I'm glad to meet you," DuBuclet said with all the good manners that he said he rejected, but no submission. "And may I ask you what your interest is in this matter?"

Terrence nodded at me. "I'm with him."

DuBuclet reached for his coat, and Jarik handed it to him.

"Well, then, I seem to have brought my old tired eyes up here for nothing. That is, if everything has been resolved." He turned to me. "Has everything been resolved?"

"Not everything," I said. "Johnny was about to tell us more about Judy Terrano and the DuBuclet family secrets."

For the first time my words seemed to sting Johnny. DuBuclet turned and faced him. Johnny shrank from his gaze. I wondered what DuBuclet's eyes were doing behind the sunglasses. "What were you going to tell us?" he asked.

Johnny seemed to have lost his voice.

"Come," said DuBuclet.

"I was going—"

DuBuclet held out his hand and stilled him. "To tell him to fuck off?" He turned to me with a calm, gentle smile. "That's generally his response when he's asked something he's either unprepared or ill-equipped to answer."

"Listen," I said. "A nun and a priest are dead, Robert and Jarik snatched my partner from in front of my house, Johnny held a gun to Terrence's back and threatened to shoot him—"

Terrence interrupted. "Let's get out of here."

I stopped and looked at him, questioning.

"Come on," he said, and he turned and walked into the hall. Something in his face made me think I should follow him.

I glanced at Lucinda and she shrugged. DuBuclet watched me through his dark glasses. Robert, Jarik, and Johnny watched me. I shoved my gun into its holster and followed Terrence into the hall, Lucinda close behind me.

Robert called after us from the kitchen, "Our guns?"

I yelled back, "Pick them up at the District Thirteen police station."

We stepped outside. The sun-warmed breeze blew against

my face. It felt like the caress of a sick old man. I turned on Terrence. "What was that about?"

He looked away and said, "Shoot the fucker in the head if you want. Or I'll shoot him for you," he said. "But William DuBuclet is a great man. A great man. Kill him if you've got to, but don't disrespect him."

TWENTY-SIX

I TUCKED THE GUNS we'd taken from DuBuclet's follow-ers into my trunk, and we drove to Penang Malaysian Restau-rant. A waiter brought *roti canai* and *popiah* to the table. Lucinda told us about her abduction from outside my house. She'd managed better than I had, punching Robert in the kid-neys before Jarik smacked her face, but the result was the same—a trip in a Lexus SUV to places we didn't want to go.

"You get any idea what they're up to?" Terrence asked.

Lucinda thought about it. "They kept me in the room, door closed most of the time. The little I heard had to do with money. They had a couple of arguments about it and a couple of ex-cited conversations. The rest was too quiet for me to hear."

Terrence shrugged that off. "Young guys are always going to want to make a buck." He took a bite of the *roti*. For a big man, he ate delicately.

"This wasn't about a buck or two," Lucinda said. "This was major money. Joe was right to ask Robert what they were expecting from Judy Terrano. They're acting like something big is coming their way."

Terrence picked up a teacup, sipped from it. "Guys like them aren't going to see big money, not in this lifetime."

The waiter brought more platters of food—mee goreng, Hainanese chicken, and Malaysian buddhist delight. The *roti* was crisp and brushed with melted butter. The mee goreng played sour flavors off sweet and bitter. But my mouth still held the musty taste of the air in the house where we'd found Lucinda.

I reported what William DuBuclet had said about his dead son, Judy Terrano, and the Bad Kitty Lounge. I described Tony Jr., sitting in a wheelchair, clapping his hands like the world was putting on a show for him.

"So DuBuclet, the killer, and Judy Terrano all tie back to the late sixties and the Bad Kitty," Lucinda said.

The past is right here between you and me, DuBuclet had said. "Yeah," I agreed. "Old blood and new blood."

"Why isn't the relationship between Judy Terrano and Anthony DuBuclet part of the public biography of the nun?" Lucinda asked. "Why doesn't anyone else know about their son?"

I shrugged. "I'm guessing Judy Terrano started a new life after the cops gunned down Anthony and she asked DuBuclet not to publicize the kid or the rest of it."

"And what did DuBuclet get in return?"

Terrence swallowed a bite. "His grandson."

"Why would Judy Terrano give up her son?" Lucinda said.

Terrence looked hard at her. "That's naive, and you don't look naive. Her child was the son of a man the cops shot like an animal. She was a black single mother, twenty years old.

The kid had extra needs. DuBuclet had the money to take care of him."

Lucinda shook her head. "It's not naive. I can't imagine giving up a child, no matter what."

"You haven't lived where I've lived," he said.

Lucinda raised both hands like she was surrendering to him and pushing him away at once. "Yeah, and you haven't lived where I've lived. It doesn't mean a damn thing."

Terrence's voice remained calm, but I knew he'd won that voice only by fighting for years against his dead brother's ghost. "It means everything."

"Umm," I interrupted, "maybe we can find out more about DuBuclet's son and Judy Terrano when they were hanging together at the Bad Kitty."

Terrence nodded and looked squarely at Lucinda. "Anyone in your neighborhood who can help us with that?"

She closed her lips tight.

"Fine," he said. "We'll go talk to some folks in mine."

TWENTY-SEVEN

WE DROVE BACK DEEP into the South Side, staying mostly on side streets until we reached a place Terrence knew called The Shack. It occupied the first floor of a three-story brick building. The first floor was painted white, and the brick face had hand-painted signs advertising ICE COLD BEER, WINE & COLD DRINKS, SNACKS, POOL, and CHICAGO MUSIC NIGHTLY. It was a sad-looking place, burglar bars over the windows, more bars over the air-conditioning units to guard against hot neighbors on hot summer nights.

We parked in a lot next to the building and Terrence led us inside. The barroom was warm and smelled like whiskey. Two men sat apart on stools at the bar. They had gray hair and tired skin. Their clothes hung loose on them. An old bartender stood opposite them, waiting for others to come in and soften their lives with whiskey. The sound system probably cost more than the four walls that surrounded it. It played a high complaining drawl that sang, "All my love in vain" over an acoustic guitar.

The bartender's face brightened when he saw Terrence. "Hey, Terrence, long time," he said.

"Hey, Dennis." The men formed fists of their left hands and bounced them off each other's. "How you been?"

"Living, just living," said the bartender.

"Can't ask for more."

The bartender peered around Terrence at Lucinda and me. "Who're your friends?"

"Friends is all," he said. "Thomas around?"

The man's grin faded. "Okay, be that way. He's upstairs." He gestured toward a door at the other end of the room. The door had a sign that said STAFF ONLY.

"How's he doing?" Terrence asked.

The bartender repeated, "He's upstairs," like that was an answer.

We climbed two flights of stairs in a dusty stairwell. At the top, Terrence knocked on another door. When no one answered, he knocked again.

"What?" said a cracked voice.

"Terrence Messier," Terrence answered.

A long pause. "What the hell you want?"

"Come for a visit," Terrence said.

The door opened. A man about my size, plus thirty years, stood in the doorway. He wore loose-fitting gray cotton pants, belted around his middle, and a faded flannel shirt. He held a baseball bat in one hand. His voice erupted, "Don't ever come here unless I invite you." He glared past Terrence. "And don't ever tell your friends about me. Don't bring them around." The bat looked like it had hit something sharp and metal. It was stained dark by age or blood or both. He held it like he was thinking of using it on Terrence's head.

Terrence brushed past him into the room. Now the man looked like he might use the bat on Lucinda and me. We stood where we were.

"Well?" he croaked at us.

"Well?" Lucinda answered.

"Well, get the hell inside," he said.

We stepped through the doorway and the man closed the door behind us. Terrence turned. He had a big grin. The man laughed. He dropped the bat on the floor, and he and Terrence swallowed each other in a hug. "Thomas is the funniest man I know," Terrence said.

"Yeah, hilarious," Lucinda mumbled.

"Also the best singer."

"Once maybe," the man said, wistful. "Once I could sing."

The man led us through a hall to a living room. There was an assortment of chairs and couches, a couple of end tables. Three guitars—two electric, one acoustic—rested on guitar stands. They gleamed like the man had spent the morning polishing them. A double window was open to the afternoon breeze, but heat, piping from the steam radiator, made the room hot. The apartment smelled like the whiskey from the bar two floors below. Even with the heat the place was comforting.

Terrence introduced Lucinda and me as private detectives, leaving out our pasts as cops. He introduced the man to us as Thomas Stetler, owner-operator of The Shack and former front man for the most popular Chicago blues band never to cut an album. Stetler went to the kitchen and brought us glasses of iced tea.

We talked about the connection between a dead nun and a family as old and tough as the dirt under the city. Stetler knew little about Judy Terrano and DuBuclet's son but he grinned when I mentioned the Bad Kitty Lounge.

"Me and the band played in that house a couple of times," he said. "We played in some wild joints over the years, joints as far from the law as here to St. Louis. But we never played in another joint as wild as the Bad Kitty. You could do anything at all in that place, and excuse me for saying so"—he looked quickly at Lucinda—"when I say anything, I mean anything. You had to love a place like that, but you couldn't live there. At least, I couldn't. Some kids did, though. Black, white, Chinese, Mexican, they all was welcome. I think they had a Sioux Indian there for a while. The place was hot as a wire. I think I've got a picture of it around here somewhere."

He stood and left the room. Terrence, Lucinda, and I exchanged glances but we said nothing.

Stetler came back with a faded photo album. He sat in a chair and removed two color photographs and handed them to me. The first showed a group of five guys standing with guitars, a trumpet, and a saxophone on the white front steps of a red two-story house. I recognized a much younger Thomas Stetler in the middle of the group, looking as proud and full of sex as a rooster. The steps led to a porch recessed into two side wings, each with large windows. Above the porch was a flat wooden roof and, above and behind the flat roof, an open door that made the roof into a second-story balcony. Pink curtains, which could have been purple before the photograph faded, covered the windows.

The other photograph looked like it was taken inside on the second floor, facing down a hall toward the door to the balcony. The hall carpet was vibrant pink. A very fair-skinned woman with blond hair sat on the carpet, her arms supporting her from behind, her breasts jutting forward, her blouse un-buttoned but covering her barely, her legs dressed in the shortest of skirts and open like a dirty book.

"That's Louise," said Stetler. "I ran with her for a while. She was a hot wire, too. Too hot. I had to get away."

"The Bad Kitty burned down in 1969?" I asked.

"Yeah, summer of '69. Terrible thing. Two young couples was upstairs at the time. They burned with it."

"How did the fire happen?" Lucinda asked.

"Arson. The whole West Side had burned. The riots, you know? No one would've noticed the fire at the Bad Kitty, except for the dead kids."

I asked him, "Who would know about Judy Terrano if she hung out there?"

He thought about the question for only a second. "Louise would."

"She still around?"

"Yeah, lives a few blocks from here. Back then, she got heavy into drugs and went out on the streets. Shit, she's probably still walking them even if it takes a cane. No one's stopping her till she's lying in the ground, if then."

We finished our iced tea and pried ourselves out of his comfortable chairs. When Stetler showed us to his door he picked up the baseball bat and tapped its sweet spot against his palm. "Come back and see me anytime," he said.

TWENTY-EIGHT

"SURE, I KNEW JUDY Terrano," said the woman. "Couldn't forget her. No one could. Don't know what ever happened to that girl."

So at least one ex-streetwalker didn't know that Judy Terrano had become the Virginity Nun. "She's dead," I said.

"Happens to the best of us." She wore a green cardigan sweater and had an afghan blanket spread across her lap. Her skin looked bad, her hair stringy, but her blue eyes were clear and sharp. A Marlboro hung from her lips. "So why are you investigating a dead old party girl?"

"Family interest. There's a little money involved, and everyone wants to make sure it goes to the right relatives." One lie was as good as another, I figured, though Louise Johnson's eyes lit up at the mention of money. I added, "I saw a picture of her when she was eighteen or nineteen. She was a knockout."

Louise Johnson took a deep drag from her cigarette, held it in until the smoke must have burned, and exhaled. "Judy could take her pick. Hell, even if a boy was with another girl, Judy could walk into the room and he'd climb out of bed and follow her like a puppy. And the girl who was left in bed alone? She'd understand. Half the time she'd get out of bed and go after her like a puppy, too."

I thought about DuBuclet's son, shot dead in his boxer shorts. "How about Anthony DuBuclet?"

She laughed and she fingered the business card I'd given her. Her fingers looked surprisingly young. She touched my hand with them. "Yeah, Anthony was one of them. He was a good-looking boy. A charmer. Angry and dangerous. Do you know whose bed he got out of so he could chase after Judy?" She gave us a proud smile. "That's right. Louise Johnson's very own." Her smile fell, and she inhaled a long drag from her cigarette. "But he was no good in bed. Too rough. I hated to see him leave me, and I loved to see him go."

We sat in her basement apartment at the kitchen table. The apartment looked decorated to offset the life she'd led on the streets. The furniture was plain, a lot of brown and beige. She'd taped newspaper comic strips onto her refrigerator next to old pictures of kids who probably were family members. A coffeepot percolated on the counter. Two bottles of Bacardi Gold, one empty, the other half full, stood next to the coffeepot. There were bread crumbs on the kitchen table. Even an ex-hooker has to make toast.

"Judy fell for Anthony?" Lucinda asked.

"You could say that, yeah. Far as I know, Anthony's the only one she ever did fall for. She fucked with no more sense than I did. Young or old, boy or girl, black, white, or yellow. But when she got together with Anthony, that was it. It was love, or else she just liked banging with a boy that used his dick like a fist."

"Did you know she was pregnant when Anthony died?" I said.

She raised her eyebrows. "No, I didn't know about that. Boy or girl?"

"Boy."

"Thank God. The world couldn't handle another Judy Terrano. She drove us all wild." She inhaled from the cigarette again like it was oxygen and she'd spent a long time under water. The cigarette paper glowed orange and burned to the filter. She tamped the butt in an ashtray, then lifted the blanket from her lap. She went to the counter and brought back four coffee cups, the pot of coffee, and the bottle of Bacardi. She poured half a cup of coffee for each of us and topped off one of them with rum. She handed the bottle to Lucinda, who poured half an inch into her cup before handing it to Terrence, who did the same. He offered me the bottle but I waved it away.

Louise looked at me hard. "I never trusted a man that wouldn't drink with me."

Terrence said, "If he takes one drink, he'll finish your bottle."

"No problem with that," she said. She took a long drink of her spiked coffee and gazed at me. "But I'm so fucking lonely I'll talk to anyone. Even you. You know where Judy's boy is now?"

"Yeah, he's with his grandfather," I said. "Did William DuBuclet ever come around the Bad Kitty?"

She laughed. "Hell, no. Back then William DuBuclet was a fighter, and the Bad Kitty was a place for loving. That man wouldn't've known what to do there. It was a dump building in a dump neighborhood. I guess the owners couldn't rent it or didn't try. But then the kids started to move in and it became everything the rest of the city wasn't. No cops. No limits. If you liked someone you could spend time together. If you wanted to experiment, you could experiment. If you were curious, you could find out anything you wanted to know. I found out a lot in that place."

"Yeah," I said, getting impatient. "Sounds like paradise. Drugs and sex and no bedtime."

She picked up on the sarcasm but laughed. "Yeah, it was all of that." She shook another Marlboro from its pack and hung it in her lips.

"How did it get called the Bad Kitty?" Lucinda asked.

She lit the cigarette and took a long deep drag, then looked at me, her blue eyes narrow, and smiled. She answered, "It was a joke. The Black Panthers were big news, and the Bad Kitty was another choice—loving, not shooting."

"Where exactly was the place?" I asked.

"On Fourteenth, a little west of Halsted. There were a bunch of run-down, empty houses and then the Bad Kitty. Never been another place like it." You could hear the rum in her voice. "I'd live there still if I could. But it was too much, too much. It's probably good they burned it down. If they hadn't I would've died a long time ago. But I can tell you I would've died smiling." She took another slug of rum and coffee.

"You say it's good 'they' burned it down. You mean the rioters?"

"Hell, no. The rioters didn't burn it. The riots happened a year earlier. The man that owned it started the fire. For the insurance money, I think, or because he didn't like the house as a squat, or both. Or maybe he was just mean."

"What was the man's name?" Lucinda said.

"Been a long time"—she shook her head—"a lot of Bacardi and a lot of faces and names since then." She drank from her cup, finished it, smiled. "First name was Bartholomew. Don't remember his last. He was circumcised. His boys, too. I know that for a fact." She leered at me. "A lot of the girls that hung out at the Bad Kitty knew it. I figure the girls must've kept the building from burning for at least a couple months."

"How about Judy Terrano?" said Terrence. "Was she screwing the owner?"

Louise Johnson squinted at him. "You need to know this because you're executing a will?"

Terrence smiled like she hadn't challenged him. "Just curiosity."

She shrugged. "I don't know if she was or wasn't," she said. "I wasn't paying a lot of attention usually. But let's say, yeah. Why not? Judy was screwing everyone else. The daddy and the boys liked to come by. The daddy didn't like the squatting, but there wasn't much he could do about it. No one there had any money for rent even if they wanted to pay it, and the cops had their hands too full to worry about a house full of kids who were busy fucking each other. So the daddy and his boys made a good thing out of a bad deal."

"So much for paradise," said Lucinda.

"Every paradise has got its snakes," the ex-hooker said. "That's part of what makes it paradise."

Lucinda asked, "Any reason that someone from back then would want to harm Judy?"

Louise Johnson squinted at her, then at Terrence, then me. "This isn't about a will."

I showed my palms. "Not just a will. Judy Terrano was killed."

She considered that. "The Bad Kitty Lounge was a long time ago. What's it got to do with anything?"

"That's what we're trying to find out," Lucinda said.

"Would anyone want to harm her?" I asked.

"Sure," she said and she finished off her spiked coffee. "Judy was there the night the Bad Kitty burned. She saw them light the fire. She testified against the family in court. And then she disappeared."

TWENTY-NINE

"THAT'S A SPOOKY WOMAN," Lucinda said as we sped north again.

"Sad woman," Terrence said.

"She's protecting someone," I said, "and maybe protecting herself."

"Could be," said Terrence.

I checked my cell phone. It said I'd gotten a call from my home number. That would be Corrine. She'd left a message on my voice mail. I knew what she would've said about me in the message, and I knew she would be right—I was late and I was screwing up again. I turned off the phone and tucked it back in my pocket. I would listen to the message later. It would still be true, probably truer than it was now. I would face Corrine later, too. I might even face myself.

I accelerated.

"Where are we going?" said Lucinda.

"To the Bad Kitty Lounge."

She looked at me like I'd lost my mind. "The Bad Kitty's long gone."

"Nah," I said. "It just looks different. Bigger, probably thirty or thirty-five stories high, lots of polished steel and glass, underground parking, maybe a doorman to help you carry your packages."

Lucinda and Terrence exchanged glances.

Ten minutes later we pulled up in front of a construction site. The building rose a full thirty-five stories from the street. Workers halfway up the side were framing plates of thick, reflective glass into a steel framework. A tower crane lifted another sheet of glass high into the air. Blocked by construction barricades, a wide driveway curved down under the building to a parking lot. There was no doorman yet, but the two-story, glassed-in lobby said there would be one soon.

"Wow," said Lucinda.

"Man," said Terrence.

They weren't looking up at the building, admiring its fine modernist lines, and they weren't looking at me, admiring my act as Joe the Clever Clairvoyant. They were looking at the big sign posted outside the building. The sign showed three images. One was the building as it would look when completed, with a caption: "City Living at Its Best." A second was a man and a woman lounging in a white bed with drapes open to a plate-glass window showing sparkling city lights on a clear Chicago night, also with a caption: "Urban Luxury and Comfort." The third was a handsome woman's face. She smiled warmly, decently. Under her portrait in italics were the words, "Come home to Stone Tower," and a tag that said the woman was Dorothy Stone. A painted scroll at the top of the sign said, "Lakeview

Commercial and Residential Real Estate Development—Your Kind of Living."

I read the sign and said nothing. I'd seen the building before in architectural renderings framed on Mrs. Stone's office walls, and Eric Stone had asked me to keep the family name out of my report when I turned Greg Samuelson over to the cops because he wanted to avoid bad publicity as the family started to sell the condominium units.

We got out of the car and walked into the fenced-in construction area. The ground was a mix of sand, asphalt, and the clay soil that had supported the city for two hundred years. A group of five Mexicans, four in yellow hard hats, one in orange, stood by an electrician's van, looking at a blueprint. We went to them and I asked where we could find Eric or David Stone.

They gave me blank looks.

Lucinda spoke. "*Con permiso, dondé esta Eric o David Stone?*"

The guy in the orange hat grinned at her. "Try the site office." He pointed into the building.

We walked through the concrete cavity that would become the lobby. Huge vertical supports rose through a network of steel rebar and more concrete. Water had pooled on the floor, and the place had the dank cold feel of a cave. In six months it would cost a million dollars to walk through that lobby and go upstairs to a condominium.

Bare bulbs lighted the way past the concrete columns to a temporary office. I knocked on the door. No one answered, so we let ourselves in. The office had a central room with a metal desk and several chairs. Architectural blueprints and diagrams of plumbing and electrical systems were tacked to the walls. Four doors led to smaller rooms, one with a photocopier and office supplies, the others with desks, computers, and file cabinets. A quick check of the desk in the main room showed it was used for reception and nothing else. We split up and searched the other rooms with desks.

The file cabinets in the room I searched held more diagrams and construction specs, building permits, permitting guides, and sheets of numbers that made no sense to me. One drawer held paper plates, plastic utensils, and a six-pack of Michelob, minus a can. Another held a folder of photocopies of construction contracts and, behind it, a folder of land titles and deeds. I took the folders to the desk and sat down. A screen saver played repeatedly across the computer monitor, showing a German shepherd fetching a throw-toy tossed from a beach into Lake Michigan. At the end of the video, the dog charged back onto the beach from the water, shook off, and ran to the camera. Its eyes were ferocious. It looked like it would drop the toy and bite the lens.

The contracts folder showed that LCR had committed over twenty million dollars to the first stages of the building that would become Stone Tower. I put down the papers and shook the computer mouse. The German shepherd disappeared and I got a blank screen with icons. I started with one for NetSuite. Nothing showed dangers of bankruptcy, obvious signs of number juggling, or evidence that the Stones were siphoning funds from their project and hiding them in the Caymans, at least nothing to eyes that were used to calculating the loose change I kept in my checking account. But a spreadsheet showed the sale prices of the condo units in the buildings. They started at

$450,000 for less desirable one-bedrooms and climbed to $2.7 million for luxury penthouses. Plenty was at stake.

I turned back to the folders. The one with deeds and titles was thick with photocopies of papers that ranged from the late 1800s to last year. I started leafing through them when a man stepped into the doorway. He was short but powerfully built the way short guys who spent long evenings at the gym are powerfully built. He wore jeans a size too tight, a flannel shirt layered over a long underwear shirt, and a tool vest. He carried a hard hat. He didn't worry me much. But the German shepherd at his side did. The dog had ferocious eyes and looked like it had just dropped its throw-toy. It glared at me like I was dinner.

The man stepped into the room, the dog at his side. "What the hell are you doing?"

"I'm interested in buying one of the penthouses," I said, "but I'm worried about the riffraff I might have as neighbors."

His eyes got almost as ferocious as the dog's. "What are you—?"

"What do you think I'm doing? I'm searching your office."

That slowed him momentarily. "Why?"

Explaining that a dead nun had hung out in a house that had stood on the spot where he was constructing a residential high-rise seemed too complicated. "I'm a private detective," I said and I reached for my wallet to show him my license.

But when I moved, the German shepherd read the man's nerves and growled. I stopped moving. The man smiled. "Keep your hands where I can see them."

I nodded.

The dog growled again.

"Who are you?" the man asked.

"I was reaching for my detective's license," I said. "I'm Joe Kozmarski and I'm working a case that involves Mrs. Stone and her sons Eric and David."

"My aunt and my cousins," he said like there was power in the name Stone. I suppose there was.

"I came here looking for Eric and David."

"They're not here."

I shrugged. "I should've tried them at the Loop office."

"They're not there either," he said.

"Then if you'll hold your wolf, I'll catch them at home."

He shook his head. "I'll call the police. And then I'll call my aunt." He stepped toward the phone on the desk.

But he stopped when a deep voice spoke from behind him. It said, "Sit." Terrence filled the doorway, his Smith & Wesson in his hand, his gentle eyes on the dog. The dog had turned at the sound of him entering and it looked at him with its head cocked to the side.

Then it sat.

"Good girl," he said and he stepped into the room. He pointed his gun at Mrs. Stone's nephew. Lucinda followed him into the room. She pointed her gun at him, too.

I got up from the desk. The dog growled, then looked at Terrence. Terrence turned his head a quarter to the left and eyed it. It stopped growling. "Sit," Terrence said to the nephew. The man glared at him but he sat at the desk.

Terrence asked me, "Did you get what you were looking for?"

The financial statements might be important but I didn't really know what I was looking for. "Sure," I said.

"Then why don't you and Lucinda take off. I'll sit here awhile with Mr. D cell."

"How will you get home?"

"Look at me," he said, and he opened his arms wide enough to hug a football team. "Do I look like I'm helpless?"

He chose a chair, glanced around the room, and picked up the folders I'd left on the desk. We left him there reading, the German shepherd lying at his feet, Mrs. Stone's nephew glaring at him silently from across the desk.

Lucinda and I found our way out of the concrete cavern. We walked outside into the late afternoon sunlight. I looked up at the sky. The construction crane held a giant sheet of glass directly over our heads. The glass rose into the sky, swung toward the sun, and disappeared into the shadows of the building.

THIRTY

WE WOUND THROUGH THE afternoon traffic toward the western suburbs. An El train shot along on the tracks beside us, then slowed for a station as gently as a bird landing on water. The faces in the train windows and in the cars and trucks on the highway were dull, consumed by the day that had passed. I glanced at Lucinda. Her face had the same dull expression but I knew better. I also knew better about the people in the train, cars, and trucks. Some of them were thinking murder, whether or not they ever got around to picking up the kitchen knife. Others were racing toward tragedy, though they kept their speed just below sixty with a foot covering the brakes.

As we neared the suburbs, the on-ramps flooded the highway with cars, and I cut around a pickup truck. I said, "There's big money in the Stone Tower project. I saw the papers."

"No surprise."

"I suppose," I said. "What did you find?"

"Employee records. The Stones seem to have hired every one of their relatives to the tenth generation."

We put back on our dull faces.

Then Lucinda said, "I'm glad we're doing this." She kept her eyes on the road but her voice got soft. "You know, working together."

"Yeah," I said. "Me too."

"It feels good." She glanced at me. "To be together."

Working with her felt to me like I was betraying Corrine, even if Corrine had walked out on me more than a year ago. "Yeah," I said.

"You know, whatever comes of it or doesn't, this part is good," she said.

I nodded and we rode together in silence.

David Stone's daughter, Cassie, answered the door. She'd changed clothes. Her little black skirt looked designed to make you wonder if she was wearing anything underneath. Her T-shirt exposed a belly with a stud in it.

"Don't you ever get cold?" I said when the door opened.

"You're silly," she said.

"Is your father or uncle here?" I asked, then added, "Or your grandmother?"

"Sure, Grandma's here. You just missed Dad and Eric." She turned and put a little wiggle into her black skirt.

Lucinda raised her eyebrows at me and mouthed, "You're silly."

We followed her inside. She led us through the front foyer past the pulsing fountain, across the living room, and to a paneled reading room. Mrs. Stone sat on a sofa with a lamp on either side, reading a magazine called *Country Gardens*. She had on a red wool dress and wore a strand of pearls. She had kicked off her shoes. She looked more like a rich lady enjoying her leisure years than the head of a family erecting thousands of tons of concrete, glass, and steel.

As we entered the room, her granddaughter drifted over to an unlit fireplace, and Mrs. Stone peered at us over the top of her reading glasses. "Ah," she said with a smile that was one part pleasure and three parts disdain. "Mr. Kozmarski again—and a lady friend."

Lucinda gave her the same. "Lucinda Juarez."

Mrs. Stone tipped her head toward her, then said to me, "And you're not accompanied by bleeding killers this time?"

"I dropped mine off at the police station. The only ones you'll need to worry about live under your roof."

"I feel we're quite safe then," she said. "When you went to the police, were you able to avoid mentioning our name?"

"I was," I said, "but I don't know why I bothered. I don't know why Eric even asked me to. The cops are a step behind on this but they'll catch up, and when they do they'll look at you. They'll look in your windows. They'll look through your desk. They'll have experts look at the hard drives on your computers. You'll be dead center." I hit hard and wildly to see how she would take a punch. I didn't worry a lot about hitting her. She looked tough enough.

She laid the magazine on her lap. "What in the world are you talking about?"

"I'm talking about Stone Tower. It's about to come tumbling down. Once the police look at you, the state attorney will freeze your assets and buyers will stop showing up in your office looking for three thousand square feet and a view. Then, if another corrupt family like yours doesn't come and finish the building, the city will tear it down, and in twelve or eighteen months weeds and grass will take over and the lot will look like the prairie it was two hundred years ago. Personally, I think it'll be property improvement."

She looked vaguely amused, not what I was hoping for. She turned to Lucinda. "Would you please ask Mr. Kozmarski to explain himself?"

Lucinda smiled at her politely. "Tell us about the Bad Kitty Lounge."

Mrs. Stone looked stunned but only for a moment. She glanced at her granddaughter. "Would you pour me a Scotch and water and offer drinks to our guests?"

Cassie narrowed her eyes at her, then gave us an ironic little curtsy and said, "May I offer you a drink?"

"Water," Lucinda said.

A glass of bourbon with or without ice sounded right. "Water," I said.

She wiggled her black skirt out of the room.

"Even in a family like mine, we shelter the young," Mrs. Stone said.

"The young at thirty-five?" I said.

"You can add a few years to that, though she'd appreciate the compliment," she said. "Some people remain forever young, especially if their families shelter them."

Lucinda said, "The Bad Kitty?"

Mrs. Stone nodded. "Yes, the Bad Kitty. What do you wish to know?"

I asked, "Did you own it when it burned?"

"Yes." Her voice trembled. "September 20, 1969. The saddest day of my life."

"Sadder for the four kids who died," Lucinda said.

Mrs. Stone looked at her sternly. "Hard for every mother who lost a child."

"What child did you lose?" Lucinda sounded disgusted.

"They arrested my son."

"Is he in jail?" I asked.

She blinked her eyes and shook her head. "Oh, no. He's been out for eleven years. It was David."

Now, I blinked. Lucinda didn't. She said, "Then you really didn't lose him, did you?"

Mrs. Stone looked at her hard. "You don't have children, do you?"

Lucinda said nothing.

"He was gone for twenty-seven years. Yes, I lost a son. Every day he was in jail, I lost him."

I asked, "How much was the Bad Kitty insured for?"

She shook her head. "Not a penny."

"Come on," Lucinda prodded.

Mrs. Stone looked outraged. "The building was uninsured."

"Then why did David light the fire?" I asked.

She spoke like she was weary from telling the story. "We argued in court that the fire was an accident and we've never changed our argument. Not once. Not when the prosecutor offered a plea bargain that would have released David in fifteen years. Not even when David knew that he could get life if he refused to bargain. The building had no gas hookup. We used kerosene for heat. David had installed a new tank on the day of the fire."

I shook my head. "Why did you heat the building if you weren't renting apartments?"

With the tight smile she said, "I don't know where you're getting your information. We'd rented one of the basement apartments and a studio on the second floor. For pennies, really, not enough to pay for the kerosene. But yes, the rest of the apartments were open."

She looked at me to see if I accepted her explanation. I didn't know if I did, but I nodded.

"In the trial," she went on, "the prosecutor said David used the kerosene as an accelerant. Three of the kids who died were black—the boys and one of the girls. The other girl was white. It was a bad time to be black in Chicago and a bad time to be the white owner of property in a black neighborhood. Some of the black rights groups got the story and turned the accident into a white-on-black crime. But if—"

"William DuBuclet's group?"

Again she looked surprised but recovered fast. "Yes, William DuBuclet's group in particular. With him threatening violence, the prosecutor had little choice but to pursue my son." She glanced at the doorway, seemingly impatient for her drink. "But if you'd known David, you would never—"

"What's your connection to Judy Terrano?" Lucinda asked in the politest of voices.

Again Mrs. Stone wobbled. Again she glanced at the doorway. "You don't know?"

We gave her blank looks.

"Before the fire, she and David were lovers."

I wobbled, too. "That's not what I heard."

"What exactly have you heard?"

"David, Eric, and your husband extorted sex from the girls who hung out at the Bad Kitty."

She laughed at me. "Who needed to extort it? The girls needed no persuasion." She eyed us. "Excuse me if I'm overly comfortable with my husband's infidelity and my sons' sexual adventures, but that was a long time ago and my husband has been dead for fifteen years. I've had time to forgive. If my husband failed me at home, he at least built me a very nice house."

I nodded. "You've come a long way from heating buildings with kerosene. I also heard that Judy Terrano and Anthony DuBuclet were a couple. Did I mishear that, too?"

She stopped smiling. "No no. After the fire, Judy took up with him. She was at the house with David on the night of the accident, and it devastated her, too. I think she also was lost that night. Everyone there was lost—and everything."

"Did she testify against your son at the trial?"

She frowned, tight lipped. "Yes."

Lucinda spoke gently. "I imagine that her testimony angered David and the rest of your family."

Mrs. Stone kept her eyes away from ours. "It hurt David. As much as going to prison hurt him, that hurt him more. But it was a long time ago."

"Wounds like that are never old," Lucinda said, as if she knew from experience.

"No," she said. "I suppose not."

I said to Mrs. Stone, "A wound like that might make somebody want to hurt someone."

That restored her. She looked at me coldly. "If you think David or anyone in this family would harm Judy, you don't understand us at all. We've always thought of her as part of the family, and she always knew that we cared about her."

"Why would you?"

"She's been with us through good and bad. You don't easily give up on someone like that." Her eyes misted and I wondered how many tears she'd shed to get so tough.

Cassie Stone returned with a tray and four drinks. She passed them around, and when she handed me mine she gave me what she probably considered a sleepy-eyed, sexy gaze. Then she wiggled her little black skirt and winked. It was a naughty wink from a naughty child.

THIRTY-ONE

WE DROVE BACK TOWARD the city in the first dark of the evening. The wind had picked up from the north. A sheet of newspaper blew across the entrance ramp to the Eisenhower Expressway. It told of someone dead or dying or getting rich or losing everything, someone at a moment that changed a life or a thousand lives or more. It disappeared under the tires of the Skylark.

I said, "So David Stone burns down the Bad Kitty Lounge and forty years later Greg Samuelson burns Eric Stone's Mercedes."

Lucinda looked at me for more.

I had nothing more. "I'm just saying."

She asked, "So Samuelson was sending a message about the earlier fire when he torched the Mercedes?"

"Maybe. Or maybe he was just upset that Eric Stone was screwing his wife."

"Yeah." She nodded.

We rode silent in the thick traffic.

Then Lucinda said, "The old lady's involved."

"Mrs. Stone? I don't think so. Definitely Eric and David, though."

Lucinda thought about that. "Judy Terrano testified against David Stone but could she have said more if she'd wanted to? Could she also have testified against his mom and dad? I mean, if the fire wasn't an accident . . . if David's mom and dad put him up to it."

"If and if," I said. "Then why testify against David?"

"She was mad at him? The police already had him cold? The police pressured—"

"Why kill Judy Terrano now? Why shoot Greg Samuelson? Why are DuBuclet's thugs running around with their guns drawn? What's his interest?"

"Hell, I don't know," Lucinda said. "But it all goes back to the Bad Kitty, doesn't it?"

"Yeah, I think so."

Lucinda shook her head, frustrated. "Why kill each other over a forty-year-old pile of ashes?"

I glanced at her. For a moment, we locked eyes. "It's no longer a pile of ashes," I said. "It's a luxury tower worth millions. Or it will be soon."

"Enough money to kill for," Lucinda said.

"Maybe," I said.

We drove and thought some more. I didn't get anywhere. I glanced at Lucinda and she shrugged.

I flipped on the radio. It played the Rolling Stones' "Midnight Rambler," a middle-aged song that still sounded young. Then the news came on. A reporter said the police had Samuelson in custody but they had charged him only with misdemeanor arson. I figured that without gunpowder residue on his hands they were doubting his guilt. If they found no other evidence tying him to Judy Terrano's body, they would need to set him free. The reporter didn't say any of that. The DJ came back on and said that our afternoon of Indian summer was over. A cold front was blowing in. By the weekend we might see snow.

Lucinda said, "You want to get dinner again?"

It couldn't happen. "I've got to get home to Jason."

"He's invited."

"Corrine's with him."

"Oh."

I didn't know what to say to "Oh."

I dropped Lucinda at her house ten minutes later. As she got out, she looked at me long like she was unsure if something she once saw in my face was really there.

"I'll call in the morning," I said.

She gave me a tight-lipped smile and closed the car door.

Before pulling from the curb, I turned on my cell phone. It told me I had missed two calls from my home number. Corrine. No messages. I called my house. The phone rang four times and the machine picked up. I listened to my voice asking me to leave a message, hung up, and dialed Corrine's cell phone. She answered, "Yeah?"

"Hey," I said, trying soft. "I just tried you at my house. Where are you?"

"That's hilarious," she said. "Where are *you*?"

I said, "I'm sorry—I screwed up."

"That's not enough, Joe. It never was, and it's definitely not now."

"I know," I said.

We both let my admission hang. Then she said, "Where are you?"

"Five, ten minutes from my house. Where are you?"

"At your house. Where do you think I am?"

"You didn't answer my phone."

"That's because it's *your* phone. *Yours*, Joe, not *mine*. As in *your* nephew, not *mine*."

"Technically he's a distant cousin—my mom's sister's daughter's son."

She hung up on me.

A couple of blocks from my house, a restaurant called Lannie's sold rotisserie chickens and sides of potato latkes and oversteamed carrots and green beans. I called ahead for an order, then walked into my house with food that could warm bodies and minds in the coldest of countries. Corrine sat at my kitchen table with her coat on and her car keys in her hand. Jason's bedroom door was closed with Jason behind it. I set the bags on the table, unfolded their tops, and looked at Corrine.

"Sorry," I said again.

She didn't return my look. She stood and started to the door.

"Corrine—" I said.

She turned halfway, slowly, unwilling to face me, impatient to go. "What?"

I'd said her name not knowing what else I would say. I thought of saying thank you. I thought of making a crack about how good she looked from behind. But I said, "I love you."

She turned the rest of the way and faced me. She shook her head sadly. "You sure don't show it."

"I try," I said.

"No, you don't. Or you don't try hard enough." She turned and opened the door.

"Stay," I said.

With her back to me, she asked, "Why?"

It was a simple question but again I had no answer. I said, "It would be nice."

She stood at the door, her back to me, and her body started shaking. A sound came from her that was part laughter, part sob. Her keys fell from her fingers to the floor. After a while, she turned and faced me again. "No," she said. "It wouldn't be nice." But she closed the door and walked back to the kitchen table, took off her coat, and sat. She left her keys on the floor.

I set the dining room table while she watched. She glanced doubtfully at the pile of rehabbing tools that I'd left out, so I carried them to the kitchen counter and made a new pile.

Then I went and got Jason. He stuck close to me in the hall and pulled his chair close at the table. I served the chicken and we ate. No one said anything. Jason glanced nervously at me. I nodded at him and glanced nervously at Corrine. Corrine kept her eyes to herself. I waited for Lannie's chicken to work its magic. When nothing happened, I waited for the latkes to do what they could do. Nothing. I didn't expect much from the steamed vegetables.

I said to Jason, "What did you and Corrine do today?"

He shrugged. "Not much."

"Not much for eight hours?"

"Nine and a half," Corrine said without looking up. "Technically."

Jason offered, "We went to one of her landscape customers' houses in Lincoln Park."

"Good," I said. "Did they have a nice garden?"

"I don't know. She left me outside."

I looked at Corrine to see if that was true. She reached for a latke and said unapologetically, "There was a bookstore next door. Jason was perfectly happy waiting outside."

That wasn't the point but I knew better than to say so. "Glad it worked out." I spooned carrots onto my plate. I asked Jason, "What did you and Corrine talk about?"

He shrugged.

"Come on, you were together for nine and a half hours."

Corrine mumbled to her plate. "You're pressing your luck."

He shrugged. "She taught me a song called 'All Men Are Liars.'"

I looked again at Corrine. This time she returned my look. "It's by Nick Lowe. It's a good song."

"I know you're mad at me but taking it out on an eleven-year-old?"

"Jason's a bright kid. It's not too early for him to hear the truth." She gave me an innocent smile.

"It might be true, but you don't need to tell it to him."

Corrine turned to Jason. "Is your uncle making sense?"

Jason shook his head.

"It's my house. I don't have to make sense."

Still smiling, Corrine stood and carried her plate into the kitchen.

Jason took a bite of latke, chewed slowly, swallowed. He sipped from his glass of milk and said, "I like Lucinda better."

A moment later the back door swung open and then closed.

I jumped up from the table and went after Corrine.

I caught up with her on the sidewalk in front of my house. I reached for her, but she stepped away. "You need to decide what matters to you, Joe, what you really want."

"I want you," I said.

She gave me a grim smile. "I know about you and Lucinda."

My face felt heat. "What? How?"

"You think Jason and I really talked about nothing all day?"

"I—" Since my night with Lucinda, I'd been thinking of how to explain it to Corrine. I still had no way to explain it.

Corrine warmed a degree or two when she saw I was speechless. She touched my lips with a finger and said, "We've both screwed up, but I'm tired of that, you know?"

"Yeah," I said. "I do."

Then she surprised me. She said, "I'll leave my door open tonight. If you want *me*, you can come over once you get Jason to sleep."

"Really?"

She leaned in and gave me a quick kiss. "Really."

Then she was gone.

I stood for a couple of minutes in the cooling night. I stared up at a dark, starless sky and sucked a breath all the way in and blew it all the way out the way Corrine had taught me to. The air felt good in my throat, good in my chest, and according to the guide Corrine read to me I should have felt like I was living life at the fullest. But I felt confused. Corrine had given me a chance to have everything I thought I wanted—to have her. But I didn't know what to do. I needed to decide what mattered to me, but I knew that more mattered to me than I could have.

When I went back inside, Jason was gone from the table, his bedroom door closed. Above my plate he'd placed a gift for me, something he must have found at the bookstore while waiting for Corrine. It was a bobblehead of Mahatma Gandhi.

THIRTY-TWO

AT 11:45 P.M. I left a note for Jason on the kitchen counter. It included more promises that I would be back by morning to make breakfast and start giving him a stable life.

Corrine lived in a new town house two miles north of me. The ceilings were low and the walls were thin, but she didn't keep rehabbing tools on her dining room table. Her lights were off when I arrived but the front door was unlocked. I went in past furniture we'd shared when we'd lived together and through household smells that had been part of the air I'd breathed. I found my way up a narrow staircase to her bedroom.

Candles were burning on her bedside tables. Corrine was lying in bed between them, her eyes closed. I sat on the edge of the bed and she stirred. A faint smile formed on her lips. "Do you want me?" she said.

I kissed her. "I do."

She sat and pulled the sheet around her. She wore nothing else.

"I've missed you," I said.

"Me too."

"I'm sorry about Lucinda—"

She shook her head and said, "Shhh."

She got out of bed. Her body, which I'd held and which had held me for hundreds of nights but then had been apart from me for hundreds more, stood in front of me.

I reached for her but she shook her head again. She said, "I'm going to take a shower." She glanced at her dresser. "Put on some music and pick a nightgown for me."

"I can manage that," I said.

She kissed me, went into the bathroom, and closed the door. A moment later the shower turned on.

I went to her stereo, looked through her CDs. Chaka Khan—too much beat. Verdi's *Requiem*—no. Nick Lowe—definitely not. Chet Baker—just right. I put it on.

Next I went to the dresser. A winter nightgown—no. A silk camisole that I'd given to her four years ago—yes. I pulled it out, and something heavy and hard fell against the inside of the drawer.

A gun?

Corrine didn't like guns.

I dug past the T-shirt and removed the object. It was sky blue and looked like a cross between a dolphin and a manatee. It had an on-off switch at the tail end. I tucked it back in the drawer as fast as I could and went to Corrine's bed, sat, and waited. The shower was still running. I wondered if I should join Corrine. Maybe that's what she wanted. But if she did, why did she ask for music and a nightgown?

Too late—the shower went off.

I sat and waited. I glanced at the dresser drawer, went to it, and looked over my shoulder at the bathroom. I dug through the nightgowns and pulled out the sea creature. How exactly did Corrine use the thing? It was none of my business. Her private life was hers, not mine. I should put it away.

I pushed the switch. It purred like a kitten.

I pushed the switch further. It purred like a sack of kittens.

I glanced at the bathroom door, switched the thing off.

It kept purring.

I tried again.

It sounded like an overexcited cat.

I switched it all the way on and all the way off. It stayed on.

Corrine was making sounds in the bathroom like she was about to come out.

I stuffed the thing into the drawer, and slid the drawer shut. It rattled against the wood.

"Shit!"

"What?" Corrine asked from the bathroom.

"Nothing!"

As the bathroom door opened, I grabbed the sea creature and stuffed it into the top of my shirt. It slid down my chest.

Corrine stood naked in the bathroom door. Her skin shimmered from the steam of the shower. She'd never looked more beautiful to me.

"Wow," I said.

She stood waiting for me. I slapped my belly as if men always slapped their bellies when beautiful women offered themselves to them.

"Are you okay?" she said.

"Yeah," I said. "Be right back." I shuffled out of the room.

I made my way to the kitchen and yanked the creature out of my shirt. Where the hell should I put it? I opened the refrigerator. The vegetable compartment? Jesus, no. The freezer?

The microwave? No no. I put it in the kitchen sink. It rattled against the stainless-steel basin. I grabbed it and stuffed it into the garbage disposal. The rubber back-splash seals held it firm and quiet.

I stumbled back into Corrine's room. She was sitting naked on her bed, the camisole beside her, and she didn't look happy.

"What are you doing, Joe?" she asked.

"I needed a glass of water," I said.

She rolled her eyes but didn't question me.

So I went to her.

She hesitated but then she stood and faced me.

I touched her neck and her breasts. I let my hands slide down to the inside of her hips. All my troubles seemed to recede.

"You're sweating," she whispered.

"Yeah," I admitted.

She stepped closer and kissed me. I held her to me and breathed in the scent of her newly bathed skin. She unbuttoned my shirt and reached inside, running her fingers over my shoulders and chest. She whispered, "I've missed you." Chet Baker sang "Let's Get Lost." I let my shirt fall from my shoulders to the floor and pulled her to me.

A grinding noise erupted two rooms away. Plastic snapped and crunched. Metal clashed against metal.

We ignored the sound.

Chet Baker sang.

The grinding got louder.

Corrine pulled away. "What the hell is that?" she said.

I shrugged. "I'm not sure, but I think your vibrator just turned on your garbage disposal."

THIRTY-THREE

AT 2:00 A.M. I was back at home in bed, with the bobblehead Gandhi next to me on the bedside table. The wind hissed through the branches of the elm tree outside my window. I tried to steer my thoughts from the hundreds of ways I'd blown it with Corrine. If Gandhi could handle the life he lived, why couldn't I handle mine? If the elm tree swaying outside could face the cold wind year after year, why couldn't I face myself?

I turned the bobblehead so it would watch over me while I slept.

I didn't sleep.

Images of Corrine shook me when my mind started to drift. Thoughts of other women only made things worse. Cassie Stone's wiggling skirt spiraled me outward when I slipped from consciousness. Louise Johnson's fingers reached like a creeping vine and touched me. Lucinda looked at me searchingly as she got out of my car. I wanted Corrine with me. I wanted Lucinda. I wanted Cassie Stone's wiggling ass. I wanted an eighteen-year-old wild child who grew up to be a famous nun and then died. I wanted Louise Johnson's fingers touching my skin—

I shook awake, sat, and turned on the light.

Gandhi leered at me.

My phone stood on the night table next to him. I wanted to call someone to save me from myself.

But it was late. Too late to call Corrine and tell her—what? I was sorry? I wanted her? I loved her? I would buy her a new vibrator?

Too late to call Lucinda.

I picked up the phone, dialed, and listened to two rings before an answering machine picked up. Terrence's recorded voice said he wasn't home, but I could leave a message and he would be glad to get back to me. I said, "Hey, it's Joe, calling to see how the visit to Stone Tower turned out. Thanks for springing Lucinda and me."

I hung up. I figured he was out hustling or partying or maybe he was lying in the dark with his girlfriend in his arms, listening to his phone ring without the least desire to pick it up.

I looked at the phone. I had no excuse to call anyone else. I turned out the light and let imaginary women do what they wanted with me until they got tired and left me alone. When they did, I dreamed of a tall building swaying in a huge wind. No one seemed scared that it would fall. Men and women sat at their office desks while the building rocked like a tree in a storm wind. Mothers and children walked on the sidewalk below, blanketed by the shadow of the swaying building, exposed to the sun as the building tilted away, then shadowed again. The elevator knocked against the sides of the shaft like a pendulum trying to break free. The men, women, and children went about their business unconcerned. No one was scared. No one but me.

IN THE MORNING JASON and I signed a sheet of paper he'd brought home from school. On it, he promised that he understood the school's zero tolerance policy toward violence and that he would behave peacefully on all occasions. I promised that as his parent or guardian I understood my responsibility to help him follow school policies.

We shared a breakfast of frozen waffles and stepped out the back door into the swaying shade of the elm tree. During the night the temperature had dropped below freezing. The morning air felt sharp and clean. The sun shined bright through the swaying branches but I kept my eyes on the ground.

When I drove Jason to school, the Gandhi bobblehead bobbed on the dashboard. I positioned him so he leered at Jason instead of me. Jason socked me on the arm as he got out of the car. "Fists to yourself," I said, and he laughed.

I drove downtown and dialed Lucinda on my cell. She sounded like her night was as rough as mine. She didn't mention Corrine and I didn't either, but her voice was cold. She said she was heading back to the newspaper archives to keep digging.

Next I called the District Thirteen police station.

When Stan Fleming came to the phone, he said, "Let me guess. You found another dead priest."

"None this morning."

"It's still early," he said. "Keep trying."

"How's the case against Samuelson looking?" I said.

"Fuck Samuelson."

"That bad?"

"Worse. Examiner sees nothing linking him to the nun or to the priest in Terrano's bathtub. Plenty of fibers on Terrano but they match her clothes and rugs. And now Samuelson's got a fancy lawyer shaking his head every time we try to interview him and arguing with the judge to get him released from custody if we're not charging him. The lawyer's got a high price and a record of getting what he wants."

"Where did Samuelson find money to pay for a lawyer like that?"

"Didn't need any of his own. A community group stepped up and is paying the tab."

"Why?"

"Hell if I know."

"Who's the group?"

"That's enough from me. Why should it matter to you?"

"Are they led by an old chunk of Chicago history named William DuBuclet?"

"Damn it, Joe! How did you know that?"

I thought about the cost of telling Stan everything. I told him a piece of it. "DuBuclet's son was friends with Judy Terrano in the late sixties. It ended badly."

"Yeah? So what?"

"So DuBuclet and the nun shared a secret from back then. A big secret, I think—one worth killing for. I think Greg Samuelson figured it out and threatened to go public with it. So the killing started. Judy Terrano. The priest. Samuelson took a bullet in his face—not enough to kill him, but enough to keep him quiet for a while."

"You know, I really could use specifics—like what this secret is."

It involved the fire at the Bad Kitty Lounge, I figured, and the millions of dollars committed to the construction of Stone Tower forty years later on top of the ashes of the old building, but I didn't know what else.

I said, "I'm working on it."

THIRTY-FOUR

I FIGURED SAMUELSON KNEW the details about the fire at the Bad Kitty Lounge, details that could shake the Stones' hold on the land where they were building Stone Tower.

But he wasn't talking.

Who else knew the details?

Judy Terrano had known.

But she was dead.

DuBuclet probably knew.

But, like Samuelson, he wasn't talking.

Judy Terrano's old friend, Louise Johnson, seemed to know more than she'd told me.

But she wasn't talking either.

The priest I'd found dead in Judy Terrano's bathtub might have known at least some of the details, enough to draw him into her room.

Dead.

Who else would know?

Maybe someone at Holy Trinity.

The crime scene tape was gone from the church entrances. The forgiving and forgetting would take longer, maybe a life-time or more. I opened the heavy steel doors to the sanctuary and stepped into the end of morning Mass. A couple dozen parishioners—all women—sat in the pews, some still bundled in the dark wool coats they'd put on against the cold, though the inside of the church was warm enough. A priest stood at the front. He was in his young fifties and dressed in black, swinging a censer, chanting in Polish. I sat in a pew in the back and closed my eyes.

When the priest finished the service, he came down the aisle to greet the parishioners. The women, some with tears in their eyes, got up and clasped his hands, and he seemed to re-assure them that the hardest days at the cathedral would pass. They shuffled out through the steel doors until only the priest and I remained. He considered me, then came and sat by my side.

"Does something trouble you?" he asked.

"Yeah," I said. "Can you do anything about a dead nun?"

He shook his head with practiced sorrow. He must have been hearing a lot of this from people who had known and loved Judy Terrano. "She's with God now," he said, "and she's at peace."

"I've gone to too many funerals to believe it," I said.

"Nonetheless—"

"If a guy dies after ten years of cancer, you can call it peace. But when a woman gets choked to death with her clothes pulled up to her shoulders, don't call it peace and heavenly re-wards."

The priest said, "Death is nothing to a woman like Sister Terrano. It opened a door to a bright beginning."

"Bright, huh?"

He nodded. "Brilliant."

I stared at his eyes. "I'm carrying a Glock," I said. I lifted my jacket to give him a peek. "If I took it out, pointed it at your forehead, and put my finger on the trigger, and you looked into its barrel, would you say death is brilliant?"

He didn't squeal, but he squirmed and sweat broke out on his forehead. "I hope so. Do you plan to shoot me?"

"Me?" I barked a laugh. "No no. I'm sorry, I've had a couple of rough days."

He gave a feeble smile and mopped his brow with a handkerchief. "Yes, we all have."

"Just skip the consolations, okay?"

"Sometimes they're all I've got." He stood.

I said, "What happened to the hundred ninety thousand dollars that Judy Terrano skimmed from her charities?"

The priest flinched and sat again. "Who are you?"

I handed him one of my cards.

He looked it over, then glanced at me nervously. "There can be authority in one's sins as well as in one's redemption."

"You can justify anything that way."

"Justify, no. Accept and forgive, yes."

I shook my head. "It's a cop-out."

"It's the oldest story in the book. Mary Magdalene . . . Augustine . . . Amazing Grace—all the converted sinners. Why would you expect faith to be clean?"

"Not clean. But a little less bloody."

"The blood of Christ is the purest—" He gave me another nervous glance. "Skip it."

I said, "What did she do with the money?"

"There are stories. I don't know if they're true—"

"Try them on me."

"Why do you want to know?"

"I want to find the killer, and I can't do that unless I understand why she got killed."

"Greg Samuelson didn't do it?"

"The police haven't charged him and they won't."

He looked at me, doubtful. "If that's true, it will go a long way toward consoling the congregation."

"What stories did you hear?"

"Sister Terrano was more experienced and worldly than many nuns. She had a background in political activism and her motives, beliefs, and actions were never quite orthodox."

He was avoiding my question, so I asked again. "The stories?"

He hesitated, then said, "The rumor is that she had a child—out of wedlock—before entering the Church, and she was using the money to support him."

I nodded. "There've got to be worse sins than that."

He shrugged. "For a nun advocating teenage chastity? Her credibility would have been shot if the press had found out."

"So much for the authority of redemption."

He sighed. "That's only if the penitence is sincere and complete."

"Hers wasn't?"

"There were other rumors—involving her relationship with a group whose beliefs are at odds with Catholic teaching. Questions about her financial dealings continued after the audit revealed the missing hundred ninety thousand dollars."

I figured the group was William DuBuclet and his followers. "Do you have access to her records?"

He shook his head. "The police have most of them. They took her computer and files. I don't know what's on them. After the audit, the church asked Greg Samuelson to oversee her accounting and to act as a second set of eyes on her expenses and the donations she received."

"You say the police have *most* of the records. Could I see what you've got?"

He frowned, but he stood and I followed him up the aisle and through the door to the narrow hall that led to Judy Terrano's office. He let us into a small office with a desk and a computer. He opened a series of documents, selected one, and hit the Print command. He handed me the eight pages that scrolled out of the printer.

The printout showed an annual summary and detailed listing of the funds Judy Terrano had received from donors over the past eighteen years. The funds totaled twelve million dollars and change. A Mrs. Arthur Fenton had bequeathed more than a million when she'd died. A number of national and local companies had contributed anywhere between two and twenty-one thousand dollars a year. Mrs. Stone first wrote a check for ten thousand dollars the year that the records began and most recently had written one for thirty-five thousand dollars. Most of the list named small donations of fifty or a hundred dollars. One man had contributed fifteen.

There was one unexpected donor. For more than a decade the ex-hooker Louise Johnson had donated between thirty and a hundred dollars a year. When I'd talked with her, she'd said that she didn't know where Judy Terrano was, but for ten years she'd been saving pennies and nickels for her. She'd kept donating her money while living in a cheap basement apartment and drinking Bacardi. I saw only two reasons why she would pretend she'd lost touch with Judy Terrano: She had something to gain if she kept quiet or she had something to lose if she talked. Greed or fear. Someone would pay her off or someone would hurt her.

I handed the priest the printout. "Have you met many of the private donors?" I asked.

He glanced at the sheets of paper. "Most of the smaller donors live in the neighborhood and attend services here. The larger donations come from all over the city and country. Some of the donors have visited. Some met Sister Terrano on her travels or saw her on TV and wrote a check."

"How about Louise Johnson?"

"Louise, yes." He smiled. "She's an exception. She rides the bus in every Sunday. She seems to live modestly but she's been generous with the little that she has. She became very attached to Sister Terrano and the work she was doing."

"Do you know what drew her to this church?"

"I do. One of the other donors brought her the first time."

I considered the names I'd seen on the list. "Who was that?"

"It was one of our largest private donors, Dorothy Stone."

I laughed.

The priest looked at me uncertainly. "Mrs. Stone and her family have been extremely generous."

I shook my head. "I don't think so."

"They've given more—"

"Thank you," I said. "You've helped a lot."

I found my way out of the church. The sky outside was graying, heavy, and cold. It looked like snow. I turned the key in the ignition of my car and cranked on the heat. The Gandhi bobblehead bobbed on the shuddering dashboard. Forty years had passed since Louise Johnson hung out at the Bad Kitty with Judy Terrano, Anthony DuBuclet, and the Stone brothers, but they still formed a tight little community, living and dead. I wondered if Mrs. Stone would invite Louise Johnson over for tea and a slug of rum when winter came.

THIRTY-FIVE

I SPED DOWN THE Kennedy toward the Loop, then out the
Dan Ryan and into the South Side. Twenty minutes after leaving Holy Trinity, I parked three doors up from Louise Johnson's apartment. A couple of kids in winter parkas walked
past. They were a year or two older than Jason and they should
have been in school. They were smoking cigarettes and trying
to look tough.

I buzzed Louise Johnson's apartment but got no answer. It
was 10:30, time for a tall glass of Bacardi and orange juice unless she'd drunk so late last night that morning wouldn't start
until noon.

I buzzed again.

Maybe she'd run out of rum and gone to the store. Maybe in
her retirement she drank her breakfast at a local bar. Maybe
she was making the rounds at the city's churches, donating her
pennies and nickels.

I held the buzzer.

Nothing.

THE BAD KITTY LOUNGE

The kids in parkas disappeared around a corner. I rattled the outside door. The tongue bolt gleamed in the gap between the door and the frame. A hard shove would splinter the frame, but I hated to expose the building to the cold air and to any twelve-year-old thugs-in-training who were prowling in it. I slid my car key into the gap and worked the bolt until it slid partway into its casing, far enough for me to ease the door open.

The entrance hall smelled of cooking and garbage. Loud music played against a crying baby. I went down a half flight of stairs into the hall where Louise Johnson lived and stopped outside her apartment.

Her door was open.

There's nothing worse than a door that's open when it should be closed and locked. It might mean nothing. I knew that. Before I quit drinking, I sometimes stumbled home and left my door open all night while I slept on the floor. And some buildings are so friendly that people leave their doors open in case the neighbors want to visit. But I hated that open door.

I knocked but got no answer. I didn't expect one. I knocked harder. Then, because I had to, I pushed the door open further and stepped inside.

The apartment looked the same as the last time I was there, with the same plain, brown furniture, the same two bottles of Bacardi and the coffeepot on the counter. The only difference was the rum bottles were empty now and Louise Johnson wasn't sitting at the kitchen table.

I wanted to leave the apartment and go back outside into the cold air. But I walked into the hall that led from the kitchen toward the bedroom. No matter how hard Louise Johnson had scrubbed it, the hall smelled sour and the carpet showed old water stains. Three framed, studio-style portrait photographs hung on the hall wall. A fourth frame leaned against the wall at the floor. The cardboard backing had been torn away, the picture removed.

I stepped past a bathroom into the bedroom and switched on the light. Louise Johnson was lying on the bed, her head on a white lace pillow. A bullet hole pierced her brow. The wound was clean, mopped so the skin around it was free of blood. Only the smallest hole remained, with a lip of pale flesh punched inward. She looked as pretty as a body in a gift box.

Her mouth was closed, and her lips formed a vague smile. Her eyes were closed, too. Black flecks dusted her chin, cheeks, and the pillow under her head. Over a blouse she wore the green cardigan sweater she'd had on when I'd last seen her. She wore nothing else. I watched her chest for the slow heave that marks the breathing of deep sleep, but I knew there would be none.

"Damn," I said, and the word felt dull in my ears.

I searched the bedroom, more or less. The closet had clothes and shoes but no bundles containing the memories of a hooker or of the life she had led as a girl, no secret diary. I opened the top drawer of her dresser. It was full of underwear, far more than any five women could need. That did it for me. I closed the drawer, left the room, and walked back into the kitchen.

The coffee cups we'd drunk from a day earlier were gone— clean and back in the cabinet—but a couple of empty glass tumblers stood in the sink. That probably meant she'd been drinking with company yesterday evening or today, some time after Lucinda, Terrence, and I left. The company could have been her killer. I left the glasses where they were.

The cabinets and drawers held the assortment of dishes,

glasses, silverware, and boxed and canned foods that you would expect to find, except an unopened case of Bacardi Gold was in the cabinet under the sink. Louise Johnson was a well-provisioned drunk. The refrigerator was empty except for a quart of milk, a pound of butter, a couple of frozen pizzas, and a twenty-five-pound bag of ice. I sat at the kitchen table and stared at the kitchen cabinets, the counters, the stove, the refrigerator.

I got up and looked closely at the refrigerator door. Lines of grime blocked out two white rectangles against the surrounding surface. I wondered if photographs had filled the white spaces the last time I'd been in the room. If they had, they'd smiled and smiled at me, and I'd drunk Louise Johnson's coffee and ignored them. They'd whispered from the past about a time when Judy Terrano and Louise Johnson throbbed in the heat of a burning city, and I'd all but put my thumbs in my ears and hummed.

I spent as much time in the kitchen as I could justify, then went back to the bedroom and did what I needed to do.

Louise Johnson's dead body was too neatly arranged. It was too clean, except for the black dust on her cheeks and chin. Her killer was sending a message, just as Judy Terrano's killer had sent a message by scrawling the words BAD KITTY on her belly.

So I touched her lips. They felt tough and dry as thumbs. I pulled them apart. I pried her mouth open with my fingers. The muscles in her jaws resisted. It seemed like the ligaments would snap and she would yawn so wide she could swallow the room and everything inside it, but her mouth came slowly open. It exposed a tongue, purple and swollen in death, and on the tongue and teeth and pasted to the walls of her mouth were ashes and, mixed with the ashes, bent and browned bits of burned photographic paper.

I dug them out with a finger. The pieces broke apart in my hand.

The ashes were the burned remains of Louise Johnson's past, I figured, a past that she'd kept alive every time she'd looked at the photos on her refrigerator or passed them in the hall—until a slug ripped into her forehead and stopped time, stopped everything. That probably meant she'd shared that past with her killer, and her killer meant to burn the evidence of it. Or, since the ashes were in her mouth, meant to do more than burn it—meant to make a point by burning the evidence. The killer was silencing Louise Johnson and erasing her past, or some of it. The killer had yanked off pants that Louise Johnson had yanked off thousands of times for twenty or thirty dollars a pop. The killer was saying Louise Johnson was a whore with no other past or future.

Who was the message for?

Maybe the answer was in the burning itself. Forty years ago, David Stone had burned down the Bad Kitty Lounge. Three days ago, Greg Samuelson had burned Eric Stone's Mercedes.

I wiped my hand on the bedsheet, trying to remove the stain, but the soot streaked across my palm. So I went back to the kitchen and washed my hands in the sink until they were red and smelled like the dish soap Louise Johnson kept next to the case of rum in the cabinet, and I washed them some more.

Then I called Lucinda.

Her cell phone rang until voice mail picked up. She must have been deep in the archives, reading about a city that no longer existed but haunted us still. Or else she was ignoring my call because she was angry with me for failing to split from Corrine.

I left a message telling her about Louise Johnson, her nickel-and-dime contributions to Judy Terrano's charities, her dead body displayed as carefully as a store-window mannequin, and the ashes of photographs in her mouth—ashes of a child or of children who had laughed from pictures on her refrigerator and hall walls.

I wondered how silent the child or children had to be, though. William DuBuclet knew that you can't wipe out the past. You might not always see it, but it's there and it might even talk to you if you listen closely enough. I said to Lucinda, "When you get done with the newspapers, will you go to the county clerk's office? Ask them if they've got any birth records naming Louise Johnson as mother."

I hung up and called the District Thirteen police station.

Stan Fleming didn't sound surprised when I said I was standing in an apartment with another dead body. He sounded depressed. "Jesus, Joe, you stay away from me when I've got a cold. You're dangerous."

"I find them dead. I don't kill them," I said.

"What's the address?"

I told him and he sighed. "Why are you calling me? That's way outside the Thirteenth. Call nine-one-one."

I told him about the connection between Judy Terrano and Louise Johnson, the short version. And I told him about the ashes in Louise Johnson's mouth. I left out the finger I'd stuck inside and my feeling that the ashes had left a mark that I would never get rid of.

"Second thought, don't call nine-one-one," he said. "Wait for me there."

"Uh-uh," I said. "I'm walking out the door as soon as we hang up. But I figured you might want to take a look before other homicide cops get their hands on this."

"You figured right. Where are you going in such a hurry?"

"I've got a friend I need to see."

"Does he wear a hooded black robe and carry a sickle?"

"No, he wears a cape and blue leotards."

"Hey, your private life's your private life."

"An academy dropout. He was too good for the department."

"Oh, one of those guys."

"Yeah, one of them."

"Well, shake this superhero's hand for me and tell him I'll send him a postcard when I'm retired on pension."

"You'll never find him to get his address."

"Yeah, he's one of those guys."

"Hey, Stan?"

"Yeah?"

"Greg Samuelson still under lock and key?"

He laughed bitterly. "His lawyer sprung him an hour ago. He paid bail on misdemeanor arson and walked out of the hospital on his own feet. They say he looked like living death but he refused a wheelchair."

A shiver ran down my neck, but I said, "Time line's too tight for him to have gotten here and killed a woman, isn't it?"

"Unless he's another superhero."

THIRTY-SIX

THE PARKING LOT NEXT to Terrence's apartment building was littered with dry weeds, cans, and a rimless tire. A sign at the McDonald's at the other side of the building said WELCOME TO MCDONALD'S. So I parked there. Seagulls that had flown inland to find shelter from the cold lake-wind stood on the pavement, eyes narrowed, looking like they might freeze into statues and spend the winter there. I stepped over a thigh-high wall onto the sidewalk leading to the front of the apartment building. A couple of gulls fought over the remains of a Filet-O-Fish sandwich that someone had chucked against the fence.

When I'd visited before, Terrence had taken me up the back stairs and through his back-porch garden. Now I went to the front door and saw why he liked the back way. There was a hole where the doorknob should have been, and the rust and wear on the rest of the door said that no one had locked it for years. In the foyer, a dirty ceiling lamp gave just enough light to show two old metal chairs and walls that someone once had cared enough about to cover with flowered wallpaper. A narrow elevator waited for passengers with its door open, its floor about a half-foot higher than the lobby floor, its light off. I took the stairs. Gang graffiti covered the walls up to the first landing, then disappeared, though someone had spent sweet minutes with a girl named Janika on the second landing and had left a message on the wall explaining what they'd done in more detail than Janika probably would have liked.

The graffiti stopped in the stairway up to the third landing. I knocked on Terrence's door.

No one answered.

I knocked again.

Maybe Terrence was out hustling and would return in the afternoon. But I'd called him four times since leaving him at the Stone Tower construction site and he'd never picked up. Anyway, a dead hooker with a bullet hole in her forehead and ashes in her mouth made me anxious to see my friend. I knocked a third time.

No answer.

I tried the doorknob. No luck. Terrence had three locks on his door, two of them Medecos—too good for me. I went to work on the lousy one. After a few minutes I felt the bolt slide into its housing. I tried the knob again and the door swung open.

I grinned, though the two unbolted locks worried me enough to make me pull my Glock out of its holster.

I stepped inside and called, "Terrence?"

A noise came from the kitchen. I went toward it silently. The apartment was cold the way only the inside of an unheated building can be cold, colder than outside where the dim sun still shined.

I came to the end of the hallway, leading with my gun, and stepped around a corner into the kitchen. A gray creature fluttered wildly into the air. I jumped back. It was a seagull.

I shouted, "What the hell are you doing here?"

It landed on the kitchen table and stared like it was wondering the same about me.

The cold apartment made no sense. The seagull made no sense. I kept my finger on the trigger and stepped into the living room. Four seagulls stood on the floor. One held a long, thin strand of something that looked like uncooked beef fat in its beak. It peered at me as if I might take its lunch. Another gull pecked at something small and wet and white. The giant plate-glass window that had separated the living room from the back-porch garden was gone, shattered outward onto the wooden decking. Cold air blew into the room through the gap. I stepped out through the window frame. Spots of blood trailed over the broken glass to the outdoor stairs. I would need to follow those spots, but first I stepped back inside.

Another gull flew through the room and landed at my feet like I might give it a fish. I kicked at it and it leaped into the air and fluttered out through the broken window.

I went from the living room toward Terrence's bedroom. I hoped I would find him sleeping, a pillow hugged over his head to muffle the knocking of a worried friend. I hoped the plate-glass window had been broken by someone dancing wildly during a late-night party. I hoped the blood on the wooden decking came from a seagull that had flown too close to the jagged glass that jutted from the window frame.

But I knew better.

I stepped into Terrence's bedroom.

I smelled him before I saw him—a sharp, salt odor of blood

and urine. The giant man was lying on the floor next to his bed, his head by an open gun cabinet, a gaping hole in his belly. His gentle eyes were gone. Blood craters remained. A seagull stood on his chest and dunked a bloody beak into the hole in his belly. It tugged and came up with a strip of flesh. I yelled and ran at the bird. It flew onto Terrence's bed, carrying the bloody flesh, dragging it over the bedcover, streaking the cotton red. It eyed me fearfully. It knew I was a thief. It cocked its head back and quivered as it drew the flesh into its gullet.

I swung my gun at it and fired. The bird's middle disappeared in a blaze of meat, blood, and feathers. The seagull's head defied everything I thought I knew about the physical laws of the universe—it bounced toward me on the bed as the blast and roar of the gunshot filled the air and made the building shudder. The head came to a rest at the side of the bed, its eyes still open, staring at me accusingly, Terrence's torn flesh edging from its beak.

My body shook.

I didn't trust myself.

I crammed my Glock back into its holster and sank to the floor next to Terrence.

He was as big in death as he'd been in life. I could hardly believe that when he'd fallen the whole building hadn't come down under him. His eye sockets stared at the ceiling like he was amazed by how far and hard he had fallen. I reached for him but stopped. His size could paralyze you, and that didn't change now that he was dead. I closed my eyes and reached, put my fingers on the side of his neck. It was still warm—not as warm as the neck of a living man but warmer than the cold room. How long had he been dead? As far as I knew, a man his size might stay warm for days, like a cooling planet with a molten core.

I fought to think clearly. What had happened here?

The door to the gun cabinet was open, emptied of the arsenal I knew Terrence had kept in it. If I figured right, Terrence had been reaching for the cabinet when the killer entered the bedroom. He had spun and the killer had shot him in the stomach. The blood on the wooden decking outside the living room probably meant that Terrence had managed to get a gun out of the cabinet before being shot and had wounded the killer. But the killer was in good enough shape afterward to empty the cabinet and carry its contents out the back.

I got myself standing and looked around the room. The window faced the empty parking lot and other apartment buildings beyond it. I walked around the bedroom, taking it all in. Terrence had a couple of small abstract nudes in frames over the head of the bed. The furniture was heavy, big, made of wood and steel. Two framed photographs stood on the dresser. One, fading, was of his younger brother, the brother shot by the cops. The other was of a woman with perfect black skin and tightly curled graying hair, cut so short you could see her scalp. Her irises were so dark they merged with her pupils. She had on a red turtleneck sweater. Terrence's girlfriend, Darlene.

In front of the dresser I picked up a small metal disk from the floor. It was as wide as a dime, but heavier. Its bottom was smooth and the dirty gray of lead. Its top was brass and, in the middle, a perfectly round edge formed a crater. It was a big-caliber slug. The hole in Terrence's belly was a big-caliber hole.

Stan Fleming would want to see the bullet. He might need it to catch whoever killed Terrence and the others.

I held it to my nostrils. I touched it to my lips. I fought an impulse to put it on my tongue and swallow it. I put it in my pocket.

The dresser drawers held clothes, nothing else. The table next to the bed had magazines. I went to the closet. More of the big man's clothes hung on the bars.

There were four boxes on a closet shelf. I lifted them. Two had gloves, hats, boots, and winter clothes. The others had high school football trophies, a diploma, and old photographs. I put the boxes back on the shelf, stumbled out of the closet, and sat on Terrence's bed. The seagull head shifted on the mattress. I opened my hand to swipe it away, then lowered my arm and left it there. I looked at Terrence's body and he seemed to recede from me.

I needed a drink. I needed to rest on a stool in a bar that smelled of old whiskey and wood. I needed to go away. The destination didn't matter. It was the trip itself, the leaving behind.

I got up and walked into the living room, wondering if I should fight the urge or drive to one of the places I knew that poured a tall shot and tolerated you when you got beyond reason. But I never got to choose. I stopped hard.

David Stone was standing in the living room. He held a large caliber pistol. It was pointed at my belly.

THIRTY-SEVEN

HE LOOKED AS SURPRISED to see me as I was to see him. "What the hell are you doing here?" he said. Like I was a seagull in the kitchen.

I stared at him. "I've been asking myself that a lot lately." I took a step toward the front hall.

He moved between me and the hallway and wiggled the gun barrel at my belly. "What the hell are you doing?"

I looked at him up and down. The band on his ponytail had come off and his hair hung wild. But if Terrence had shot him and the blood on the wooden decking was his, he didn't show it. He had no obvious holes in him.

"No," I said, "what the hell are *you* doing? My friend's lying dead in his room and I'm going to take a wild guess—if I sniff the barrel of your gun, I'll smell cordite. And there's a dead hooker lying in her bed about a mile from here and I'll bet you killed her, too. A nun and a priest are in the morgue and, who knows, maybe if we poke around your car and your house we'll find a thing or two that links you to them. What am I doing? Who cares what the hell I'm doing! What are *you* doing?"

His face went ashen and he stepped backward as if my crazy, angry words were blunt weapons and I was swinging them at him. I stepped toward him and reached for my Glock. But he held his gun toward me, his hand shaking, and fired. The shot went past me and tore a hole in the wall. The sound of it almost knocked me over.

I stopped and panted.

He stared at me wide eyed as if *I* had the gun and was shooting it.

"Okay," I said, calmer. "What now?"

He needed a moment to think about that. "Your gun." He caressed the trigger of his pistol with his finger.

I nodded but said, "Last time I reached for it, you shot at me."

He thought some more. "Take off your jacket. Slow."

I opened my jacket, exposing the gun, and started to slide off the sleeves.

"Stop," he said.

I did, and he came to me and removed my gun from the holster. My sleeves cuffed my hands behind me. Unless I kicked his knees or bit him, he had me. He backed away with my gun, and I slid my jacket onto my arms again.

He gestured at Terrence's bedroom. "In there."

"You going to shoot me, too?"

He pointed his gun at my belly. I walked into Terrence's room.

He came in and glanced around like he'd left something behind. He saw the remains of the bird I'd shot, spread across the top of the bed—feathers and blood, an intact wing, and two orange feet. "What the fuck?"

"A seagull."

He gave me a look.

"You don't want to know."

He must have figured that he didn't because he went back to looking around the room. He went to the gun cabinet and peered inside. He retraced the search I'd made, though he didn't bother with the closet and he never glanced at Terrence. Whatever he was looking for, he didn't find.

"Need help?"

He gestured toward the door. "Out."

He marched us around the apartment, looking for something that didn't seem to be there. In the kitchen the seagull stood on the table. Stone pointed his gun at it but it stared at him blankly and he left it alone.

"Okay, let's go," he said, and he steered me back into the living room toward the broken window.

It was cold out there. I shook my head. "I've had enough. If you want to put the gun away and tell me your sad story about why killing four people wasn't your fault, I'm curious to hear it. If not, you can leave on your own. I'm tired—"

He lowered his gun and shot at the floor and this time the shot was no mistake. A five-inch hole splintered the wood in front of my feet. The blast of the gunshot roared through the apartment.

Sweat broke inside my shirt and between my legs. "What kind of noise does it take around here before the neighbors call the cops?"

He raised the gun and pointed it at my chest. "You ready now?"

"Let's go," I said. I stepped through the window frame into the freezing air.

I went lightly, quietly, afraid I might make him pull the trigger again. But then my cell phone rang inside my jacket. I raised my hands, half expecting the noise would make Stone shoot me in the back.

"You want me to answer?" I said.

He thought some more. "Give it to me."

I gave him the phone. He looked at the display. "Lucinda?"

"My partner," I said.

He dropped the phone on the deck and ground it to pieces with his heel. "Not anymore."

He directed me down the stairs past the cases of bottles and the bicycles and tricycles. The spots of blood continued all the way down. At the bottom of the stairway, Stone's silver Mercedes was parked in the trash-filled alley.

"You drive," he said.

I slid into the driver's seat and he got in beside me and stuck his gun in my ribs.

The car crunched over beer cans and cardboard boxes in the alley. I swung it onto the street and drove past the McDonald's. My Skylark sat in the parking lot and I wished I was in it. If I left it long enough, maybe the seagulls would finish eating scraps of Filet-O-Fish and French fries and devour it, too, rust and all.

"Where to?" I asked again.

"The Dan Ryan. South."

"Did Terrence wound you before you shot him?"

He looked at me hard.

"I don't want you bleeding to death," I said. "Not in your car. Not on this fine leather upholstery—"

"Would you shut the fuck up?"

"Sure," I said, and I drove onto the Dan Ryan and headed

south out of the city. I merged into thickening traffic, swung two lanes to the left, and accelerated. If the speed worried Stone, he didn't show it. "So how is Greg Samuelson trying to take Stone Tower from you?"

Stone shoved his gun harder into my ribs. I took a hand from the wheel and pulled the barrel away from a rib bone. "Shooting me at eighty miles an hour would be bad for both of us."

He put pressure on my ribs again but let me breathe.

"Samuelson's definitely trying to play you. When he went to your mother's house after he walked out of the hospital, he wanted to confront you—he wag going after something big, big enough he was willing to risk his life again after you'd shot him. He could've killed you if he'd wanted to. He could've killed everyone at the table. But that would have ended the game right there, and no one would've won. I figure he wanted money—big money. The kind of money only rich guys like you usually see.

"You know what I don't get, though? What's with Samuelson's wife and your brother? Why's she screwing him if Greg is about to take his money? And why's he screwing her if her husband's extorting you? You got any ideas?"

"I've got the idea that I wish you'd shut up."

"Yeah, you said. But who knows? Maybe it's love. Stranger things have happened—"

I grabbed the barrel of his gun and shoved it toward him and up. With my other hand, I cut the wheel, and swung the car across two lanes, then back. The trick almost worked. His body bounced off the passenger-side door and if he'd squeezed the trigger, he would have made himself a sunroof. But he reached into his waistband and came up with my Glock and pointed it at my head.

I let go of his gun.

He said, "Don't do that again or I'll shoot you, eighty miles an hour or stopped."

I forced a smile. "Fair enough."

"And shut the fuck up."

I nodded. We drove for a while quietly. Overhead signs said the expressway would split into the Dan Ryan to the south and the Skyway toward Indiana and the southeast.

"The Skyway," Stone said.

I nodded again. "So you made two mistakes."

He growled, "Shut up."

"Right. When you shoot a man in the head, shoot him in the brain. A jaw shot will make him ugly, but it won't kill him. You needed Greg Samuelson dead. That's your first mistake. Your second mistake was the priest, not that it could be helped. You needed to search Judy Terrano's room, and there he was, poking around. Did you find what you were looking for? I don't think so. If you'd found it, all of this probably would have stopped and you wouldn't have killed Louise Johnson or Terrence, and I wouldn't be driving your car—which, by the way, handles beautifully—"

"If you grab again, I'll shoot you."

"I don't want the gun. I want to know what you were looking for in Judy Terrano's room. And why you killed her to begin with. What did she know that threatened you? Something about the fire at the Bad Kitty Lounge? What did she have?"

"You've got the ideas. You tell me."

I thought about it. "A photograph? You stripped Louise Johnson's photos off her refrigerator and walls. So why not a photo? I don't know what you were looking for in Terrence's apartment but why not a photo in Judy Terrano's?"

"Sure," Stone said. "Why not?"

"It would have to be a pretty good photo for you to kill four people—a photo that would get you in a lot of trouble."

"It would," Stone agreed.

He watched my face like I was becoming more interesting to him but he hated me all the same. A sign on the shoulder of the highway advertised an Indiana Welcome Center a mile ahead, just outside the city limits.

I said, "Not a photo."

"No?"

"No photo is worth four lives."

"How much are four lives worth?"

"Depends on whose. Your life, about ten bucks. Mine, about twice that on a good day. Most people's, a whole lot more. I figure you were looking for a document of some kind." I thought about the folder of titles and deeds that I'd seen at Stone Tower and that Terrence was reading when I last saw him alive. "Something that tells what really happened at the Bad Kitty Lounge."

"Would that kind of document be worth four lives?"

"To you, maybe."

He shook his head like I amazed and saddened him. He pulled his gun from my ribs and regripped it so that he could hold the barrel and smash the butt on my head. "You don't know when to quit," he said.

I held my arm to protect myself from a blow, hit the brakes, and slid onto the shoulder of the road, jamming the transmission into Park.

He watched me with a weird, patient sadness.

Then he raised the gun.

I dived across the seat for him, reaching for his throat, his face, his eyes. He brought the gun butt down on me. I threw my left hand up to deflect the gun but it went through it like I was a ghost. Before the pain, I felt the metal sink into my skull. Then I felt the pain. My vision narrowed and went black, and a small bright red thing the size of a maggot floated across the dark field, and I thought in that final crazy moment that it looked like it might work as fishing bait. Then the red maggot disappeared, and all was dark and cold and very deep.

THIRTY-EIGHT

I OPENED MY EYES. I was riding in a car. I wondered how I'd gotten there, buckled tight into the passenger seat. The cold October sunlight cut through the windshield. Someone or something had cracked my head. Pain shot down my neck into my shoulders, and nausea flooded my belly and chest. I closed my eyes and the world was a blue veined darkness.

I opened my eyes and a street sign said COLUMBIA AVENUE. It meant nothing, said nothing about where I was going or why. Overhead, dozens of telephone wires extended up and down the street. More wires crossed the street and segmented the long wires into squares and rectangles as if someone had stretched the first yarns on a loom to make a blanket that would shelter me from the sun. The asphalt on the street was old and cracked, repaired with snakes of black tar. A woman with an Afro stood by a bus-stop bench, wearing tight shorts and a sleeveless halter top that showed her belly and most of her breasts. She shivered and glared as the car rolled past.

"Where—?" I said.

Like magic, a ten-legged water tower rose on the roadside. Block letters on the water tank said THINK HAMMOND.

Hammond, Indiana.

People told jokes about Hammond, Indiana.

Before I could remember them, the world gave itself back to the blue veined darkness.

I opened my eyes. The car had stopped. A man was pulling me from the front seat. I helped as much as I could. Why not? He seemed friendly enough. I fumbled with the seatbelt but it was already unbuckled. I fumbled with it anyway. The man slapped my hands away. I slapped his hands. He reached under my arm and lifted me. He yelled at me and slapped my face. I lunged at him and connected with his chin. He stumbled backward.

I got myself out of the car and onto my feet as he came back for me. My legs didn't like standing. Maybe with one-sixth of earth's gravity they would like it. I tumbled onto the man. I had thirty or forty pounds on him but he held me up and we danced some steps on the pavement. I looked at him eye to eye. His hair was long and wild. His eyes were fierce.

"Not my type," I mumbled, and tried to push him away.

He didn't resist. He let me fall.

The cold pavement cleared my head. I kneeled on it and stared at him. A huge sky with a horrible sun framed his raggedy face.

"Stone," I said, "I'm going to kill you."

He grinned.

I dragged myself to my feet, swayed, and steadied myself. He didn't take any chances. He drew his pistol and pointed it at my chest.

He directed me toward a brick building with a giant open

garage door. Scraps of sheet metal and a trash bin full of bent pieces of rebar stood on the sidewalk in front. The gaping space inside the building was dark. Sparks wheeled into the air from whining, ripping, pounding machines.

I stumbled inside in front of Stone's gun. A dozen men worked the machines. They wore T-shirts, work boots, and blue jeans stained black with oil. Their faces were creased and lined, sweaty from the heat of their tools. They fed sheets of metal into the teeth of saws, carted slag in wheelbarrows, and opened the door to a fading green monster of a processing furnace that rose almost two stories to the ceiling. We were thirty or forty yards away from the furnace and the heat swelled over us.

"What is this place?" I managed to say.

Stone guided me into a dark hall at the back where the air felt cold and smelled like grease and damp soil. "'Metalworks,'" he said.

"What are we doing here?"

He didn't answer. He led me to an office, used a key to let us in, and flipped on the light. He shoved me and followed me in.

"Sit down," he said.

There were a couple of worn office chairs next to a metal desk with a fake wood-grain top. File cabinets stood next to the desk and a water cooler.

I went to the water cooler, helped myself to a cup, and did as I was told.

"What are we doing?" I asked again.

He busied himself with a coffeepot that stood on a battered credenza, then turned to me. "This is where you disappear."

THIRTY-NINE

I THOUGHT ABOUT THE furnace. I thought about disappearing. I said, "It looks like it would hurt."

"Not for long," Stone said. "Give me your wallet and keys."

I gave them to him. "You going to rob me before you kill me?"

He shook his head. "The wallet gets burned separately. So do your shoes and belt, but you can keep them for now."

"You're learning. You weren't so careful with Judy Terrano and the others."

He adjusted the coffeepot under the drip filter, then sat on his desk facing me. "I didn't kill Judy."

"No? You started with the priest?"

"I didn't kill him, either. Or Terrence Messier. Or Louise Johnson."

My head hurt every time I moved it, but I shook it at him. "I suppose you didn't light the fire that killed the four kids at the Bad Kitty, either."

He gave me a half smile. "That one's more complicated."

"You want to know what I think?"

"Not really."

"I think you lit the fire and Judy Terrano testified against you and sent you to jail, and when you got out you waited eleven years for an excuse to kill her. Everything goes back to the Bad Kitty, but now the building's gone and Stone Tower is rising on the land where it stood, and that's your excuse. I saw how much your family has invested in that building. What? Twenty or twenty-five million so far? More? Judy Terrano could show what really happened at the Bad Kitty and then you would lose it all. That's enough to kill for."

"A nice story," he said. "How do you explain the others?"

"What's to explain? The priest was in the wrong place at the wrong time—if he hadn't been searching Judy Terrano's room, he'd still be alive."

"Could be," he said.

"Louise Johnson knew Judy Terrano when they hung out with you at the Bad Kitty. She still knew her. She probably knew her secrets and how much they were worth. If she called you after I visited her yesterday, you would have worried about what she knew and what she might want from you."

"That wouldn't stand up in court, but it sounds reasonable."

"And Terrence went with me to Stone Tower yesterday. We ran into one of your cousins. Terrence kept him busy when I left to talk with you at your house. But you weren't at your house. Where did you go? To the construction site to deal with Terrence?"

He shrugged.

I thought again about Stone's cousin surprising me as I looked through the file of property deeds and titles. I thought about Terrence picking up the papers as Lucinda and I left and about him sitting down and reading them like they were a good book. Maybe the deeds and titles meant nothing, I thought. Maybe. "Who owns the property where you're building Stone Tower?" I asked.

He looked surprised, then resigned. "It doesn't matter now," he said. "Everyone thinks Judy Terrano was a saint, but she was a hypocritical cunt. She blackmailed my dad. Made him sign over the deed. You think that sounds like virtue?"

He'd lost me, or almost. *She blackmailed him. Made him sign over the deed.* Judy Terrano owned the land?

If so, that meant what? She saw David Stone burn down the Bad Kitty and guessed or knew that his father was involved in the arson? Then she took the land in exchange for what? Her silence in court?

I answered, "I don't know. I think it could be justice."

He threw up his hands. "Then you're as bad as she was." He stepped past me toward the coffeepot.

I said, "You needed her copy of the title to the land. That's what you were hunting for when you killed her, and that's what you were hunting for when you killed the priest. Who has it now?"

I should have seen his gun butt coming. If he hadn't already hit my head with it once, I might have seen it. I was sitting on a desk chair, and then I was tossing through the air. I didn't hurt. I didn't have time to. I was flying and I wondered when and where I would land. I never knew. I was unconscious by the time I hit the floor.

FORTY

I WOKE UP ALONE on a gray carpet. I was getting used to waking up alone on the floor. I looked at my watch. The face was cracked, the hands frozen at 2:35. I listened. The metalworks was quiet. Instead of sending out for a bag of campfire marshmallows and holding a party, Stone seemed to have decided to wait until the workers went home before making me disappear.

I pushed myself onto my hands and knees. Nausea sank into my belly and I lowered myself back to the carpet. I breathed deep and exhaled, breathed deep again. Breathing exercises—Corrine would be proud of me.

I pushed myself to my hands and knees again. Nausea circled through me and centered in my belly. It was no use fighting. I crawled to a garbage can and emptied my guts. Then I collapsed to the floor, panting.

I listened. A voice was speaking somewhere—a calm voice, no rush, no worry. The voice went quiet and I heard footsteps.

I struggled to get up. If I could find something to swing at

Stone when he came back, I might have a chance in a hundred of getting out of the metalworks alive. If I could get to the wall next to the door and surprise him, I might have a chance in ten.

Steps approached outside the door.

Stone's voice spoke. "Hey, Jerry—"

The voices were friendly but the friendliness was lost on me. All I knew was David Stone and a guy named Jerry were coming for me. It wasn't worth struggling. I closed my eyes and sank onto my stomach.

"How'd it go?" the guy named Jerry asked.

A key turned in the lock but Stone didn't come in. He laughed at Jerry's question. He said, "She says before she'll do it, I've got to go to a doctor and get a checkup. She says she's heard something about me."

Jerry laughed, too. "So you go to the doctor?"

"What do you think?" Stone was coming to kill me but first Jerry wanted to chat with him about his love life.

"You went to the doctor," Jerry said.

It went on like that. I opened my eyes and listened. Jerry didn't seem to be part of the plan to kill me. I wondered if he would help me if I yelled. I wondered if Stone would push the two of us into the furnace together.

I pulled myself up the side of the desk until I was standing. I worked myself toward the desk chair. The pot of coffee that Stone had made was still steaming on the cabinet next to the desk. I got the pot and set it on the desk, then sat in the chair behind it. I ran my fingers through my hair and tried to put a casual look on my face.

Stone was saying, "I wanted to kick him in the balls when he stuck his finger in me."

Jerry laughed. "You didn't do it, did you?"

"Who do you think I am? Of course I didn't. I think doctors are saints. I said I wanted to. I didn't say I did it."

"So you shake his hand afterward?"

"Yeah, I shook his hand."

Jerry gave Stone a moment, then said, "Fag."

Flesh cracked against flesh and a body struck the thin office wall, shaking it.

"Hey! I was fucking kidding," Jerry yelled.

"Go home," said Stone. "And put ice on that."

Footsteps moved away from the office.

The knob turned and Stone walked in, inspecting his knuckles. He glanced at the floor where I'd been lying, then saw me at the desk. He grinned. "Hey, look who's up."

"Only a little wobbly."

He laughed at that. He felt good about himself. He had me where he wanted me. He drew his pistol again, swung it around loosely, and leaned in over me. "Yeah," he said almost gently. "You're wobbly. Very wobbly."

He was right. He could get rid of me in any of a dozen ways and no one would ever know what had become of me. One day a tenant in a million-dollar condominium at Stone Tower would admire the crimson tint of the glazing on a steel countertop that had my blood in it. That would be the closest anyone would ever come to bringing flowers to my grave.

So I reached for the coffeepot on the desk, and I swung it at his face. There was no reason that he shouldn't duck. But he didn't. He leaned over me and laughed at me. The glass pot smashed against his cheek and the scalding coffee washed over him.

He screamed, "Fuck!" and lurched away.

The broken glass opened a gash on the side of his face. The

coffee steamed on his skin and mixed with his blood. He tried to cover his face with his arms. He windmilled and swung his hands. A terrible burn was in him and he couldn't get at it. But his gun stayed in his hand and it pointed at me, at the floor, and at the ceiling. I knew I should take it away from him but I wanted out—out of the office, out of the metalworks, out of Stone's life.

I moved to the door, opened it, and stumbled into the metalworks without looking back. I never wanted to see Stone again.

No one else was in the building. The machines were turned off, but gauges and a warning light on the processing furnace said that it stayed hot and ready whether or not anyone was there to use it. The giant garage door was down. But a standard door stood next to it. I made my way to it.

A man stood outside with a woman. They were at the curb, next to a brown BMW. The driver's door was open. The woman must have jumped out when she'd seen the man coming out of the metalworks. The man had a cut lip. He might have had a broken nose. I figured he was Jerry. The woman was David Stone's daughter Cassie. She was holding a white towel to Jerry's face but it wasn't doing a lot of good. He was bleeding on himself and on her, too. She was talking quietly to him.

They looked at me as I came from the building like a wounded soldier. I went to them. Cassie's eyes were misting. Stone had loosened the teeth of his daughter's boyfriend.

Cassie recognized me and gave me a nervous smile.

"Your dad's a monster," I said.

She said nothing to that, but she reached toward my forehead and lifted the hair from it. She looked me in the eyes like she wanted to kiss my bruises and make them better.

"Thank you," I said, and I moved her away from the car. I

climbed in. She and Jerry looked confused. The keys were in the ignition. I started the car and threw it into drive, ripping away from the curb before they could stop me.

At the end of the block I made a U-turn and accelerated back toward the metalworks. Cassie Stone and Jerry stood on the curb and watched me come without stepping into the street to block me. But as I passed the building, David Stone stumbled out of the door and over the curb. If I'd turned the wheel an inch, I could have gotten him.

FORTY-ONE

THE CLOUDS OVER COLUMBIA Avenue had grown thick as the sun dipped west. The dashboard said the time was 4:48. Darkness would come early. The lighted billboards, the business neon, and the streetlights would glint against the black sky.

An auto-body shop sign swung on its chains, blown by a wind from the north. I whipped around a slow-moving truck, passed a scrap yard called Otto's, a tool and die shop, and Thompson's Self-Storage, then accelerated over some railroad tracks and blew through a stoplight turning red. Chicago wasn't even a ghost in the distance.

I glanced at my face in the rearview mirror. A fiend stared back. Eyes that had seen fire. A face that had felt blunt metal. Lips that had kissed an oily carpet like it was a breast. I tilted the mirror away.

The next stoplight turned red. I stopped behind two cars and closed my eyes, slapped my cheeks, opened them again. No rest. Not yet.

I closed my eyes again.

A blast ripped me awake.

In the rearview mirror, the back window looked like crushed ice.

Another blast.

The back window collapsed into the back seat. David Stone's silver Mercedes stood a car length back. A hand stuck out of the driver's side window. It was holding a pistol. The pistol was pointing at me.

I hit the horn, cut the steering wheel, and stomped on the accelerator. The BMW spun its tires and shot into the intersection. A pickup truck swerved and missed me. An SUV behind it fishtailed. I cut hard to the side. The SUV tapped the back panel of my car, slid past, and I whipped across the rest of the intersection.

Stone's Mercedes pulled into the oncoming lane and accelerated. The car closed on me. I held the accelerator to the floor. His gun came out of his window and blasted.

I threw the BMW to the left at the next corner as a line of cars came into the intersection. Stone tried to follow, couldn't. At the next corner I turned left as he raced down the street, then turned left a third time before he came into view. I completed the square and turned back onto Columbia Avenue. If I was lucky, Stone would have turned right where I made my third left and would be cruising slowly past driveways and alleys, looking for a brown BMW with a missing back window and a cowering driver. I watched the mirror and drove. No Mercedes. No pistol sticking out of a car window. Just a bunch of tired men and women driving home.

A laugh came from my chest. It hurt to laugh. But it was a good hurt. You can hurt like that only if you're living. I laughed and I accelerated around the other cars and passed a building that housed sanitary district offices and then a block-long oil products depot. I laughed until I realized tears were running down my cheeks, and then I sped up some more.

I don't know how many blocks I drove like that, half-blind with the shock of being alive. Cars and trucks got out of my way, blew their horns, skidded to a stop.

Then a cop's icy blue lights appeared in my mirror and a siren filled the air.

I grinned like an idiot and pulled to the side.

The cop strutted to my window. He was thin and had a wisp of a goatee, a moustache, and wire-rimmed glasses. He'd parted his receding red hair in the middle. He looked like a librarian in a bulletproof vest.

I smiled at him. "I can't tell you how glad I am to see you."

He didn't look glad to see me. His eyes moved over my bruised and filthy head. He glanced back at the shattered pieces of the rear window. He said, "You were going seventy in a thirty-five-mile-an-hour zone."

Bless his heart. He was going to give me a ticket. I laughed again. His fingers touched his service pistol, ready to draw and shoot if I turned out to be the nutcase I sounded and looked like.

"Officer," I said, "I swear I wasn't going a bit over sixty." I couldn't help myself.

Sweat beaded on his brow. "Would you please keep your hands where I can see them and step—"

A burst of gunfire cut him off. The side of his face exploded into flesh and teeth and blood.

I dove for the seat.

I waited for more gunshots.

None came.

I crawled out the driver's side door. Nothing remained of the cop, nothing that mattered.

Cars were stopping. Their drivers watched like I'd done the shooting.

I got so close that I felt the heat of the cop's body leaking into the cold afternoon, and I wished he was far away, at home with a wife and kids, sitting behind a desk at a library, anywhere but here. There wasn't anything I could do to put him back together.

I climbed back into the BMW, sat, got out again. I eased the dead man's nine-millimeter from his belt. The steel was ice cold.

I got into the car and shifted into drive. The tires spun on the roadside gravel and bit. Something thumped under the rear wheel. The cop's foot.

The clip in the nine-millimeter was full. That meant fifteen rounds. They could put fifteen holes in David Stone. I drove up Columbia Avenue after him. If I figured Stone right, after shooting the cop he would have pulled into a parking lot and waited for me to pass. He would be planning to slip in behind me again and kill me.

So I cruised in the right-hand lane past a cast metal manufacturer and a gas station. Stone kept out of sight. I crept past a used car lot and Hank's Auto Wreckers. I could have waved a red flag and painted a target on the hood. Stone wasn't there. Three cop cars sped in the other direction. An ambulance followed, though it could do nothing but carry the pieces to the morgue. When an overpass for the Illinois-Indiana Skyway appeared, I figured Stone must have spooked himself and given up on me. I sped up and crossed under the viaduct.

But as I came back out into the daylight, the rear passenger window imploded and a bullet blew a hole through the inside of the car roof. Stone's car whipped onto the street from behind the viaduct. The car closed on me and the hand with the pistol came out of the driver's side window.

I reached over the backseat and fired.

A spiderweb of cracked glass appeared on his windshield. His car weaved and the hand disappeared inside it. I figured I'd hit him. But the car straightened and closed on me again.

I accelerated through a yellow light and turned onto a cross street, following signs to a Skyway on-ramp, Stone's car right behind. We sped onto the highway and the wind howled in the cavity where Stone had shot out my back window.

The Mercedes moved up on my back bumper, the cracked web of a windshield charging like a clouded eye. Stone couldn't possibly see through it. I raised the nine-millimeter and put a second web in it. Then a black object punched a hole in the glass from inside his car. Stone was beating the windshield with the butt of his gun. Sheets of broken glass fell onto the hood and whipped away in the wind.

The Mercedes moved toward the back of my car and hugged it like Stone wanted to lock bumpers. No window separated us. Ten feet divided us. His eyes stared at me in the mirror. He lifted his gun over his steering wheel and pointed it at my head. I yanked the steering wheel to the side as he pulled the trigger, and the BMW rocketed across two lanes. The blast shook the air.

Stone swung his car after me. I sped past an SUV, swung back, and slowed so the SUV blocked me from behind. I rolled down the window as Stone accelerated next to me. I aimed and shot. The passenger-side window of his car blew in. He raced forward eight, nine, ten car lengths, then slowed, and the Mercedes wobbled left and right in its lane. The other side window came down and he started firing. A bullet dug a trench in the hood of the BMW. Two bullets went through the bottom of the windshield and shredded the passenger seat. I fired back and killed anything that was sleeping in his trunk.

The Mercedes flew forward and cut around the side of a semi. I went after it, hung in the draft of the big truck, swung from side to side, and looked for Stone. He'd disappeared. I swung side to side again, chose left, and accelerated, the nine-millimeter in my hand.

I flew past the front of the truck.

Stone was gone.

A minute later, a roadside sign welcomed me to Chicago. I kept my nerves and didn't shoot it.

Stone was gone, charging back into the city, and I was driving at twenty over the limit in a car with blown-out windows and bullet holes in the metal body. Every cell phone on the highway between Hammond and the city limit must have called 911. If I was smart, I would pull over to the shoulder, put my hands in the air, and wait for the cops to cuff them. But my skull had taken too many knocks to be smart. I shoved the accelerator to the floor and wove through the traffic.

Stone's Mercedes didn't show itself until Eighteenth Street. The car was on the exit ramp and I was in the middle lane, going eighty. I hit the brakes, cut the wheel, and slid past the guardrail onto the ramp.

Stone saw me coming and cut around a van into the cross traffic.

I went after him.

He zigged and zagged and then drove north. He didn't shoot at me. I didn't shoot at him. I cut into oncoming traffic, pressing the horn, and tried to pull even with him, but I could have been honking at a moving wall. The cars came at me and I cut back in behind Stone. We behaved as politely as possible for two guys driving bullet-pocked cars, until Stone sped through a changing light and left me behind.

I stayed calm. I knew where he was going.

A couple of minutes later, I parked the BMW next to his empty Mercedes at the Stone Tower construction site.

The BMW dashboard clock said the time was 5:21. Construction had ended for the day an hour earlier or more. I got out and looked the Mercedes over. It was a pretty car if you didn't mind broken windows or punched-out upholstery. Or blood smeared on the front seat. Not enough blood to slow Stone but enough to make him mad.

Stone had his own gun and mine. He knew the building, inside and out—every steel beam, copper wire, and PVC pipe. He could be waiting for me anywhere, watching me now, taking his time until I stepped against the barrel of his gun.

I white-knuckled the dead cop's nine-millimeter and walked into the building.

FORTY-TWO

I YELLED, "STONE!"

The concrete lobby absorbed the sound. I yelled again anyway. "Stone!"

No one answered.

A draft blew a packing receipt across the floor. Shadows lined the lobby and the edges of a dimly lighted corridor. I moved into the shadows, figuring I would live or die there. A pool of water stood on the floor and, a little past it, a stack of slate tiles. Then the temporary offices appeared. Stepping into the light seemed like a bad idea. If Stone was as good as he seemed to be, he could be standing twenty feet from me and there would be no movement, no glint off the polished steel of a handgun.

So I stood next to a concrete column and peered at the door from the dark before I stepped into the light.

The door was locked.

I threw my shoulder against it. The office was thin plywood, nailed to a flimsy frame. The wall shook. But the door stayed shut.

If Stone hadn't known where I was before, he knew now. I ran back to the shadows, caught my breath, and peered into the dark some more.

Nothing moved. Nothing glinted.

I charged across the corridor and threw my shoulder against the door again. The door and the frame broke into the office and I fell forward, rolled, and scrambled over the top, waving the gun around the reception area, ready to shoot man, woman, or child, anything that came at me.

I went into the inside room where Stone's cousin and his vicious German shepherd had interrupted me as I'd looked through the folder of deeds and titles. I returned to the file cabinet and looked for the folder.

It was gone.

I clambered back over the broken door and sprinted into the shadows. Then I stepped deeper into the building.

The corridor led past a door to a big room that looked like it would be used to house utilities. At the end of the room a heavy security door led outside. I stepped through it to the back of the building.

The back lot was a scar of dry clay soil with four Dumpsters parked against the side of the building and a chain-link fence and gate limiting access to trucks delivering construction materials. An elevator rose almost twenty stories along the outside of the building—a steel framework structure with two steel-cage elevator cars. Anchored to a concrete base behind the building, a tower crane rose higher than the elevator, higher than the building itself.

Stone stood behind one of the vertical struts that supported the crane. He'd trapped himself between the building and the fence. But he didn't look worried. He shot at me. I ducked behind the security door and he shot again. The slug dented the metal door frame. I waited, then poked my gun out and shot blindly at the place where I thought the crane stood.

Four, five, six shots, maybe more, pounded into the security door as if Stone figured he could bore a hole through it to me. I wondered if he could.

I cracked the door open and yelled, "You've got nowhere to go!"

He answered with four more shots.

I waited, swung the door open, shot twice at the place where he'd been standing, and ducked back inside.

He didn't shoot back.

I cracked open the door.

Nothing.

I waited, peered through the gap.

Stone was climbing a series of ladders that rose through the interior of the latticed steel tower crane.

I stepped outside and called to him, "What the hell are you doing?"

He stopped, midway up a ladder, pulled a gun from his belt, and fired.

A bullet sank into the clay at my feet. I ducked toward the door.

Another shot. Another *twock* of clay.

I glanced out. He was climbing again. I aimed the nine-millimeter and fired. If the shot hit anything, it was too soft to make a sound. I fired again and he fired back.

A few yards from me, the door to one of the construction elevator cages was open. I ran to it and punched the lever to go up. Gears ground as the car climbed a track.

The car rattled and the metal whined for oil.

Then Stone's gun fired and steel banged against steel.

Gears didn't bang like that.

Another gunshot, another metallic bang, and the steel mesh wall of the elevator dented in.

Another shot. A strand of mesh tore and a slug fell to the floor.

I threaded the mesh with the nine-millimeter barrel and shot.

Stone didn't seem to mind that we'd exposed ourselves to each other's shooting. But I did.

I punched another lever. The elevator stopped between floors.

Stone shot and metal banged against metal.

I slid open the cage door, slipped through the bottom, and dropped to concrete. A bullet dug into the floor. I spun and shot.

That got Stone climbing again.

He went up ladder after ladder until he reached the operator's cab. It was a tinted glass box. Above it, an American flag whipped in the wind. He got into the cab and a moment later the cable hanging from the long working arm started retracting. I'd figured he'd climbed the crane because he'd had nowhere else to go, but he was acting like there was no place he would rather be. The cable reeled into the working arm, and a steel I-beam rose from the dirt lot behind the building. It went into the air the way smoke rises, hovers on a down draft, and rises again. The beam passed about twenty feet from me and rose into the darkening sky. The working arm of the crane swung toward the building, like a second hand on a giant clock speeding toward home. The beam accelerated as it approached. I looked up as it struck. High above, a plate of reflective glass exploded under the impact, and slabs, heavy enough to cut a man in two, rained down the side of the building.

The working arm swung out again, then in. Another plate of glass exploded and rained down.

Another.

Stone was destroying the building.

The working arm swung farther from the building and the cable lowered until the I-beam was even with me. The trolley that held the cable rolled toward the operator's cab, stopped.

The I-beam turned in a gust of wind, then straightened. I pointed the nine-millimeter at the crane cab window. The working arm swung toward the building.

The beam closed on me. I squeezed off a shot and then another. I was shooting at the clouds.

I dove to the floor as the beam smashed into the concrete column where I'd been standing. The steel rang like a huge bell. The beam broke from the cable, fell to the concrete floor, and rang again. Then the beam bounced over the side of the building and disappeared far below into the brown earth.

I got up on one knee and fired the nine-millimeter at the crane cab.

The glass on the cab exploded. Stone sat in the open sky with a pistol pointed at me. He fired three, four times. I ducked behind a column, waited, spun into the open, and shot at the cab.

Too late.

Stone was scrambling down a ladder.

WHEN HE STEPPED FROM the last section of ladder onto the concrete base, I was waiting for him behind a pile of scrap.

He ran into the open from the steel framing, looking for me, his gun pointing everywhere except at me.

I took my time.

As he peered up at the floor where he'd tried to crush me with the steel beam, I stepped out, aimed for his chest, and fired.

His body fell back and hit the concrete.

He didn't get up. Didn't move.

I wanted to keep shooting him until the clip in the nine-millimeter ran dry. Then I would keep pulling the trigger just to hear it click. That seemed about as crazy as smashing a skyscraper with a steel beam, so I tucked the nine-millimeter in my belt and went to him.

His chest had stopped heaving. His left arm was bent back and away in an unnatural pose of the dead. I watched him like he was a curious monster, safely asleep in a cage—until I noticed he had no blood on his chest or his belly, none on his face either, except the gash where I'd hit him with the coffeepot.

I grabbed for my gun, but his eyes opened and his right hand rose from the concrete with his pistol in it, pointed at my forehead.

I put my hands in the air.

He sat up and squeezed the trigger.

But a gunshot rang from across the dirt lot. Stone spun. When he came back around, pain and shock had put a horror mask on his face. A patch of blood spread from his left shoulder toward his belly.

He turned toward the end of the building. Lucinda stood there. Her pistol was pointing at him. She looked as stunned as he did that she'd shot him. Stone steadied his gun and fired at her. Her gun arm flew sideways and her pistol soared from her hand and hit the building wall. Stone swung his gun at my face and stumbled toward me. I reached for the nine-millimeter.

From behind me a burst of automatic gunfire cut him down. His body flew back. His gun flipped into the air, fell on the concrete next to him, bounced and bounced again and came to a rest against a steel strut. He landed on the concrete slab, dead—he had to be dead this time.

Another burst of automatic gunfire tossed his body across the concrete.

The shooting stopped, and I went to him. His body and legs had dozens of holes in them. His head was blood and splintered bone. I pointed the nine-millimeter at his chest and fired. I knew better. I knew I would have nightmares about shooting a corpse. But I fired.

When the shock and the sound passed, I looked at the building behind me. Perched inside a third-floor gap, DuBuclet's helpers, Robert and Jarik, cradled light assault rifles. Robert nodded to me with a grim smile. Then he and Jarik disappeared into the shadows.

FORTY-THREE

LUCINDA SAT ON THE dirt by the side of the building. She'd gotten her gun and had it in her lap. I ran to her and she looked at me with sad eyes.

"I froze," she said.

I looked at her wounded arm. "How bad is it?"

Her leather jacket had a hole in the sleeve. A trickle of blood was running down her arm and dripping from her fingers. She lifted the arm, looked at the hole, and grimaced.

"I froze," she said. "I shot him. Then I froze."

"You saved my life."

"I've never frozen before. I was afraid I'd hit you."

"Can you take off your jacket?" I said.

She stood and held her arms open to me. I undressed her like a child, unzipping the jacket, slipping the sleeve off her left arm, gently sliding off the other sleeve.

The wound had soaked her cotton shirtsleeve with blood. I tore away the cloth. The bullet had taken the flesh off the outside of her arm. Blood flowed freely but it would stop on its own or with a few stitches. I ripped away the rest of the sleeve, folded it, made it into a compress. She held it against the torn flesh and I draped her jacket over her shoulders.

I said, "How did you know where to find me?"

"You weren't at the Stones' house or office."

"But how did you know I would be with the Stones?"

She looked at me like I was missing the point. "You were too close."

"Yeah, so you froze—so what? How did you know?"

"Birth records. You sent me to the county clerk's office. Louise Johnson had a daughter in 1970."

"Yeah?"

"The father was David Stone. The daughter was Cassie."

"David Stone and Louise Johnson?"

"And daughter Cassie. I figured he had to be involved one way or another. So I went looking for him."

That explained the photos missing from Louise Johnson's refrigerator and the frame in her hallway. The photos probably were of Cassie. David Stone had burned them and stuffed the ashes in the mouth of Cassie's mother. I figured that Louise Johnson had kept quiet about her connection to Judy Terrano because a deal she'd struck with the Stones when they'd taken her daughter must have included a vanishing act. I wondered what she got in return. Rent money and a monthly case of Bacardi?

"Thank you," I said, because what else do you say when someone saves your life? Then, "How about Robert and Jarik? Did you bring them with you?"

"I've no idea where they came from. But I get the feeling

that William DuBuclet knows everything that happens in this city and where and when."

I thought about Robert and Jarik knowing I was helping Stan Fleming almost before I knew it myself. "I've got the feeling you're right."

I glanced at David Stone's dead body, flat against the concrete like gravity was pulling him toward his grave. "We should call the police," I said. "You have your phone?"

She nodded down at herself.

I fished her cell phone out of the inside pocket of the jacket. She looked at me with those sad eyes. "I never freeze."

I leaned over her and touched my lips to hers, kissed her. She dropped the compress, reached, and pulled me toward her. She breathed me into her like I was life itself. Then she pushed me away.

She looked at me, wild-eyed.

"It's okay," I said.

Her voice was bitter. "Why is it okay? You could have died. I could have."

"I didn't. You didn't."

"Well, it's not okay."

I had no answer for that. I sat on the dirt across from her and watched her. She looked away. I knew of nothing to say to her, nothing to say to myself. So I dialed 911 on her cell phone. I told the operator where we were and asked her to send an ambulance for Lucinda and the cops for David Stone and everything else. The operator told me to stay on the line. I hung up.

I went back to Stone. His long hair was pasted against his bloody head, all but a few strands, which blew in the wind like dry grass. His body had the shape of something that had been broken inside. I started at his collar, patting his shirt. His pants pockets were damp with blood and urine. They held his car keys, his wallet, and a lighter. My wallet and keys, too.

I groped his legs, then rolled him over. My Glock stuck out of the back of his waistband. I stuck it into my shoulder holster, then started again from the top.

Nothing. If he had the file of land titles and deeds that Terrence and I had seen in the Stone Tower office, he'd eaten it.

I returned to Lucinda and wiped my hands on the soil until they were filthy but dry. She still wasn't looking at me, so I called Stan Fleming at the District Thirteen station. By the time I'd given him directions to Stone Tower, sirens filled the air.

FORTY-FOUR

FOR THE NEXT THREE hours we had a big enough crowd in back of the building to hold a block party. The cops rigged floodlights that shined a jaundiced yellow over the dirt and reflected high into the night from the mirrored glass. The paramedics convinced Lucinda to let them take her to the hospital. The medical examiner poked and prodded David Stone's body, then put it in a bag. A forensics team did a scavenger hunt for bullets and shells. I told my story a half-dozen different times, but none of them included Robert and Jarik. Along with Lucinda, they'd saved my life. But they'd walked away afterward. I figured I should respect that, though it could cost me plenty. The cops didn't like my knowing nothing about them.

Stan Fleming came onto the dirt lot as the others finished with me, so I told my story again. He gave me a long stare when I said I didn't know who had finished off Stone. When the stare didn't break me, he said, "DuBuclet?" as if he'd read my mind.

"Does it matter?"

"Of course it does."

"They were ahead of us on this. They knew it was David Stone."

He looked at me hard. "All the more reason I want them in my hands."

"You're going to arrest them for bringing down Stone? You should be shaking their hands and pinning little medals on them, but you won't and they don't want your medals anyway. They definitely don't want to shake your hand. They don't want to be connected with you. They don't trust you."

Stan shook his head. "Ask me if I give a shit."

I stared at him.

"I'm not arresting anyone yet," he said. "But I want to know what happened from everyone involved, separate and to-gether."

"They won't tell you a thing. They'll deny they were here."

"They'll talk to me."

Stan had a toughness that made me wonder if he was right. But DuBuclet and his followers were tough, too. "I'll tell you what you want to know," I said.

I gave it all to him, everything I knew and everything I sus-pected. I told him that David Stone had burned the Bad Kitty Lounge in 1969 and had wasted half his life in jail for lighting that one match. I told him I figured that after the fire the Stones had struck a deal with Judy Terrano involving her court testimony, making promises that involved the land where the Bad Kitty Lounge had stood and where the Stones now were building a luxury condominium tower. I told him I figured Greg Samuelson was trying to extort the Stones for a piece of the Tower and got himself shot for the effort. I told him about the loose connection to the priest in Judy Terrano's bathtub and the close connection to Louise Johnson. I told him he could find Terrence's body in his apartment.

When I finished, Stan nodded but looked unhappy. "So why did David Stone put the ashes of the photographs in Louise Johnson's mouth?"

"The guy was into burning. Had a long history of it."

"Maybe," he said. "And why did he take off her pants? Why did he strip Judy Terrano?"

I shrugged. "He was a monster."

He shook his head. "That's not an answer."

"It's the best I've got," I said.

He thought. "So this was about a square of muddy real estate with ashes on it?"

It was about everything, I thought. Sex. A kerosene fire. Four dead kids. Race riots. A history of blood and sperm and sweat as old as the city or older. Ash that would stay in the air for as long as the city existed and we all would breathe it and live in it. It was about the hope that in a few rooms in an all-but-abandoned building on the southwest side, the violent history of the city could go to sleep and the kids who visited could have happy dreams. Like the Bad Kitty Lounge, it was about anything you wanted it to be about. It might even have been about love.

"It was about money," I said. "Millions of dollars. But basically, yeah—it came down to mud and ashes."

AROUND NINE O'CLOCK A young cop drove me out through the chain-link gate, past the news vans and cameras, away from the blood, and back to the McDonald's parking lot where

I'd left my car. The seagulls were gone. But next door, four police cars and an ambulance lined the curb outside Terrence's building. I knew what they were looking at inside and I never wanted to see it again.

I got in my car and pulled into the street. Jason's Gandhi bobblehead danced on the dashboard. I ripped it off the vinyl, threw it against the front window.

I yelled for a while. I don't know what I said.

At the next stoplight, I looked at the passenger-side carpet. Gandhi gazed up at me without an angry bone in his bobble-head body. I picked him up and put him back on the dashboard.

"It's okay," I said to him. "It's going to be all right now." And I drove home.

FORTY-FIVE

LUCINDA'S HONDA WAS PARKED at the curb in front of my house. A yellow light glowed inside. I pulled into the alley, walked back, and climbed into the passenger seat.

"Hey," I said.

"Hey."

"You going to live?"

"They swabbed my arm with iodine, taped on some gauze, and told me to get a tetanus shot tomorrow."

"Not even a kiss to make it feel better?"

"Not covered by my insurance. The doctor said the biggest injury will be mental. He said I should get counseling."

"So are you going to do it?"

"That's why I'm here."

"Me? I can't even figure myself out."

"That's why I figure you're the one I should talk to."

"Hmm. So what do you want to talk about?"

She looked at me long. "Dinner. I'm hungry."

"That's not going to help you mentally."

"If you don't feed me, you'll really see crazy."

"Come inside."

We walked through the alley to the back of the house. The night was black and bitter cold. The elm tree hung overhead in the dark like an old, bent tower from a time before men made buildings of steel.

We went up the back steps and into the house. The kitchen was bright and smelled like slow-cooking meat, roasting vegetables, and baking bread. It smelled like a place where no one has ever heard of guns, and people spend cold October days bringing in the harvest and eating themselves fat. Mom sat at the kitchen table with Jason, playing cards. She acted like she didn't hear us come in. Jason looked up and smiled. I nodded at him, and Lucinda gave him a little two-fingered wave.

We put our coats on the counter and washed our hands and faces in the kitchen sink. Lucinda had on a ripped, blood-stained shirt and had a thick bandage on her arm. Her face was bruised where Robert and Jarik had hit her. Her eyes were wild and hungry. I figured I looked about the same.

A pot of *bigos* simmered on the stove next to a loaf of warm bread. That and a tumbler of bourbon, filled to the brim, no ice, would have sent me to heaven. I poured a glass of water for Lucinda, one for me, ladled *bigos* into two bowls, and brought the bread to the table.

Mom slapped down her cards, looked at me, looked at Lucinda, and looked back at me. Anger and worry spread across her face. "What happened to you?"

I tore a chunk of bread, dipped it into the broth. "Lucinda got shot in the arm. I took a couple knocks on the head." The heat and salt of the bread soothed me like no medicine could, easing a weight in my chest and in my head. I looked at Lucinda.

She was lost in the food, too. I stabbed a piece of sausage with my fork and tipped it toward her. "The best therapy," I said.

She smiled as she chewed.

Mom glared at me. "You invited me for dinner at six. It's a quarter to ten."

I tried again. "Lucinda got shot. I—"

"If you'd been here for dinner, no one would have shot her and no one would have hit you on the head."

Her glare broke me every time. "I'm sorry, Mom."

"Okay then," she said. She got up and made an ice pack for my head and searched my closet for a shirt to replace the one Lucinda was wearing.

"We saw you on TV again," Jason said, like I'd become a rerun of a favorite show.

"You shouldn't watch so much TV," I said. "There's nothing good on."

Mom looked at me, concerned. "Is it over now?"

"Yeah," I said, "it's over. All but the funerals."

Mom nodded, content, and crossed herself. "May they all rest."

Jason squirmed but then brightened. He turned to Mom. "Did you know that a single aphid can have five million babies in a summer?"

She laughed. "God bless her, that must hurt. I hope they're all daughters."

At 10:30, Jason went to his room to get his overnight bag. He would spend the weekend at Mom's house. I would spend it nursing my head.

After I got them into Mom's car, I went back into the kitchen. Lucinda was cleaning the dishes.

I got close to her. "How are you doing?"

"Better," she said. "Not great, but better."

I watched her rinse a bowl and smiled. "You look like a mess."

She grinned. "You too."

"I feel like it."

We looked at each other for a while, quiet. Then I held my hand out, inviting her to come to me.

She stayed where she was. "I froze because you were standing near him," she said. "I was afraid I would hit you."

"Thank you."

"But I wouldn't have hit you. It was a safe shot but I couldn't take it."

"You took the one that mattered."

"I don't like what you do to me. You make me freeze. Damn it, I can't be in the same room with you without feeling like I might freeze."

I reached for her. But she pulled away from me, grabbing her coat.

I said, "You make me freeze, too." Like it was an excuse, an apology—like it was the most romantic thing I could come up with, my way of saying I wanted her.

She dropped her coat on the floor. "Damn it, Joe!" She came to me. She said, "We could be happy together, the two of us."

And I said, "Yeah, I think so."

"What about Corrine?" she asked.

"I don't know. What about Corrine?"

"What are you going to do about her?"

"I don't know," I admitted.

"You'd better figure it out quick." And she kissed me.

I pulled her toward me but she didn't come. She removed her lips from mine and stared at me. I thought I saw pain and desire in her eyes. She must have seen them in mine.

"Figure it out real quick," she said. She picked up her coat and put it on.

"Where are you going?" I said.

She said nothing.

"Don't go," I said.

She went.

AFTER A WHILE, I slept. I dreamed of falling towers. I ran from strut to strut, propping them with bricks and boards. The bricks and boards slipped like gravity meant to flatten everything that was standing or had ever stood. I propped the towers until I was dead exhausted and then I stood to the side and watched them fall.

I woke in the dark. My mom had asked if it was over and I'd said it was. But I knew that wasn't true. I fished for the phone and dialed.

"What?" Lucinda answered.

"Get up."

"Why?"

"Let's go talk to Greg Samuelson."

"It's a quarter after two."

"Yeah. Let's finish this."

"What the hell?"

"He has Judy Terrano's copies of the Bad Kitty papers."

"How do you know?"

I didn't. Not really. I said, "As Judy Terrano's assistant he could have seen the land title every time he went to her file cabinet. When he realized that the Stones were building on the Bad Kitty plot he saw a chance to get rich. He told them he had the deed and would expose the Bad Kitty history if they didn't pay him a price. So David Stone shot him in the mouth—a warning shot, telling him to keep quiet about the Bad Kitty. They couldn't afford to kill him, though—not if he really had the deed."

Lucinda was silent. Then she said, "I'll be dressed in five minutes."

FORTY-SIX

WE DROVE WITHOUT TALKING through cold, empty streets to Samuelson's condo. The clouded sky was heavy and unmoving. Cars, parked along the curb, looked like the steel carcasses that would remain in the dark at the end of the world. Lucinda shivered and rubbed her hands in front of the heater vent like it was the last ember. I put a hand on her thigh and felt the heat grow through her jeans. I wondered if that heat could warm the world with or without the sun.

She put a hand on top of mine and I decided there was hope.

It was 3:10 A.M. and only one light was on in the condo complex. It was in Samuelson's condo, like he was expecting us.

I rang the buzzer and we waited for the intercom to crackle. There was no answer.

I figured Amy Samuelson was at the Stones' house, comforting Eric as he cried into an overstuffed pillow for his dead brother. I figured Greg Samuelson was high on painkillers, sitting in his kitchen like one of the living dead.

I hoisted myself over the security gate, dropped onto the

brick walkway outside the condo, and let Lucinda in. We climbed the stairs to Samuelson's door. Someone had tacked a piece of plywood over the glass panel that I'd punched out when I'd come to visit the last time. A gentle tug removed it. Lucinda reached inside and the door swung open without a noise.

We drew our guns and stepped into the front hall. The light came from the kitchen deep inside the condo. So did a soft sound, a chair moving back from a table. We moved silently toward the sound.

Then Lucinda stopped, grabbed my arm, and pulled me into the living room. Slow, heavy footsteps were approaching. Lucinda hugged the wall, out of sight, her gun raised so close to her face she could have kissed it. I hugged the wall behind her, the same.

A tall man in a black overcoat and sunglasses stepped past us in the hall. William DuBuclet. In his right hand he held a nine-millimeter, in his left a manila folder. Without looking at us or breaking his slow pace, he said, "Good evening, Mr. Kozmarski, Ms. Juarez."

We stepped into the hall, our guns pointed at his back. "What are you doing here?" I asked, though I figured he'd come for the same reason we had.

He continued toward the door. "An old man like me—I hardly ever sleep," he said, as if that was an answer. He reached the door.

I trained my gun on the cross formed by his spine and his shoulder blades. "Stop," I said.

He opened the door. "You're not going to shoot me," he said. "I need that folder."

He turned and faced us, his gun hanging loose at his side, the most relaxed man I'd ever seen. "This folder is mine," he said. "It's mine to take care of my dead son's child and per-haps change the world he lives in a little bit."

"What's in the folder?" I said.

DuBuclet hesitated, then said, "A will, a letter, and a deed." He gave a bitter smile. "Being of sound and disposing mind and memory, Judy Terrano gave ten percent of her assets to the programs she'd set up to sell chastity to unsuspecting girls. The remaining ninety percent would go to her one and only child, Anthony DuBuclet Jr. That is, unless her will disap-peared. Then who knows what would have happened? Someone else, like the Stones, might have stayed rich or, like Samuelson, gotten rich."

"The letter?" I said.

"Signed by Judy Terrano, David Stone, and David's father, Bartholomew. Dated January 12, 1970. It tells a story about a bad night when a building burned down. David and his father went into the building with cans of kerosene. David's mother sat in a car outside. David was arrested that night. For keep-ing the rest of the family out of it, Judy, who saw it all, got four thousand dollars a year. Not much even then, but the Stones hadn't made their money yet. She also got title to the land where the building had stood. Probably no big loss to the Stones at the time and just a point of principle to Judy. The deed transfers the ownership of the land to Judy, but with a provision—ownership would revert to the Stones if she ever spoke publicly about her relationship with them."

I said, "Samuelson stole these from Judy Terrano before she died and was blackmailing the Stones?"

DuBuclet shrugged. "She would have been killed anyway. They'd started construction using the titles on public record and wanted the land back. Judy was in the way."

Lucinda said, "So now you'll get the land?"

He shook his head. "My grandson will."

She shook her head, too. "With you as guardian, deciding how the profits get spent."

"Naturally."

I thought about the cash hidden in Judy Terrano's room and the cash DuBuclet had Robert and Jarik deliver to me and realized that I'd been wrong about the nun taking payoffs. She was doing the paying and DuBuclet had passed some of her money along to me. "Judy Terrano supported her boy for years, didn't she?"

DuBuclet gave a single nod. "Some years better than others."

"And she supported you, too?" Lucinda said.

DuBuclet didn't deny it. "Judy Terrano was a great woman. The best I've ever known."

"So was or wasn't she extorting the Stones when she got killed?" I asked.

DuBuclet sighed. "As far as I know, Judy never in her life extorted anyone."

"But you just told us what was in the letter," I said.

He flashed a quick, impatient smile. "She wouldn't call that extortion. She spent her life finding people who had too much power and reallocating it to those who had too little. What you call extortion, she would call fairness." Another flash of the smile. "I personally would have to agree with her."

"Because it put power and money in your pocket," Lucinda said.

Again, DuBuclet didn't deny it.

I asked again, "Samuelson stole her papers and was going after the Stones' money for himself?"

A single nod. "But I think the money may have been of secondary interest to him. He started blackmailing them only after his wife began her affair. Call me old-fashioned, but I think love and jealousy got him started. And a fierce anger."

Lucinda gave him a smile of her own. "And what kept *you* in this? Money?"

He nodded again. "The money is rightfully my grandson's. As for me, I'm only trying to take care of the people who matter to me."

I pointed my thumb toward the kitchen. "Is Samuelson—?"

"Dead," DuBuclet said without feeling.

"Did you kill him?"

"He was already dead." He stood for a time, waiting for us to ask other questions. When we didn't, he turned away and stepped outside into the cold, adding, "I believe he died a long time ago."

Lucinda and I listened to his footsteps go down the stairs from Samuelson's condo. Then I nodded toward the kitchen. "Do you want to see?"

She shook her head no—little shakes, little more than a tremble. "You think we should?"

"No," I said, and we let ourselves out.

In the dusty heat of my car, under the dull glow of streetlights, Lucinda asked, "Did DuBuclet kill him?"

"I don't know," I admitted.

"Do you want to do anything about it?"

I thought for a while. "No," I said. "You?"

She shook her head.

We sat for a while, quiet.

Lucinda asked, "If Terrence shot the person who killed him and the wound was bad enough to leave a trail of blood down the back stairs, why was there no blood on David Stone when you ran into him in the apartment?"

"I don't know," I said.

"Why would he put the ashes of Louise Johnson's photographs in her mouth?" she asked. "Why would he strip off her pants? Why would he pull up Judy Terrano's dress and scribble on her stomach? None of that feels right."

Stan Fleming had asked the same questions. I gave Lucinda the answer I'd given him. "He was a monster."

"Didn't anyone ever tell you? Monsters aren't real."

"Then what *is* real?" I asked.

She looked at me with the eyes I'd seen when I'd told her I wasn't sure if Corrine and I were through. Hurt eyes. Eyes that looked a little crazy. "Anger is real," she said. "Jealousy is. Love is."

"I know where you can find all that," I said.

"Yeah?"

I nodded. "In someone willing to crush anyone who threatened what was hers."

FORTY-SEVEN

THE HIGHWAY FELT LIKE a ghost road with long empty stretches and then twenty-ton trucks blasting through the cold and dark. It took us to a suburban off-ramp and smaller ghost roads, minus the trucks.

At the Stones' house, the lights were on but I knocked hard enough to wake the sleeping.

No one was sleeping. Eric Stone opened the door, wearing jeans and a sweater, looking haggard. Amy Samuelson hung onto his arm.

"Yeah?" Stone said like he'd never seen me before.

I didn't break the news about Greg Samuelson to his wife. I stepped into the house, Lucinda behind me. Stone made no effort to stop us.

We walked past the front-hall fountain. It pulsed like an open artery. We went through a series of rooms to the living room. Cassie Stone sat on the couch in a little yellow dress, haggard, too, smoking a cigarette, two empty wineglasses on the table in front of her.

"Where's your grandmother?" I asked.

"Can't you leave her alone?"

"No," I said.

She reached for one of the wineglasses and sighed when she saw it was empty. She turned her eyes on me. "In the pool," she said.

Swimming at 4:20 A.M. on the night that her son died.

Lucinda and I went through more rooms to the breakfast nook and opened the glass door to the pool. Soft lights showed a Plexiglas ceiling and poolside tropical plants in pots.

Mrs. Stone swam in the pool, wearing a black swimming suit. Lucinda and I stood by the side and watched her. At eighty years old she was an extraordinary swimmer. But she was a wounded creature. Torn skin hung from her left shoulder, emerging pink from the water, reddening when it touched the air, and submerging again. Terrence had managed to shoot her before he'd died. David had come in later to pick up after his mother.

Mrs. Stone touched the pool end, turned, and started back. If she felt pain, she didn't show it.

We went to the close edge of the pool. When she approached, she reached for the pool gutter and lifted her head into the air. She caught her breath, started to pull herself out of the pool, and grimaced. Lucinda reached for her but she said, "No." She struggled but managed to get herself onto the pool deck. She stepped close to me, the water running off her and her blood darkening her shoulder, sliding down her breast, streaming into her swimsuit.

She looked at me like I'd done her a wrong. "No one wanted the land," she said. "No one but Judy. She wanted nothing else. My husband insisted that we give her money, too, because he thought we should, because it seemed like the right thing to do. She only wanted the land. So we gave it to her. But as you can imagine, when the area began to revitalize, I needed to have it back."

"No," I said. "I can't imagine killing for that."

Her eyes glinted. "Not for fifty million dollars? Not a woman who'd seduced the person you loved most in the world? Not a woman who sent your child to jail?"

I didn't know the answer but I said, "No."

She laughed at me. Blood and pool water staining her skin and streaming down her legs onto the pool deck, she laughed like I was a liar. "I did nothing you wouldn't do," she said. "Judy and Louise needed to be exposed for what they were."

"And Terrence?" I said. "The priest? What did they do?"

Her toughness broke but only for a moment. "They shouldn't have gotten in the way."

LUCINDA WENT WITH HER to get her dressed. I sat in my car and waited.

I wondered if Mrs. Stone was right. If a bag of money so big that it could light up the sky for the rest of my life hung over my head, what wouldn't I do for it? What would I do if someone took away a person I loved the way Judy Terrano had taken her husband from her bed and her son from her house? I'd warned William DuBuclet what I would do to Robert and Jarik if they hurt Lucinda, and I wondered if I meant it.

I stared out at the dark. Morning was still an hour to the east, brightening the waves on the cold Atlantic, glowing on other cities.

Something tapped the windshield more lightly than a fingertip. Another tap. Another. Snow had started falling. Quieter than death. Whiter than stars and gentler.